D0956655

A NOVELIZATION BY JOHN SHIRLEY
MOTION PICTURE STORY BY DAVID CALLAHAM
MOTION PICTURE SCREENPLAY BY
DAVID CALLAHAM AND WESLEY STRICK
BASED ON **DOOM** FROM ID SOFTWARE

POCKET **STAR** BOOKS
New York   London   Toronto   Sydney

This book is a work of fiction. Names, characters, places and incidents are products of the author's imagination or are used fictitiously. Any resemblance to actual events or locales or persons, living or dead, is entirely coincidental.

An *Original* Publication of POCKET BOOKS

A Pocket Star Book published by
POCKET BOOKS, a division of Simon & Schuster, Inc.
1230 Avenue of the Americas, New York, NY 10020

Doom, the movie novel © 2005 by Universal Studios
Licensing LLLP.
Doom, the movie © 2005 by Universal Studios.
Doom, the game © 2005 by id Software, Inc.
All Rights Reserved.

ISBN-13: 978-1-4165-0995-0
ISBN-10:   1-4165-0995-X

This Pocket Books paperback edition October 2005

10 9 8 7 6 5 4 3 2 1

POCKET STAR BOOKS and colophon are registered trademarks of Simon & Schuster, Inc.

Manufactured in the United States of America

For information regarding special discounts for bulk purchases, please contact Simon & Schuster Special Sales at 1-800-456-6798 or business@simonandschuster.com.

*For all those brilliant guys at **id***

My nerves are made of steel, my nerves are made of steel, my nerves are made of steel, my nerves are made of steel, my nerves are made of steel, my nerves are made of steel . . .

—Monster Magnet, "The Right Stuff"

Thanks to:
  Ed Schlesinger

  The producers, director, designers, and writers of
  Doom, the movie

ONE

A DARK CORRIDOR, deep underground. A single shriek, quickly cut off. The sound of running feet, coming closer . . .

Pounding down the corridor, Dr. Todd Carmack couldn't see his pursuers, couldn't hear them, couldn't smell them, not here—but he knew they were behind him, gaining ground on him and the other five scientists.

Oh yeah: the things were solid enough, loud and reeking enough, and murderous enough—one of them had stood over him, as he lay on his back in the lab, dripping drool on him, gnashing its teeth in anticipation, a lab technician's raggedly severed arm still clutched in its talons. Carmack had pulled the limp, semiconscious Dr. Norris onto him, putting Norris between him and that thing—it had to go through Norris's body first, and that had given Dr. Carmack a moment to scramble away and start the headlong flight down this corridor. But Norris's sobbing screams still echoed around Carmack's skull—they seemed to echo down the corridor and up through level on level of the labs; despairing screams shivering over the archaeological digs, reverberating across the poisoned surface of the planet Olduvai.

Legs and arms pumping, sweat streaming down his face, Carmack figured he was going to die of a heart attack before he got to that heavy door. He was sixty fucking years old, for God's sake. His thudding heart was trying to climb out of his chest; and every breath slashed his lungs like the scalpels he'd used on the subjects in the lab.

He seemed to see the terrified eyes of the lab animals, now, coming out of the darkness ahead . . .

Ten more strides ahead, a fluctuating pool of light waited, threatening to cut out with the flickering of the fluorescent bulb illuminating the door: the door to safety. If there *was* any safety on this goddamned planet.

He risked a look over his shoulder, saw the other scientists running in and out of the intermittent shadow; a middle-aged woman in a white lab coat, Dr. Tallman, was several strides behind Carmack.

His assistant, Dexter, a spindly awkward man, face contorted with terror—was taking up the rear, slowing down now, hobbling, clutching his left leg. A cramp. And then something swept blurrily from the shadows to one side, a dark, strangely rippling arm encircled Dexter's waist and jerked him screaming into the darkness. A blink, and he was simply gone . . .

Carmack stumbled, facing front and just managing

not to fall headlong, knowing he'd be weeping with fear if he had the wind to do it with. He flung himself against the door, just as the light overhead started sparking, hissing . . . about to go out.

"Get it open!" Tallman screamed, running down the hall toward him. Looking absurd sprinting in her white lab coat, as they all did. "For God's sake, Carmack, get it open!"

Gasping for breath, chest heaving, pulse hammering in his ears, Carmack punched at the small keyboard on the door's control panel, but his sight was blurry with sweat, and he had to hit CLEAR and the number combination again . . . the door, dented and marked by claw marks, clattered within itself, struggling to respond . . .

Glancing down the corridor, Carmack glimpsed a hulking black silhouette closing its claws around the throat of the last scientist in the terrified, sprinting procession, Willits—and though Willits was the biggest of them, almost three hundred pounds, he was snatched into the shadows as if he'd been a rabbit caught up by a French chef.

There was a wet crunch, audible fifty feet away—but the door was at last shuddering open, just as Dr. Tallman huffed up to Carmack.

The door stuck, only partway open.

Carmack turned sideways and forced himself through the opening, into the lab, immediately punching at the interior control panel. He jabbed the EMERGENCY CLOSE AND LOCK button.

3

"Dr. Carmack!" Tallman yelled—and shoved her arm through to stop the door closing—it slammed shut on her upper limb with a sickening crunch. Tallman gave out a piteous squeal, her trapped arm twitching.

One of the others shrilled, "—*for God's sake, Carmack!*"

It was a matter of triage, Carmack thought, floundering inwardly for justification. There was no way they could all make it.

Tallman shrieked, her twitching arm going blue—then it was dragged upward as something smashed her body about, flew ceilingward in the space left by the partly open door, smacked hard into the top of the frame with shattering force, only to immediately whip downward again, slapping the floor like the dead meat it had become. Something was wrenching Dr. Tallman's body; something else was at the others. Carmack could hear them sobbing, could hear enormous jaws gnashing, flesh wetly rending.

Tallman's arm again flapped up and down in the slot of the door, splashing blood, as if the door itself was eating it . . . and finally it severed, the crudely amputated limb falling onto the floor of the lab, the door closing most of the way.

It wasn't over. Tallman was still alive, out there, her screams alternating with begging . . . and bubbling sounds . . .

But Carmack felt a little relief, seeing the steel door finish closing—maybe he was safe now!—until something began pounding on it with jackhammer force. The door shuddered, creaking, and dust drifted from the ceiling.

Carmack recoiled, stumbled to the video-comm panel, forced himself to concentrate on tapping the keyboard, setting up a transmission to home—light-years away.

The light went green, signifying *open channel,* and he began, "This is Dr. Carmack—" He had to raise his voice to be heard over the screaming from the corridor. "—at Classified Research, Olduvai! ID 6627! We've had a level-five breach, implement quarantine procedures immediately—"

A final sobbing cry from beyond the door . . . the sound of tearing. Crunching bone. A sound—what was it? Was it the sound of flesh being gobbled down?

"—I repeat! Implement level-five quarantine procedures *now!*"

He hit the SEND button. The screen read out,

TRANSMISSION SENT.
TIME UNTIL RECEPTION:
2:56:18 . . . 17 . . . . 16 . . .

Christ, he thought, *almost three hours before they'd even get the message* . . . The pounding at the door redoubled. Almost methodical now. Thud. Thud. *Thud.*

He turned to see that the metal door was denting

inward. This room was supposed to be supremely reinforced, ultrahigh security. And he wasn't safe even here.

He turned desperately back to the comm screen.

2:56:11 . . . 10 . . . 9 . . .

And a feeling washed over Carmack as he watched the hopeless countdown. A feeling that was also a realization of his fate.

So this is it, he thought.

This is what doom feels like.

TWO

REAPER IS ON point, that hot, wet dusk on the edge of the methane fields, five miles north of the fuel-processing center. Reaper is buzz cut, clean-shaven, with sharp features, two dark slashes for eyebrows, and dark eyes as grim as his name. His real name is John Grimm; the other guys in the "Privines"—slang for Privatized Marines—called him Reaper, and by now he answers to it. Monikers are a tradition in their unit.

So the Japanese guy coming through the Amazonian rain forest after Reaper is just Mac; and after him, part of their single-file patrol, is a bulky, implacable black man, who goes by Destroyer—which'd be a nickname to induce eye-rolling if he hadn't earned it thirty or forty times; then, tall and wiry, comes Duke.

After Duke is Jumper—a red-haired soldier twitchy with nervous energy, perpetual loopy grin, and a humorous squint to his green eyes, always spoiling for a fight. His real last name is Cable—he's been there for Reaper since boot camp.

Then there's Goat. Long face and tuft of beard that goes with the name, mutters under his breath—you can never make out what he's saying—and his hands shake when he's not in a firefight. Brutally efficient when he is.

Bringing up the rear, sunken-eyed and sullen, is plain old Portman—he hasn't been with them long and hasn't earned a combat name.

Each man wears helmets with headsets, lightly armored cammies, RRTS insignia on one shoulder, United Aerospace Corporation patches on the other: *UAC Special Assignment.* Each carries an M-100 combination assault rifle and grenade launcher—they've been specially assigned for the mission . . .

Maybe not the right weapons, Reaper is thinking. Their usual arsenal is what they'd trained with . . .

Somewhere far away, John Grimm shuddered under Plexiglas. He was lying on a cushioned table, with electrodes taped to his temples, the sensors slowly rotating over his cranium scanning his brain, the military therapist having insisted . . .

"I must insist, John," she'd said. "I must insist . . ."

"They insisted on these fucking M-100s," Reaper is muttering, as Duke draws up beside him, on the edge of the clearing. Reaper slings his rifle over his shoulder, raises his right hand to signal a halt, the other hand wiping sweat from his head as he scans the tree line. Interlocked umbrella-shaped trees, branchless for a hundred feet up, make a canopy over most of the rain forest. The path leads through the clearing to the methane fields, but there is no way Reaper is going to take his men into that clearing, an ideal spot for an ambush, without checking it out first. Intel has anti-UAC guerillas heading for the general area of the methane fields, probably bent on sabotage. Maybe they'll hit this one—or maybe not.

"These rifles—I think we're in a goddamn test drive . . ." Reaper adds, swinging the rifle back into readiness again.

"We're *testing* these weapons?" Duke asks softly, looking down at his weapon. "You mean all they did was, like, fire at some targets somewhere?"

"That's what I mean. M-100 hasn't been significantly field-tested. Meaning not tested for reaction to humidity, for starters."

"And goddamn if it ain't humid here," says Duke, wiping his forehead with the back of his hand.

"We should've brought our regular ordnance, left these in the . . . Hold on, you see something move, over about three o'clock, under that tree there?"

"That tree? That's like pointing out a snowflake in a blizzard."

"That yellowish one that's leaning, Duke—look, right there, two frog's hairs to the left—"

"I make the tree, but I don't see any—wait. Yeah. There's someone there . . . I see a weapon! Let's hit cover, John."

Reaper nods and signals the others. The patrol

melts back into the underbrush—but they've been spotted and some anxious guerilla opens fire. A flock of something red and feathery takes to the air, startled by the rattling submachine gun . . . Twigs and leaves shower down close to the patrol as the SMG rounds cut through the brush.

"Anybody hit?"

"No."

"Negative . . . How many are there?"

"No telling. Portman, Duke, you head northeast, see if you can flank them, you other guys with me . . . But not you, Jumper . . ."

Reaper tensed under the glass, fitfully opening his eyes, but seeing only that day in the rain . . . Seeing . . .

"Yes, sir?"

"Jumper, I'm just a corporal, and you don't have to call me sir, goddammit . . ."

"Hey—I like calling you sir, you're such a macho hot pants of a swingin' dick."

"And you're a talented comic. Now lay some fire down over at three o'clock, do not expose yourself . . ." Knowing that was contradictory directions. Firing at the enemy would itself expose Jumper.

"Deploying . . . sir!" Jumper grins and, hunching down, slips off into the brush as another probing strafe of SMG fire chips across a tree trunk, just over their heads.

"Permission to return fire, sir," Destroyer says.

"Nah, not yet, bro," Reaper answers. "You and Portman watch my six, I'm gonna push their lines, see how far I can get before they push back . . ."

"Roger that."

Hunched over, Reaper leads Destroyer and Goat around to the right, skirting the edge of the clearing. It's getting darker: shadows lengthening, air seeming to thicken to transparent blue gel as the sun eases into the horizon. He hears stuttering gunfire from Jumper, jabbing at the guerillas' flank, hears the guerillas returning fire.

Reaper hurries, trying to take advantage of the decoy fire, and finds himself in a narrow opening in the leaf-carpeted, underbrush—

And suddenly there's a young guerilla, SMG in his hands, popping up from behind a lichen-coated fallen tree, his face drawn in fear as he fires sloppily at them—firing in sheer hysteria.

Reaper fires back, and the guerilla goes spinning backward, seeming to fall in slow motion . . .

Reaper writhed under the electrodes, wanting out, feeling trapped in the dimly sensed glass coffin—and trapped in the past. A voice from somewhere was saying, "I think he's fighting the therapy, maybe we'd better . . ."

"No," a woman's voice said, "if he doesn't relive this now, he'll relive it as repression stress, he'll snap in combat . . ."

Goat vaults the log, comes down beside the kid, gun butt at ready to smash his head in if he's still got any fight in him . . . Hesitates. Stares.

The young guerilla—not more than fifteen years

old, Reaper guesses—has been torn open just under the rib cage by the close-range burst from Reaper, and he's lying on his back twisting like a salted slug. Whimpering.

In the glass coffin, Reaper twisted his body exactly as the kid had . . .

The boy is moaning something in his own language. Reaper touches the insta-translator switch on his headset. "I'm sorry," the translator voice says, as the kid repeats himself. "Sorry I let them know we were there . . . I made up for it, Uncle, didn't I? I made them come to me . . ."

It hits Reaper that they are the ones who've been decoyed.

He puts a bullet in the boy's forehead, avoiding looking into his eyes as he does this, and heads for the clearing, touching the headset's transmission node. "Jumper—they're flanking you, we were decoyed over here, they're—"

"I've got 'em, Reaper, I can hold 'em till you get here—"

Gunfire racketing from the jungle.

"—I can hold 'em if . . . dammit it quit on me again . . ."

His voice in the headset lost in crackle for a moment.

"What? What quit on you?"

"This fucking M-100, John, it's jamming, it's—I can't get the grenade launcher to work either—oh fuck here they come . . . where's Duke? Duke! Portman!"

"Reaper—don't go out there!"

Ignoring Destroyer's warnings, Reaper breaks

from cover, sprints across the grassy clearing, risking both mines and small-arms fire—as bullets make blades of grass, just behind him, fly like cuttings from a mower.

"Duke!" Reaper shouts into the headset, "can you guys get Jumper's back?"

"Negative, we're pinned down! My rifle's only working every third round!"

Reaper tries his autorifle's grenade launcher, and he's in luck: he fires a grenade into the jungle, just where the muzzle flash had been. Sees the blast, hears a scream.

Then he reaches the line of trees, punches through like brush like a linebacker through defense, swearing, shouting for Jumper . . .

Finds him sitting up against a tree, with the upper half of his head shot almost evenly away.

Nothing left but some nose, a gaping, blood-drooling mouth.

The guerilla who did for Jumper turns, seeing Reaper running at him—and that's when Reaper's gun jams. But it doesn't matter, because he's using the butt, roaring as he smashes the man's forehead in, throws the rifle at another guerilla, draws his sidearm, snaps off three pistol shots in two faces. Those two go down, but more are coming—then Goat and Destroyer are there, firing from the hip, their own weapons choosing to work.

Reaper screams and fires and screams and . . .

                              *   *   *

"John Grimm? Are you with us?" The lady psych tech's face—a pretty girl, really, if a bit pudgy—smiling down at him. "We lost track of the memory. Stress levels too high—but I do think we made some progress. How do you feel?"

He thought: *Like I'd like to kill you and everyone in here.*

But aloud he said, "I want to go back to my unit. Take all this fucking gear off me."

Reaper was packing his bag, almost cheerful for the first time since they'd gotten back from their tour on the methane fields. How long had it been, six weeks? Seemed like a year.

This part of battle-stress therapy he liked: going on furlough. R&R.

He snorted, as he put a T-shirt in the bag, thinking: *"battle stress."* Pretty term for how you felt when you blew a fifteen-year-old kid in half, then found you'd let the closest thing you had to a friend get his head shot off because you'd misread the situation . . .

And because I agreed to use untested rifles.

The humidity had made the M-100s lock up—they all knew that could happen with cheap ordnance. And UAC was cutting corners on the weaponry. *Give me a good chaingun anytime . . .*

Sarge had trusted him with that patrol—and it'd gone south; it was his cluster-fuck, no one else's.

And that kid . . . probably had been a guerilla for about an hour and a half.

Reaper turned to look at the others, wondering if they thought he was some kind of liability, being ordered to memory therapy.

But they were just chilling in the barracks here in Twentynine Palms, California. Duke, on his bunk with his feet up on a packed kit bag, wearing only a wifebeater and his cammie pants, was squinting against smoke from the cigarette wedged in his lips as he played *Space Invaders* on a laptop. That was normal enough for Duke.

The others were getting ready for leave, too, or already packed. Portman was checking his kit for the third time to see if he'd remembered his condoms. Goat kneeling at his bunk, praying. That's what he'd been doing for a lot of the last six weeks. Praying.

Against orders, Goat had piled up a pretty good collection of human scalps, souvenirs from firefights— but he'd thrown those out, first thing, on coming back. He'd changed, after the methane fields. Something about the guerilla kid being from the same ethnicity as Goat—all too much like a cousin.

Goat had been muttering about God and praying ever since; there was a silver crucifix dangling on his chest.

The new kid—*Kid*, they called him, imaginatively enough—wasn't going on leave. He'd just gotten here: Jumper's replacement. A gangly nineteen-year-old, the Kid was sweeping the floor with an old-fashioned broom—they made him use the broom, although maintenance had sonic sweepers. He looked lost and miserable.

Mac was pitching oranges the length of the room to Destroyer, who was "up to bat," teeth bared.

Reaper thought about complaining about the mess they were making as Destroyer swung the bat, making the orange into a juicy, disintegrating ground ball spattering down the aisle between the bunks . . . but Reaper didn't feel like a hard-ass today. Let Sarge deal with it.

Behind Destroyer was a cardboard cutout of a naked girl wearing a catcher's mask. She caught the next orange on her right breast, as Destroyer whiffed one. Juice ran down her exquisitely taut tummy.

The barracks normally smelled of sweat, leather, and boot-black—but they were getting ready for R&R, so tonight it smelled of aftershave and hair gel.

"I don't fucking believe this shit," Portman said, banging his watch on the end of his metal-frame bunk. He glared at the watch, then at the clock on the wall, comparing. "Six months without a weekend, and the fuckin' transporter's five minutes late. That's five minutes of R&R I'll never get back."

"Relax, baby," Duke said, not looking up from his game. "You're on vacation."

Portman stuck his hands in his pockets, scowling, came to look over Duke's shoulders. "Why do you play those fuckin' stupid old games?"

Duke shot down another video invader with a

16

practiced snap of his index finger. "You ever play chess, Portman? Some games will never die."

Portman walked away, snorting. Duke shook his head sadly at Portman's ingrained philistinism. "This game was *layered,* man."

Mac tossed an orange up, caught it, tested its weight in the palm of his hand as he looked for a pitch opening. "So where are you going, 'Stroyer?"

Destroyer did a couple of near-light-speed practice swings with the bat, grinning as he thought about his leave. "Grover Island. Surfin'. I'm telling you man, their weather is crazy. Thirty-foot breakers."

Destroyer put his finger meditatively to his mouth, licked orange juice. "How about you, Portman?" he asked. Every so often one of them remembered to try to "include" Portman.

"I'm goin' go down to El Honto," Portman said, a dreamy look coming into his eyes, just as if he was going to talk about sitting on the porch with his dear old granny, "lock myself in a motel with a bottle of tequila and three she-boys."

Destroyer made a face at that but said nothing.

Mac pitched his citrus baseball—Destroyer swung, hit the orange dead on. It angled like a meteor across the barracks and smacked wetly into the wall just above Duke's head. Fingers dancing over keyboard and mouse, Duke didn't even flinch.

Another orange whooshed by, just missing Goat's left ear. Maybe Mac did that on purpose—being a practical joker, he probably did.

"Where you going, Kid?" Duke asked, still not looking up.

The Kid paused in his brooming. Everyone looked at him. He cleared his throat. "Me? Oh . . . I gotta stay here."

Portman made a bogus sound of sympathy. "Oh. Oh that's tragic. Grunt's been here, like, *ninety seconds*. He ain't never been in rotation."

Destroyer reached into his bag of oranges. "Sorry, Kid, you don't get R&R till you've at least been shot at . . ."

Head ducked low, Portman shot the Kid a glare. "My heart fuckin' bleeds for you. Sweep up, you fuckin' pussy."

Duke clucked his tongue in disapproval of Portman's tone. "Hey, this kid was the best marksman in his entire division. Don't listen to 'em, Kid. We're all glad to have you here." After a moment he added, "Now sweep up, you fuckin' pussy."

Everyone laughed at that, even the Kid. Okay, so not everyone, after all: Reaper hadn't laughed since the last assignment. Right now, the Kid saw, as he swept his broom into an alcove off the main room, Reaper was sitting at a table, assembling and disassembling a heavy, gunmetal black light machine gun so fast his fingers blurred. The Kid whistled in admiration at Reaper's skill.

"How fast, sir?" he asked.

"Not fast enough," Reaper said.

Reaper assembled the weapon again. His fingers,

picking up components and snapping them into place, seem to have a life of their own.

"Looks damn fast to me, sir," the Kid said.

Reaper looked at him. "Call me John, Kid. I work for a living, just like you."

The Kid smiled. But the uncertainty must've been there in his face anyway, because Reaper added, "Give it time, Kid. You'll get it."

"What about you, Reaper?" Destroyer asked, raising his voice so Reaper could hear, in his alcove, tossing an orange from hand to hand. "Where you going?"

Reaper didn't answer.

They all turned to look—they knew about the psych-tech. They'd picked up on his mood, anyway, you couldn't miss it.

You felt the burn of his bad mood like a tanning light on sunburn, Destroyer thought.

"Yeah what's it gonna be, Reaps?" Duke asked—actually glancing up from the game this time. "An armed conflict someplace quiet."

"Little relaxing jungle warfare?" Portman chimed in.

Duke grinned. "Or you gonna stay here cleanin' your piece, doing push-ups?"

Reaper winked at the Kid, picked up his rifle. "Well you know, Duke, I thought maybe I'd drop by your mom's house, wait in line."

The others laughed. Duke didn't. Reaper just stared him down.

Reaper didn't feel like letting them know that for

once he was looking forward to R&R. He figured maybe some vacation would get him into another frame of mind. Anything so he could stop thinking about Jumper. That day in the jungle.

He put the gun aside, and went to pack his duffel.

But he was wasting his time, packing for R&R. He didn't know it yet, but he wasn't going on furlough.

He was going to Hell.

In the dimly lit, spartan NCO quarters down the hall, sat the NCO himself, the guy whose men just called him Sarge. He sat on his bunk, shirtless, staring at a blank wall. Big guy. About as muscular as you can be without being pussy enough to resort to steroids. Head shaved, dark skin reflecting his indeterminate racial mix. But you could see the tattoos—he's a living canvas for tattoos muraling his massive shoulders, down his arms, across his chest: each one a souvenir of a campaign, or an invasion—an invasion of a whorehouse, in some cases.

Anybody just walking in might've thought he was talking to himself, till they noticed the headset.

"Go ahead . . ." He listened. Nodded to himself. "Access level of threat," he said. "Code black. Containment or quarantine . . ."

He was repeating what someone was saying to him, verifying, confirming it to memory.

". . . Extreme prejudice . . . Search and destroy . . . Orders received and understood."

20

Sarge stood up and shrugged into a cammie T-shirt, already on his way out the door, down the hall, his big boots ringing on the steps down to the barracks.

At the bottom of the stairs he took one step out into the barracks, and the laughter in the room ceased. Everyone looked at him with a mixture of dread and anticipation.

"Ah, *shit*," Portman muttered.

Something in Sarge's face, his whole manner clued them in to what was coming.

"Listen up," Sarge said. A voice like an electric bass on its lowest note. The Marshall amp's volume knob was on three but it could go up to ten. "Leave is canceled."

The men looked at one another. Amazement. Disgust. Wry resignation. No one with the nerve to complain, though it was obvious from Portman's expression that he'd like to. Finally, looking at those expressions, Duke had to laugh out loud.

"You got a problem, Duke?" Sarge asked.

"Me, Sarge? Hell, no. I love my job." Duke smiled sunnily. Mac grinned.

Sarge just looked back at him, his dark, deeply etched face almost expressionless.

It was time to ask the obvious question. They waited. Finally, Destroyer asked it. "Whassup, Sarge?"

"We got us a game." He looked at the Kid. "Kid—you're up."

The Kid leaned his broom against a locker. Reaper

could tell he didn't know what to do with himself after that. Just sort of stood there in the middle of the floor.

"You're in the RRTS now, boy," Sarge went on. "And what do we do in the RRTS?"

Everyone responded to that one at once: *"Pray for war!"*

Except for Goat, who only shook his head. He'd been praying along different lines.

Reaper was thinking maybe it was better this way. In some part of his mind he'd been afraid he might be a loose cannon in the civilian community. The way he'd been feeling, it might be dangerous if he got drunk.

He didn't want to spend any time in prison. Not even a civilian one.

"Fall in," Sarge told them, his eyes on Reaper as he spoke.

Portman growled deep in his throat but fell in with the others to file out of the room, heading upstairs.

"Great vacation," Duke muttered to Destroyer, as they went. "They go so quick, don't they?"

"Almost like we've never been away."

Reaper started to go with them—but Sarge stopped him with a hand on his shoulder.

"Not this time, Reaper."

"What?" Reaper was genuinely surprised.

"Take the furlough. We can handle this one."

"We got a *game,* Sarge." The term in this unit's

argot meant it was going to be tough—balls-out, hard-core tough. Yeah: maybe that was just what he needed. Something so demanding there'd be no time to think. That was another problem with R&R: you had too much time to think. "We got a game, I'm ready."

And Reaper started obstinately for the stairs.

"It's Olduvai," Sarge said, simply.

Reaper stopped in his tracks. A shiver went through him. A feeling like superstitious dread. "Olduvai?"

"Just take the leave."

"Is that an order?"

"It's a recommendation."

Reaper had been stopped for a moment by the thought of Olduvai. The personal ramifications of it. But those connections were exactly why he had to go . . .

Still. It'd be hard to be objective.

Sarge looked at him—then turned and climbed the stairs, leaving him alone to think.

But thinking was something Reaper was trying to avoid, lately.

RRTS Six, without Reaper, was crossing the tarmac in the predawn grayness. They were headed to the big, armored transport chopper, already warming up, its rotors lazily turning. It showed their squadron's insignia: a gun and knife crossed, twined by a fanged serpent.

They clambered into the large troop bay of the chopper, went immediately to their spots along the face-to-face wall-mounted jump seats.

Each one grabbed a weapon from the overhead rack—the one they specialized in, or, in the case of the Kid, the ones they were cleared for.

Destroyer grabbed an enormous chaingun—an ordinary man would have trouble even lifting it, let alone shooting the thing. Almost tubular in overall shape, with its primary handle up top, designed to be wedged against the hip while fired, it was fed with long, long chains of 10mm armor-piercing bullets.

"Any idea where we're going?" the Kid asked, getting his own ordnance down from the rack.

"Yeah," Destroyer said, slinging an extra ammo chain over his shoulder. "Wherever they send us."

The weapon itself spoke up, then—its computerized identity lock system said, in a monotone:

"RRTS Special Ops clearance verified. Handle ID: Destroyer."

Goat stood a moment, looking at the small worn Bible in his hand—then he put it in his coat pocket, so he could have both hands free to heft the double-barreled, multiround shotgun . . .

"RRTS Special Ops clearance verified. Handle ID: Goat."

Portman grabbed the plasma rifle. It was made of light, artificially hardened maxiplastics, its design bulky, jutting with attachments. When properly charged it had the power to fire ionized plasma capable of breaking down the bonds of the target's molecules. Though it looked as primitive as a triceratops, it was sophisticated, if anything this murderous could be called sophisticated. Portman chuckled, hefting the plasma rifle. It made him feel like his balls had just doubled in size.

And the weapon spoke up: *"RRTS Special Ops clearance verified. Handle ID: Portman."*

The Kid started for a chaingun, but Destroyer shook his head at him. He hadn't been cleared for the weapon yet. The Kid sighed and took the two handheld semiautomatics.

And the automatics, speaking in chorus, confirmed it: *"RRTS Special Ops clearance verified. Handle ID: The Kid."*

The Kid winced. "'The Kid'?"

The Kid was looking forward to getting a new nickname. Once he'd said as much to Duke, hinting that maybe he could earn a handle a little ballsier than the Kid. Duke had said, "Your handle's too small for you to get a bigger handle."

"He couldn't *handle* it," Portman had chimed in, thinking he was pretty cute.

"If he handles it, it better be in private. I don't want to see that in the barracks."

The Kid had kept his mouth shut about it after that.

Katshuhiko "Mac" Takaashi took the massive Combo ATS Grenade Launcher and Elephant Gun off the rack. He made a low growling *Mmmm* sound as he hefted it, like a man who's just bitten into a perfect cut of steak. This was so much better than the M-100.

"*RRTS Special Ops clearance verified, Handle ID: Mac.*"

Gregory "Duke" McGreevy lit a cigarette with one hand, grabbed his automag with the other: light, similar to a Mack 10, but chockablock with lethal rounds, it had decent long-range accuracy.

He twirled the automag, as its ID chip said, almost companionably: "*RRTS Special Ops clearance verified. Handle ID: Duke.*"

"Oh yeah," Duke said. "Say my name, baby."

A huge hand reached into the overhead rack, in one scoop—in that one hand—taking both a sniper rifle and a big 65mm pistol. He took the rifle in one hand—

"*RRTS Special ops clearance verified. Handle ID: Sarge.*"

—and stuck the pistol in his holster. "All set?" Sarge asked.

He turned to shout the liftoff order to the chopper pilot up forward . . .

"Hold it!" came a deep voice from the tarmac—someone just outside the chopper passenger hatch.

They all turned as one to see John "Reaper" Grimm entering, dressed for combat, complete with helmet.

"You sure about this?" Sarge asked, his voice soft, as discreet as he could manage in the circs.

For answer, Reaper selected his handheld machine gun: lighter than the chaingun but lethal close in, good accuracy for longer ranges—six hundred rounds max, sixty-round clips. Reliable—no matter the humidity.

"RRTS Special Ops clearance verified. Handle ID: Reaper."

Reaper turned and met Sarge's eyes. Gave out a tiny smile.

Sarge nodded. "Take us up!"

THREE

THE CHOPPER LIFTED off, carrying the squadron to the Ark Facility in Papoose Lake, Nevada.

Strapped into his harness, Reaper noticed the Kid watching him and Destroyer; modeling himself on them, Reaper figured.

Jumper had sort of looked up to Reaper, too . . . Where had it gotten him?

Portman noticed the Kid watching Reaper. He grinned. "You know, Kid, it's funny. Couple days ago I tell Sarge I could use a little pussy. Next day, he brings you onto the team."

Annoyed at Portman's constant ragging on the Kid, Reaper said, "Don't give me an excuse, Portman. No one here will miss you."

But the Kid was distracted by Goat—who was pulling a knife.

Goat's shirt was open, his scarred chest exposed. He ran a thumb along the edge of the combat knife, locking eyes with the Kid—then turned the blade against himself, digging the point into the skin. He looked down at himself, concentrating on his handiwork as he carved a cross into his skin—amongst all the other crosses scarring his chest. The chopper gave a sudden shudder, making Goat's hand jog, so the bottom of the cross came out a bit crooked. He had to start another one, to get it right. Then the chopper lurched again . . . Goat frowned. And started another cross.

The Kid stared. Had to shout over the noise of the chopper. "Fuck is he doing, man?"

Portman chuckled. "Mission log. Goat used to collect human scalps. But he's all straightened out now, aintcha, Goat?"

Goat's dark eyes flickered over Portman, then drilled the Kid. The Kid swallowed and paled.

The chopper's engine roared; the blades beat a drumroll against the sky.

Sarge glanced out the window. They were far enough away from base to get into the classified briefing. "Look in!" he shouted.

He slapped a disc into the briefing console on the bulkhead. "This is what we got from Simcom," Sarge told them. He turned the volume all the way up so they could hear over the racket of the chopper.

The VDU screen flashed, and they watched as a fuzzy image of Dr. Carmack appeared.

There was Carmack's terrified face, looking down at the minicam node on the comm-sole he'd used for that transmission. The image fluttered, resolved. Carmack's voice came across only a little less fuzzy than the picture.

". . . is Dr. Carmack at Classified Research, Olduvai! ID 6627. We've had a level-five breach, implement quarantine procedures now!" The sound of a distant pounding. *"I repeat, implement level-five breach quarantine procedures now!"*

You'd think that a face couldn't show any more terror than his did. But as he looked up at something off camera, his face contorted into something more primeval than mere terror. Like something a small animal's feeling as it's about to be torn apart by a hawk.

And then the image dissolved into snowy static.

The men in the chopper looked at one another.

"We got a quarantine situation on Olduvai," Sarge said. "They sent that message before the research team stopped responding to communications."

"Olduvai . . . ?" Portman said.

Sarge nodded. "Three-and-a-half hours ago. UAC has shut down the lab. We go up there, locate the team, eliminate the threat, and secure the facility."

"What threat?" the Kid asked.

"Goes like this, see," Duke said. "If it's trying to kill you, it's a threat."

They hung in their harnesses, absorbing the briefing—and each one came to a stop on the name *Olduvai.* They were going to that mysterious region on the planet Mars. And that meant . . .

The Kid leaned over to whisper to Duke. "We're going through the Ark?"

"Don't worry, Kid," Duke said. "You're gonna love it."

The ironic smiles on the faces of the other men, at that, didn't make the Kid feel any better. The Ark was some kind of wormhole to another world—and maybe the scariest thing was, it was an alien technology. The compound's end of the Ark had been retroengineered from something found in the digs on Olduvai, Mars. An alien doorway to an alien world.

A long trip, mostly through darkness. They were flying over the sprawling, intricate city: all that remained between them and their first destination; they flew between shimmering towers, past gracefully sweeping buildings of synthetic steel and intelligent glass glimmering with the soft light impregnated into their very girders; over interlacing freeways, chains of glowing computer-guided vehicles. There were no brake lights, no headlights, just interior lights because the cars drove themselves. They never jammed, never crashed.

It was coming up to dawn, and the chopper was almost to the Nevada teleport facility when Sarge unbuckled himself from his harness, went over to sit by Reaper.

"How long's it been?" Sarge asked, leaning close to Reaper.

Reaper reluctantly answered, "Ten years."

"You sure she's even still there?" Sarge persisted.

Reaper looked at him coldly. "You gotta face your demons sometime."

Sarge wasn't ready to drop it. Sarge had no comprehension of small talk at all. He never spoke unnecessarily—but when he did speak, he dropped a subject exactly when he was done with it, not a second before. "This better not spoil my day."

He slapped Reaper on the shoulder, stood, and moved carefully to the front—sometimes, when the chopper shifted in the sky, he looked like a man walking a tightrope. He turned to address the whole team.

"I want this spit and polish, no bullshit!" he told them. He spotted Portman listening to something on headphones. Might be music, might be soundporn. "Portman, get that crap out of your ears. LZ approaching . . ." Sarge braced himself, looking at the altitude indicator as the chopper eased down to a landing. "T-minus fifteen. Fourteen . . ."

The Kid looked out the window—they were approaching a great swatch of shadow on the far side of the town they'd just passed. The sky was graying with first light, but the ground down there was still dark. It looked like they were going to crash into that bleak opacity—but then lights flicked on, outlining the landing pad, and the chopper settled onto it.

The doors opened. Cold air gushed in; their breath steamed as they grabbed their gear and jumped out into the icy prop wash.

Nothing out there but the landing lights, and the distant sparkle of the city's skyline.

"Double-time!" Sarge shouted. "We're on the move!"

They ran across grass now, jogging over the otherwise-empty field in formation, leaving the landing pad and the chopper behind.

Where, the Kid wondered, *are we double-timing to? There's nothing out here. We're just running into the goddamned darkness . . .*

Suddenly the ground began to elevate itself, in front of them: an illuminated block of stainless steel rose up, humming, out of a subterranean shaft, in the midst of what a moment ago had been an empty, grassy field. The Kid lost his double-time rhythm in his surprise, slowing to stare, blurting, "Holy shit . . ."

Passing the Kid, Portman slammed a shoulder into him—theoretically a reminder to stay in formation but really it was about Portman getting off on slamming the Kid.

The Kid was the last one to hustle onto the elevator that would take them down—down, only to be projected upward into the sky, when the moment came.

Seeing the Kid come into the elevator at the last possible second, Sarge told him: "You hesitate, people die."

The doors irised shut . . . and the elevator dropped like stone released into a mining shaft.

Fourteen levels down . . .

* * *

Like so many other nightmares, it really started with a slick, corporate lobby. They could've been waiting to audition for a viddy commercial, Reaper thought, as they stepped out of the elevator and looked around.

United Aerospace Corporation logos were arranged symmetrically with wall-mounted plasma screens; the screens played UAC infomercials maundering on about the company's globe-spanning services.

A slender man dresssed as slick as the lobby was striding toward them, extending his hand. His face was frozen in a public-relations mask of friendliness, only his eyes showing how intimidated he was by the big, heavily armed men in the strike squadron.

Here comes the suit, Reaper thought.

"Sandford Crosby, UAC public relations," said the suit. "On behalf of UAC, welcome to the facility. If you could follow me, please."

He turned on his heel, almost spinning in place, and led the way, in a hurry. The squadron exchanged glances, shrugged, and followed.

"Has anyone passed through the Ark since the emergency?" Sarge asked.

Sandford glanced back at Sarge. "Oh, no no, Sergeant." He indulged in a carefully measured laugh. "This isn't an *emergency.* I believe what we have on Olduvai is officially a *situation.*"

Sarge snorted but said nothing.

"Should the 'situation' deteriorate," Reaper asked,

as they almost trotted down a corridor, "has a plan been drawn up to evacuate the civilians?"

He was as concerned about getting them out of his hair as much as getting them to safety. Civilians pretty much just got in the way of getting a job done. And then there was that certain civilian . . .

Sandford seemed to pick up speed, gesturing for them to hurry along close behind him. "The guys at corporate feel that won't be necessary. What you're doing for us here is really a 'fact-finding mission.' "

"Through here, please," Sandford added, gesturing toward the door with a limp hand.

"How many people up there?" Reaper asked.

"UAC employs eighty-five permanent research staff on Olduvai," Sandford replied, crisply.

They passed through the door into the Ark Chamber Prep Room. Sandford frowned, noticing that Duke, as usual, was smoking. "Please extinguish the cigarette. The Ark is an ultrahigh-frequency fusion reactor. One spark and—"

"Gettin' so you can't smoke anywhere anymore." Duke stubbed it out in the callused, blackened palm of his hand—making Sandford blanch.

Sandford guided the squadron to the base of a mirrored cylinder protected by armed UAC Security Personnel. The armed guards here were more than security guards, but less than the level of soldier represented by the squadron, and they knew it. They gave Sarge and his men flat looks that seemed to say,

I could take you. Only, they couldn't, and they knew that, too.

The Kid stared at the Ark Containment Cylinder. From there, they would be individually projected through a wormhole, across space, and onto the surface of the region of Mars known as Olduvai.

A translucent plaque hung in the air above them, containing twenty names etched into a scroll graphic.

Maybe stalling, the Kid asked Sandford, "What're all those names?"

Sandford glanced up. Clearly not liking the subject. "Oh that. That's a UAC-funded memorial to the early pioneers of the Ark, who in the pursuit of perfecting this groundbreaking and unique technology, made the ultimate sacrifice . . ."

Reaper looked at Sandford, wondering if he were serious, coming out with this PR palaver. *"This groundbreaking and unique technology?"*

A different part of the speech stuck with Portman. "Ultimate sacrifice?"

Sandford went on, reassuringly. "This was long, long ago, before they perfected the crystalline structure."

The Kid looked at the shiny cylinder awaiting him. Then at Goat and Destroyer, close beside him. He swallowed. "You . . . done this before?"

Goat surprised him by answering a direct question. "Once. Training mission." Three words. It was something.

Reaper had gone through it as a kid—but he'd been sedated. Not this time . . .

Duke slapped the kid on the back, making him stagger, and grinned. "Hope you had a big dinner!"

Sandford took a remote controller from his pocket, tapped a code, and the cylinder slid open.

They stepped through, and the curved wall closed behind them, leaving them inside a shiny metal vertical tube, with just enough room for them and a drop of mercurial liquid floating, weightless, in the center of the chamber. The light seemed to warp across its surface; the rippling interior of the drop seemed to enfold infinity. If you looked at the edge of the drop, it became the center; and the center became the edge, around and around . . .

"That's it?" the Kid said, blinking. "I thought the Ark was, like—a spaceship. Not . . ."

". . . A metaphor?" Reaper said.

The squad stared at the hovering droplet.

Reaper found himself wondering: *How big is it?* One moment the floating quicksilver droplet at the heart of the Ark seemed like something you could fit into your hand. The next moment it was bushel-sized, and getting bigger. It seemed all of those sizes. Then it seemed, impossibly, as big as a whale though it was in a room a whale couldn't fit into. A manifestation of the quantum-uncertainty realm, it was constantly shifting within itself. Interesting . . .

He smiled at himself. *The apple doesn't fall far from the tree.*

Reaper came from a family of scientists—he was clearly a black sheep, but the interest simmered in him nonetheless, and he followed science when he wasn't on assignment. He didn't let the rest of the squadron know it though . . . as far as they knew he was a stone-cold jarhead and nothing more.

Sarge gave Sandford an order then, just as if he were a new recruit. "Soon as we're through, lock down the surface elevator here for a six-hour standard quarantine."

Sandford hesitated half a second, as if not sure he should be taking direction from Sarge, then nodded. He turned to the others. "Please form two lines. In the unlikely event something goes wrong, there are exits behind me here, here—" He pointed. "And here." He paused, glanced at them—and Reaper could see Sandford wanted to get out of there. "Any questions?"

Duke held up his big-assed weapon. Asked straight-faced, "Does this classify as 'carry-on'?"

Sandford managed a thin smile at that.

Sarge cocked his weapon and walked over to the Ark. He stepped within its range of sensitivity . . .

It expanded to envelop his body in a glistening, faintly wobbling globular shell.

Until, in a flash of blue light, it condensed backed to its original size—as if it had swallowed Sarge and digested him.

Sarge was gone.

Shaken, the Kid took a step back, sucking in his

breath. Reaper grabbed his elbow. Locked eyes with him. The look said it all. The Kid swallowed, and nodded, held his ground.

Reaper clapped the kid on the shoulder, then turned and walked to the quicksilver droplet . . .

He felt himself enter its field of sensitivity—it felt like immersing himself in cold water that was instantly warm water, then icy again . . .

Suddenly the quivering droplet seemed to leap at his eyes—and there was a wall of living silver, all around him. A series of anomolous smells. The smell of a campfire; the smell of ozone; the smell of roses; the smell of death. A flash of light . . . blue— then shifting to blue-white, incandescent white . . .

Reaper felt himself dissolving, his body turning to liquid, his flesh like sugar diffused in living water, bones becoming a skeleton of ice melting down in a second—splash—then a riot of sounds: roaring and singing and piercing screams and gibbered words and thundering bits of half-forgotten symphonies; his consciousness spun in a vortex of sickening black light, striated by colors that were all wrong, just *wrong;* those colors don't exist *anywhere.* Reaper thought he saw his father fly past him, translucent and ghostly, mouthing something, trying to warn him; then the light and color shrank away, replaced by blackness rich with *feeling,* tactile sensations from some forgotten corner of his brain: a woman's soft hair brushing against his naked shoulder, a spiderweb breaking on his cheek, moss under bare boyhood feet, the surprisingly soft flesh of his enemy's throat that time in the desert when his gun had jammed and he'd had to leap on the guy and strangle him, the feeling of blood running across his wrists, a jawbone cracking against his fist, a bullet crashing into his shoulder, shattering pain—

The cryptic opacity was split by shimmering light, and he could feel himself solid and whole again—but he was falling, falling up; no, falling down; no, he was being pulled sideways, he was nauseatingly spinning, he was falling through a flash of frozen blue light . . .

Into the wormhole chamber on Olduvai, Mars.

FOUR

REAPER MANAGED TO stay on his feet as he emerged from the Ark at the UAC Research Facility on Olduvai, Mars, though the room was shifting, his head throbbed and his stomach was trying to crawl out of his body.

He turned as Destroyer came through—staggering. Destroyer gave him a sickly grin.

That shit is *fucked up*, the grin said.

The others were coming through, gulping, pale, looking like they badly wanted to throw up.

But only the Kid actually did: he took three steps, bent over, and puked. Then it was Portman's turn.

Reaper smiled at that—though his gut still convulsed inside him—because Portman was always coming on like he was so much tougher than the Kid.

Portman straightened, wiping his mouth. "Why we gotta come all this way? Why can't the UAC rent-a-cops fix this bullshit?"

The metal cylinder whirred open, and they were all stepping unsteadily down off the platform.

"Jesus," the Kid muttered, holding his middle. "Is it always that rough?"

"Believe me," someone coming into the room said, "it used to be rougher . . ."

Reaper turned to see a man who'd been grafted into a kind of sleek wheelchair—a cyberchair, a module that enclosed everything below his sternum. The cyberchair seemed to merge seamlessly with his upper half. He drifted effortlessly forward, the wheelchair apparently responding to his nervous system, and extended a hand. The wheelchair graft seemed to call for an older man, but this guy had a boyish face, curly hair, an impish glitter in his eye. "Time was," he went on, "Ark travel was susceptible to patches of, let's say, *major* turbulence."

"What's he mean?" the Kid whispered to Reaper.

"He means he went to one galaxy and his ass went to another."

"Call it a scientific miscalculation," the man in the cyberchair went on. "Unbelievable as it may seem, UAC does make the odd tiny mistake." There was a moment when they were all blinking at him, obviously thinking, *Who the hell are you?* He smiled and answered the unasked question. "Marcus Pinzerowski. Call me Pinky."

A gaunt man in uniform came toward them—some of the gauntness might've been the worry etched on his face. Reaper had never seen the uniform before. A lieutenant of some kind.

The lieutenant only glanced at the puke on the floor. "Lieutenant Hunegs, UAC Security Officer. Welcome to Olduvai. Pinky is your acting Comms officer."

42

Portman whispered it, but it was loud enough for Pinzerowski to hear: "The sparko's a gimp?" Pinky pretended not to hear.

Reaper sighed. He wanted to smack Portman—not the first time he'd wanted to do that.

Wiping his mouth, the Kid was gaping around at the wormhole chamber. A little seamier, darker than the one they'd just left. Looked like he was thinking: *So this is another world? Doesn't look like it.*

Sarge shook the officer's hand. "Sergeant Mahonin, RRTS."

Pinky handed Sarge a fistful of access cards on chains, to wear around their necks. "Access chips for the security doors." He led them into the next room—a much bigger room dominated by computer monitors, comm consoles.

Sarge—always ready to get on with it—gestured toward a console to one side. "Put us up, Pinky."

Pinky whirred over to a console, tapped touch-responsive spots on the screen. "Activating remote personal surveillance."

On the screen over the console, images appeared from the viewpoint of the digicams—fiber-optic microcameras on their chest armor. The idea was to transmit their point of view to the communications center so everyone there could see what the squadron was seeing. Most of the time, the squadron had kept the digicams turned off. You didn't always want what you did in the field on record.

Pinky stared into the screen. One of the little

43

thumbnails was just a blank outline. "Who's Dantalian?" he asked.

The squadron looked at the Kid. Mac shook his head, reached over and slapped the switch on the Kid's chest-mounted CDM. It blinked green—and his thumbnail on the comm screen lit up with an image of Mac chuckling at him.

The digicams were up, but there was a second-line of point-of-view connect. "Circle up!" Sarge ordered.

All the squadron—except the Kid—suddenly pointed their guns at other members of the team. The Kid started at this—it was a little lacuna in his training.

But on Pinky's screen, another set of images showed. "Killcams up and running," Pinky said. There were fiber-optic cameras on the guns, too, just below the barrel, so people monitoring the squadron could see what was being shot.

"People," Sarge rumbled, "this room is code red. No one gets in without our permission." He let that sink in, then went on, "Mac—stay here, secure the door. Squad, on me. Let's move it out . . ."

Mac scowled. He didn't like hanging back from the action. He came from a culture that emphasized self-sacrifice, even suicidal risk in the service of the team. But there was no questioning Sarge.

Pinky hit a tab, and hydraulic locking pins clashed, a big metal door rolled aside.

The squadron stepped into an atrium room, a

vault of cobwebbed marble archways and high, shadowy ceilings. Under the arches, along with the ubiquitous UAC logos, the infomercials chattered to themselves, dialed low volume, like lunatics who babbled on no matter what happened.

Reaper noticed rubble in the corners—loose pipes, cracks in the walls, dust. The place wasn't being maintained. One of the screens flickered like it was about to go out.

"Nice," Duke said. "Cozy. Where the fuck *are* we?"

"Couple million miles from breakfast," Goat rumbled, looking disdainfully at a clutch of UAC employees passing through, carrying digital clipboards and giving them frowning looks.

Leading them across the room to another computer console, Hunegs asked, "When can I start evacuating my people out through the Ark, Sargeant?"

Sarge shook his head. "We're at level-five quarantine. So nobody's going anywhere."

Reaper started to ask about the quarantine—there had to be some protocol to get these people out if it came time—then noticed the woman standing at the computer console.

Samantha. Samantha Grimm. Reaper's own sister.

It was an uncomfortable moment. He'd been expecting to see her here of course—just not so soon.

Portman was hitting on a couple of minor female technicians—with nice legs. "Hey, uh—we're up here on vacation, we were wondering what you ladies were doing later?" They looked at each other, amused—and not at all tempted. "We—" He broke off, seeing Samantha Grimm. Who was in a whole different league from the techs. Flat-out gorgeous—and with the absolute minimum makeup. "Hold that thought," Portman mumbled to the techs. Turning instead to Samantha as she walked toward them. "Excuse me, we're up here on vacation, we wondered . . ."

She walked past him as if he didn't exist, stepped up to Reaper and Sarge. And waited with a kind of quiet authority.

"Sergeant," Hunegs said, "this is Dr. Samantha Grimm, the UAC science officer assigned to retrieve data from the lab."

"Sergeant," she said.

"Dr. Grimm," Sarge rumbled. Managing not to react to her beauty—mostly. But his eyes flicked over her body, just once.

She had light eyes, strawberry blond hair, the suggestion of a dimple in her chin. But her expression was all business. She was just twenty-six but, Reaper knew, she was a brilliant scientist—she'd graduated from high school at the age of thirteen. She'd always had an interest in the past, in forgotten worlds. So she'd gotten her doctorate in "archaeological genetics"—almost following in their parents' footsteps, but finding her own path. She'd always looked for her own way to do things.

Her eyes met her brother's—just a flicker of reaction. Some warmth, not much. Reaper had to hand it to her—she was unflappable. They had a troubled history, and there was no room in the unraveling situation on Olduvai for family sentimentality.

"Hello, John," Sam said. She looked at the light machine gun he carried. Just the suggestion of contempt in that look. She'd never gotten over it . . .

"Hello, Samantha."

Duke took off his shades. "Hel-*lo* Samantha!" He waggled his eyebrows at her.

She rolled her eyes and looked at a printout she held in her hands, as if it were infinitely more interesting than Duke. He kept smiling at her.

Reaper gathered that Samantha was being introduced to them for reasons other than politeness. *Assigned to retrieve data?* Were they thinking that she was going along with the squadron? Olduvai he could deal with. But his sister, breathing down his neck? Uh-uh. Besides . . . Sam would be at serious risk, judging from the hints they'd had from the transmissions.

"Sarge," Reaper said firmly, "this mission is code black. We can't take passengers."

Sam turned back to him, those pretty eyes narrowing, going icy. "Excuse me, *Corporal*, but I have orders to retrieve data from the physical anthropology, forensic archaeology—*and* molecular genetics servers—"

"With respect, *Doctor*," Reaper interrupted, not

47

very respectfully, "our orders are to locate and neutralize a present threat. It's not to retrieve some"—he smiled dismissively—"science homework."

She crossed her arms. "That science homework is the core study of a nine-billion-dollar research program. You got the nine bil, fine, cough it up, pal, I'm sure UAC'll call it quits."

"Give me the address," Reaper said blandly, matching her glare for glare, "I'll send a check."

They exchanged scowls for a moment. Then she went on, "I've got an idea, why don't you ask your CO what your orders are?"

Everyone looked at Sarge, a noncom but the closest thing to their CO.

Sarge thought for a moment, then recited, "Contain and neutralize the threat, protect civilians . . . and retrieve UAC property." That contradicted what the suit had said—which was no surprise.

"We finally done here?" Sam said. "'Cause I've got a job to do."

Reaper winced. She'd checkmated him again. She always had beat him unmercifully at chess.

Sam knew what he was thinking—every little thing between them had some kind of nagging family-history resonance to it—and she gave him a chilly look of triumph. Then she turned on her heel and strode off, heading for another computer, giving Reaper's shoulder a push, as if he were rudely in her way, as she went. Reaper watched her go, thinking

48

maybe he should go after her, have everything out. Including the pecking order here.

Sarge took Reaper aside, spoke in undertones. "You *chose* this, Reaper," Sarge reminded him. "Is this gonna spoil my day?"

"There's gotta be someone else—"

"Is this gonna spoil my day?"

Reaper let out a long slow breath. "No, sir."

Sarge nodded—as if to say: *That's right, it won't.* Then he went off to talk to Hunegs.

Duke and Destroyer ambled over, Duke nudging Reaper. "Tell me you didn't let a fine-lookin' piece of ass like that get away from you, Reaper . . ."

Evidently Duke thought Sam having the same surname as Reaper meant "ex-wife."

Sighing, Reaper prudently decided against punching Duke in the nose. "She's my sister."

Duke blinked in surprise. "Really? No shit . . ."

Destroyer shook his head at Duke as Reaper walked away. "Don't do this again, man."

Duke feigned innocence. "Do what?"

"There are three sections to the labs?" Sarge was asking, as he walked beside Sam to the air lock. Hunegs was close behind her, with the squadron.

She nodded. "Archaeology, Genetics, and Weapons Research . . ."

"You test weapons up here?" Portman asked. Articulating everyone's puzzlement over the weapons lab. Not what you expected to go with archaeology and genetics.

Sam shrugged. "Mars is a dead planet. You want that stuff tested up here where it's safe—or in your own backyard?"

They were following her down a corridor. A sign on the wall said, TO AIR LOCK. "This is primarily an archaeological facility. The genetics labs are only here studying the structures of various forms of fossil life. Weapons research is in its own separate area. It has nothing to do with Dr. Carmack's work."

Reaper wasn't sure he bought that. Could be they'd found something that needed . . . special weapons. If they hadn't—why bring the squadron here?

"How many inside when shutdown occurred?" Sarge asked.

Sam considered. "Only Dr. Carmack's team. After he maydayed, we tried all the internal comm systems and the data lines, but there was zero response."

She's acts like she's really on top of things, Reaper thought, annoyed. *Hell, she probably is, knowing her.*

Though Reaper still thought of her as his little sister, he knew better than to underestimate her.

They reached the outer door to the Research Labs division. Two UAC security guards stood at the high-security door—they just managed to drop their looks of excruciating boredom as Sam walked up to the door.

Turning to the others at the door, she went on, ". . . except in one of the carbon-dating labs there was an internal phone left off the hook. The line was live to an admin station upstairs."

"Give you any information?" Reaper asked.

She looked at him with a kind of blank disbelief, as if it was just penetrating to her that here was her brother, in full combat regalia, right in the midst of her crisis.

Then she turned abruptly to the UAC security officer. "Hunegs. Play him the tape."

Hunegs took a small handheld tape recorder from his coat pocket, hit REWIND, then PLAY.

Static, as Reaper bent nearer to hear. Then a woman's voice. "Jesus please help me . . . oh God . . . Mother!" She whimpered—then shrieked. Screaming. "Keep away! Get away!" A piercing cry that made Reaper draw back a few inches, wincing. Then another order of sound entirely—the sound of something being torn apart. A gurgling . . .

Static.

Hunegs pressed STOP. Sarge grunted to himself, then turned to his men. "Any questions?"

They had lots of questions. But they knew there weren't any answers yet. A few minutes earlier, on the way in here, Hunegs had said: *"We're not sure what the threat is. We need you to find out."*

So the squadron cocked their weapons and tried to look like they were all balls and no nerves. They almost managed it, except for the Kid who was chewing his lower lip.

"Open the door," Sarge said.

Sam pushed the green button, the pneumatic bolts hissed and gnashed, the door opened.

Sarge pushed past her and headed into the air lock. The others followed—except Hunegs.

The surface atmosphere of Mars was thin, unbreathable. The labs were supposed to have breathable air but the integrity of their interface with the planetary surface could be breached, hence the air lock.

It was a small stainless-steel cubical room, just big enough for the squadron and Sam. Once the door to the Ark and command facility had sealed behind them, Goat and Portman both pulled handheld particulate scanners from their belt clasps, squinted into them.

"Magnesium, chromium, lead. Normal," Portman announced.

The LAPT in Goat's hand blinked, and chimed; he glanced at its little screen. "All clear."

Sarge motioned, and they opened the door into the corridor.

It was pitch-black out there. Their gun-mounted flashlight beams swept the darkness of the corridor beyond the air lock, scarcely seeming to penetrate it.

And Reaper took the lead, stepping out into the shifting darkness.

FIVE

THE CORRIDOR WAS cold and dark, and there were disturbing, undefined smells in it. Like something you smell as a small child on your first trip to a zoo.

Reaper could smell something reassuringly human, too: his sister's perfume—could feel the warmth of her body close to his right elbow. She'd never admit it, but she was sticking close to him in here. He wished once more he'd found a way to keep her from coming along. She wasn't even armed . . .

"Pinky," Sarge was saying, into his headset, "get us some juice down here, damn it."

There was a response from Pinky, but it was crackly, distorted. Reaper wasn't sure if he'd said yes or no can do.

Sarge didn't wait for more light; he moved down the corridor, leading the way, the narrow flashlight beam from his gun probing ahead. Their gunlights swept over bare walls—not quite bare, there were brown stains, in places: big splashes of dried blood. Wires hung from gaps in the ceiling; the occasional pipe. In the narrow beams of light the dangling wires looked like filaments of living tissue. And the darkness itself seemed to squirm, hinting at shapes just beyond classification.

When Portman spoke, he sounded like he was trying to convince himself: "Five bucks all this shit is a disgruntled employee with a gun . . ."

Sparks spat from a broken power line then, announcing the return of the juice. Reaper spotted a light switch, hit it, and an overhead fluorescent tube came on. But there wasn't much reassurance in the grim, echoing, bloodstained corridor made visible.

Reaper noticed the corridor branching left and right up, ahead . . . which way to go?

"Pinky," Sarge said into his comm, "you get us a schematic?"

There was a pause as Pinky shot them the layout from the mainframe. "Uploading to you now."

Sarge held the flashpoint uplink in his hand, angled downward; it projected a schematic of the lab on the blood-scuffed floor. They all stared at it but it seemed mostly a jumble of interlocked squares. After a moment they made out patterns—and labels: GENETICS, LAB OFFICE, WEAPONS.

"Goat, Portman . . ." Sarge ordered, ". . . Genetics. Destroyer, Kid: the office where Carmack sent the mayday . . ." He pointed with his free hand to indicate the place. "Reaper, keep Dr. Grimm safe on her salvage op. Duke and I will take the Weapons Lab, make sure the hardware's secure." He looked at each subteam as he gave them their assignment, a hard look emphasizing the inflexibility of the orders. And added, "Fluorescent powder marking as rooms are cleared."

The squadron nodded as one and after a final glance at the schematic to get their bearings set off.

In the wormhole chamber, Pinky watched a monitor displaying a layout of the labs, tracking the squadron with GTS blips tailed by their names. The guncams showed in thumbnail images across the top of the screen.

Pinky found himself wondering for the tenth time that day if they were doing the right thing. Complete and instant evacuation would've been wiser. They could return later with a larger force and get the data then. But the way things had been going, the whole base, labs and all, could be destroyed in their absence. And they had to seal off the Ark. Something might get through, otherwise . . .

Still, they might simply be wasting more lives, sending the men in—and Sam. He felt a twinge, thinking about her going in there. He should've tried to talk her out of it. But he knew that'd be like trying to talk the moon out of rising.

He glanced at Mac, leaning against the wall near the door, gun cradled in his arms. Mac was looking at the monitor, frowning, trying to decode the floor plans and blips.

"They're on the move," Pinky told him. After a

moment, looking Mac over—Mac was obviously Oriental—he added, "You don't look like a 'Mac.'"

Mac looked at him expressionlessly. Then recited his full name. "Katshuhiko Kumanosuke Takaashi."

Pinky nodded. "So . . . Mac!"

Sarge and Duke moved down their divergent corridor, toward the Weapons Lab. Wall signs confirmed they were going the right way.

Duke wondered just what kind of weapons were squirreled away down here. How much had they been tested? The M-100 in the jungle was still a fresh memory—a bad memory. If they tried out one of these weapons—and how could a weapons expert like Sarge resist?—they might find out why the damned things were locked away up here . . .

It never occurred to him to try to talk this over with Sarge. Someone else maybe, not Sarge.

Duke wished he'd been assigned to go with Reaper. Someone to talk to. One thing Sarge wasn't, was someone to talk to.

They kept on, in silence, through passages where the lights flickered; past cross corridors that led into restless shadow, where things moved—intuited more than seen. Things that snuffled and chuckled and clicked their teeth together.

Both Sarge and Duke felt the things out there. And neither one of them said a word about it.

*   *   *

Destroyer and the Kid swept the back hallway and storage rooms, marking with the fluorescent powder as they went.

"Clear," the Kid said into his headset, as they passed through another nondescript room. Trying to keep the nervousness out of his voice.

The Kid had come to the squadron right from secondary training, just a week before. But in the short time he'd been with Unit Six he'd come to look up to Destroyer. Didn't want him to know how scared he was. Destroyer was tough, all right: he could go from smiling to flinty in a heartbeat. But—despite some ribbing—he'd spent a long time showing the Kid how to field strip his weapons, in the days before this assignment. He'd given him a couple of lessons in hand-to-hand fighting, hardly hurting him at all—if he'd wanted to, he could have broken the Kid's neck—and he'd listened to the Kid talk about his family without once making fun of him for it the way Portman had. Destroyer had shown the Kid a holo-cube of his wife; had smiled at the Kid's cell-images of his girlfriend Millie. Hard-nosed moniker or not, the Kid suspected that Destroyer had a soft heart.

Unless you were the enemy.

The animal lab was freaking Portman out.

Monkeys, rats, dogs in cages, some of them alive. All of them staring at Portman and Goat as they passed. Some whimpering, some growling, some cringing in terror. Patches of bare, inflamed skin on some of the animals where the fur had been shaved off for operations, for wire inserts; stitches across skulls and bellies. Nasty. Poor little fuckers.

And there—a series of shelves with dissected animals suspended in big jars of viscous liquid: gels and solutions glowing livid yellow, blue, red. Some of these creatures were still alive, intubated and sprouting electrodes. Visible hearts beating.

Just to ease the tension, Portman considered making a joke about how maybe they'd find a goat in here with the lab animals, and it'd be one of Goat's relatives. Goat—*goat*, get it? But he glanced at Goat's grim face and thought better of it. Goat had even less sense of humor than Sarge.

Flatscreen monitors on the deserted lab's consoles streamed anatomical and genetic monitoring diagrams, MRI images, X-rays, 3-D constructs, as if ghostly technicians were there to study them. Some of the MRIs showed what you'd expect—familiar mammalian organs.

But some of them looked completely unfamiliar. Unnatural. What the hell was *that* thing? A severed head, all tubed up and twitching, it was mostly jaws, clusters of eyes. Where'd they find that? And was he imagining those eyes following him as he walked by?

He got the strange notion that he could hear it thinking. *Kill you*, it was thinking. *Want to kill you. Please. Let me. Kill you.*

58

Seemed you got crazy notions, in a place like this . . .

"Pinky, you getting this?" Goat asked, turning his guncam to take in the lab animals.

"There's another chamber to the north," Pinky prompted them.

Goat jabbed his gun that way, and Portman nodded. They headed north, going through a door into what looked like the surgery: there was a ventilator, EKG, bloodied cutting equipment, a gurney with the heaviest restraints Portman had ever seen. Something about that gurney, those suggestive restraints made Portman want to turn, run the way they'd come back to the air lock.

Get a grip, chickenshit, he told himself. He needed to get his game on. Sometimes it helped to listen to speed-metal, to something that really rocked—it seemed to throw a switch in his nervous system, turned him around so that he went from defensive to ready for action. He found his earphones, plugged them in, hit the PLAY button. Pounding music: Sado-Nation's vocalist singing:

> *There's a truth you can't avoid*
> *Listen to Johnny Paranoid*
> *Your life will end in the burning void,*
> *Shaking shaking shaking like a rock 'n' roll chord . . .*

He grimaced. Maybe not the best selection to listen to right now. He pulled the headphones off.

Above the gurney there was a railing in the ceiling, a winch system. They followed it the length of the room, to another, bigger chamber . . .

They stepped out into the echoing, circular room. And almost stumbled into a pit.

Looked to be twenty-some feet down to the bottom of the perfectly round pit. Blood splashed the floor down there. The pit's walls were lined with stainless steel.

Goat shined his gunlight into the pit, swept it back and forth. Gouges marked the steel, almost to the upper edges. The gouges couldn't be what they looked like—not in steel.

They couldn't really be claw marks . . .

"What the hell is that?" Portman asked.

"You never did time, Portman?"

"What?"

"This is a holding cell," Goat said at last.

"Bullshit." Portman didn't want to believe that—if it was a holding cell, that might mean the claw marks were, well, claw marks. The pit could be for storage of some kind. "What makes you think that?" Portman asked as he knelt by the edge, reaching out to touch the slick steel surface of the pit's walls.

A fat blue spark of electricity bit his hand, the current snapping his whole body like a whip, throwing him back against the outer wall of the surgery.

"Because the walls are electrified," Goat said, X-ing the upper wall of the room with his fluorescent powder.

Okay, Portman thought, numbly, trying to sit up and just managing it. *Maybe Goat does have some sense of humor. In a weird kind of way.*

He blew on his singed, stinging hand. "Goddammit!"

Goat gave him a hard look. He'd taken the Lord's name in vain.

In the Weapons Lab, Sarge and Duke looked curiously at the workbenches with high-tech tool-and-die equipage, the deserted computer workstations—and they stopped, almost licking their lips, at the racks of neatly labeled, stacked weapons. Mostly familiar ones, in this rack.

Sarge was looking at a secure door at the far end of the room. He crossed to it, swiped his UAC ID badge in the slot.

"So what's the deal with the sister?" Duke asked, carefully replacing the plasma cannon.

A small wall panel opened to reveal a palm print reader. "Reaper's parents led the first team of archaeologists to Olduvai," Sarge said distractedly. "They bought it in some accident up here when he was a kid. She followed in their footsteps, he didn't."

Reaper's parents had been killed on Mars, when he was young—*killed by archaeology?* Duke shook his head. Archaeologists usually died of old age—or malaria. Weird.

So Reaper had been just a kid when they died. Maybe that's why he'd gone into being a soldier. A way to deal with the predatory chaos of the world . . .

But aloud, Duke maintained his veneer of not caring about anything but partying. "Yeah, yeah, whatever, Sarge, what I meant was, *Is she single?*"

Sarge turned from frowning at the palm print reader to glare at Duke.

Then the panel spoke up, in a tinny computer-generated voice:

"Please provide DNA verification."

So this one didn't read palm prints after all—it wanted your hand so it could suck up a speck of flesh, get a DNA read.

Experimentally, Sarge put his hand into the reader. The device thought about it for a moment. Then:

"Advanced Weapons personnel palm print ID only. Access denied."

Sarge shook his head, annoyed. Both he and Duke wanted to know what was in that room. The term *Advanced Weapons* made the two oldtime warriors nearly salivate . . .

Duke found a portable plasma cannon on the outside gun rack; he slung his automag on its strap and hefted the advanced killing machine. "Jeez. They leave this shit lying around, I'd hate to see what they lock up . . ."

Gunfire.

Three bursts of small-arms fire, the distinctive

deep-throated rattling echoing to them down the corridors.

"What the . . ." Duke said. Surprised that there was contact so soon.

Sarge barked an order into his headset comm: "All units report contact."

Destroyer slapped the Kid's gun muzzle down. He broke off firing—having shot a bundle of ventilation hoses in the unevenly lit corridor.

The Kid looked at Destroyer sheepishly.

Destroyer spoke into his comm. "Misdirected fire, Sarge. Wasting ghosts." And he shoved the Kid forward, back into the patrol route.

"It looked like it was moving," the Kid said.

"There's a lot of stuff looks like it's moving down here. Including me."

The Kid knew what Destroyer meant. That kind of jumpiness got soldiers killed. And a man killed by friendly fire died for nothing.

"I thought you were supposed to be a crack shot," Destroyer grumbled.

"I hit it, didn't I?"

Feeling pretty low, the Kid walked on ahead. Destroyer started after him—then stopped at the ventilation hoses the Kid had perforated, looking up into the ceiling gap they dangled from.

Destroyer noticed something on the floor, directly under the ceiling gap. He picked it up, held it up into the light.

A lab coat—with the left sleeve ripped away. Spots of fresh blood. Maybe, after all, the Kid had shot something besides dangling ventilation hoses.

"Sarge," Duke asked, as they moved down the corridor, "remember when you said, 'Any questions?' and we all pretended like we didn't have any questions?"

"Yep."

"Uh—did you get any kind of briefing you haven't shared yet on what we're looking for here?"

"Nope. But I don't need a briefing. I got a clue what the problem is here."

"Yeah? What clue?"

"You notice the blood on the walls?"

"Yeah."

Sarge looked at him deadpan. "That don't give you a clue? The problem is something here is killing people. They get killed, here. It's a problem. They're supposed to die of old age, not get killed."

"Thanks, Sarge."

"I'm not done. We *find* what's killing them. We kill that thing. Clear?"

"Uh . . . but if we knew what it was . . ."

"You'd be better equipped to fight it, Duke?"

"Yeah."

"Bullshit. That's not why you wanta know. You wanta know because something about this place makes you feel like you might shit yourself."

See, this was why it wasn't good to try to start a conversation with Sarge. He said things like that to

64

you. Duke held on to his temper. "Sarge—you ever see me show the yellow feather?"

"No. But you never been here before."

"I just want a handle on it, Sarge."

They got to a corner, Sarge looked around it, gestured for him to follow. "Okay. A handle on it. You remember the talk about quarantine?"

"Yeah."

"You notice this is Mars . . . an alien planet?"

"Yeah. You're saying the enemy is aliens?"

"Something along those lines. Related to the damn aliens. Whoever they fucking were. Maybe. Or maybe not. Maybe it's people. Some kind of brain-fever virus. Maybe we'll get it, and I'll be killing your ass dead because it's fucking me up. Maybe that'll happen in about ten minutes. Or maybe I won't wait that long because I'm fucking sick of your mouth."

"Thanks for helping me with this, Sarge. Now I feel better."

Sarge ignored the sarcasm. "To review, we don't know what the fuck it is, except . . ."

"Except it kills people."

"Yeah. You clear now?"

"No."

"Good. Then you'll stay alert, won't you. Now shut the fuck up, Duke, before I knock your teeth down your throat."

When Samantha Grimm turned on the lights of the archaeological spectrographic lab, it looked to

65

Reaper like the place had been in use moments before: everything was left out, seemingly still in process. Computers were turned on, showing images from archaeological digs—carvings, bits of ancient bone, broken pieces of sculpture, intricately worked metal from unfamiliar machinery—rocks and fossils on workbenches, tools lying atop them. Brushes, chisels, specialized scrapers, dust blowers. Reaper looked curiously at the streaming shots of damaged sculpture, remembering some of it from his brief stay here with his parents as a child. Despite the unbreathable surface, the Olduvaians of Mars had been humanoid, judging from the sculpture.

What had happened to his parents had been explained away as some kind of accident in one of the lower, innermost digs. They'd broken into a hidden chamber and a trapped gas had affected them . . . sickness, psychosis, death . . . anyway, that was the story he'd been given.

But there had been questions, hushed up when the Grimms' son and daughter were around . . .

He pushed all that from his mind. *Focus on the job, Reaper.*

Sam was at her workstation, inserting MICDIs into the computer intake.

"How much time you gonna need?" Reaper asked her.

"Thirty minutes, tops."

She tapped the keyboard, starting the download-ing process as he set about moving some file cabinets, other equipment to block the entrance. There was something down here killing people, and he didn't want it jumping in at them—at least he could try to slow it down a little, whatever it was, while they were in here.

Sam was concentrating on the computer, but she said, without looking up: "So, 'Reaper'? As in 'Grimm'?"

"They're Marines, Sam. They ain't poets. Who's this Carmack guy?"

Click-clickety on the keyboards. "Dr. Carmack . . ." Clackity-click. ". . . is a genius. His research program will save tens of millions of lives. He's the single finest scientific brain I've ever encountered."

"Yeah." He pointed at a display of fossils—specifically at a preserved humanoid skeleton curled protectively around the skeleton of a child. "What the fuck is that?"

"That's Lucy." She turned to the fossil and pretended to introduce Reaper. "Lucy, this is my brother, John, someone else from the long-lost past."

He pretended to ignore this, but the shot went home anyway. He had been deliberately out of touch with her for years, partly because of the Olduvai thing. Partly because she had strongly disapproved of his career direction. "A sad waste of talent," was the nicest thing she'd said about it.

He thought about Lucy. "They found human remains?" They hadn't when he'd been here as a kid . . .

"Humanoid. Close to us. 'Lucy' and her child were our first find. We're bringing out more every day."

He looked at her. "You've reopened the dig?" He'd thought they were just looking at artifacts taken from the dig a long time in the past.

"Look, maybe I should have told you," she replied, looking at him evenly, "but it's not the sort of thing you jot on a yearly birthday card. Besides, it's been stabilized . . ."

He wasn't going to let her off the hook that easily. "Stabilized—what does that mean? You're saying it's *safe* now?"

"I'm saying the procedures we employ are second to—"

He held a hand up, as he interrupted. "Hold it, hold it—are you saying it's *safe*, Sam? Jesus. How naïve are you?"

She gave a soft, incredulous laugh. "You want to talk about *safe?* Like you took a *desk job.* Like you're not out there doing God knows what for God knows why. I'm a forensic archaeologist with a specialty in genetics. I go where the work is."

"That the only reason you're up here?"

"You want to know why I'm up here?" She turned back to the console, punched some keys. A readout appeared showing a massive grid and the words THERMAL IONIZATION MASS SPECTROGRAPHY.

"This," she continued, tapping the screen, "is a ra- dioscopic map of the ground around us. These are

68

outlines of building foundations. Looks like a city, right? It's not. It's a hundred times as deep and wide and high as any city we've ever known. Population of ninety, a hundred million. A megalopolis. And can you imagine the physics necessary to build the Ark? We're centuries away from this kind of quantum technology, John."

He turned to look again at the sad fossil: the bones of a mother curled in pathetic futility around the bones of a child. *So what happened to them all?* Reaper wondered.

He wondered if they were about to find out the answer—millennia later, on a reawakened Olduvai . . .

Her computer chimed to announce that the first download was complete. Sam pulled out the MICDI, inserted another. "Come here," she said.

He moved closer to the hominid display, looking at it from another angle.

Sam hit another keyboard combo, and chromosome maps appeared, strata of black and white in translucent tubes. "This is Lucy's chromosome profile. Notice anything?" He shrugged, and she added: "We both know you smoked me in biology. It's the first thing Dad taught us to look for."

His answer was as dry as the bones on the worktables. "My molecular genetics is a little rusty."

"She has twenty-four chromosomes. Humans only have twenty-three."

He nodded, counting the chromosome groups on

the display. "You don't say. So what's the extra chromosome do? I mean, what's the difference between me and her, under the hood?"

"You're human—she's superhuman. The twenty-fourth pair made her superstrong, superfit, superintelligent. Her cells divide fifty times faster, so she heals almost instantly. The fossil record indicates they'd conquered disease. No genetic disorders, no viruses, no cancers."

"So she's just naturally superior . . ."

"Not naturally. The earliest remains we found had twenty-three pairs of chromosomes. We suspect this extra chromosome may be synthetic."

Reaper raised his eyebrows. "Bioengineered?"

She smiled thinly. "Long word for a Marine. As I'm sure you also don't know, only ninety percent of the human genome has been mapped. There's plenty of room in the helix to insert stealth DNA if you could figure out a way to manufacture it."

He shook his head. "Sorry. You lost me."

She snorted. "Sure I have." Another, different kind of hesitation. Should she go there? "Does it bother you, you could've spent your life looking in a microscope—instead of a sniperscope?"

"And work up here for UAC? Sorry. I value my life too much."

It was true, he thought. *Those splashes of blood. The level of quarantine. The tapes.*

There were indications that this base for pure science would be far more dangerous than the firefights he'd been in on Earth. Maybe the strongest indication was simple hunch—the instinct of a long-time warrior:

There was death waiting in those corridors.

"Right," Sam was saying. "Like we don't all work for UAC."

He knew what she meant. The corporations had subsumed the government—except in the most cosmetic way. But he insisted, "I'm RRTS, Sam. I serve my country."

"Really. Now who's being naïve?"

Reaper shrugged. "So if they were so smart—how come they died out?"

Voices crackled in Reaper's comm. *"We got something,"* Goat said.

A dark corridor, deep underground. A single shriek, quickly cut off. The sound of running feet, coming closer . . .

It was the same corridor. The one in which Dr. Carmack had achieved his feat of sexagenarian sprinting. Where Jorgenson and several others had been torn to pieces.

Goat and Portman were moving down it now, treading slowly, approaching that same door.

"We got movement in Dr. Carmack's office," Goat said, into the comm. His voice had the hush of a man on the hunt, not wanting to scare off his quarry.

The door had been ripped open—pried, then torn back like tinfoil.

The walls and floor here in the hall, near the door, could almost have been painted uniformly red-brown, with all the dried blood. Where, Portman wondered, was the rest of the body . . . or bodies?

They eased up to the ravaged entrance—they'd seen something go through that door.

And they could hear it moving around inside the lab . . . making a sound that was almost words.

Scraping in there; rattling. Breathing. Muttering.

Weapons ready, fingers on triggers, they edged cautiously, slowly, through the torn-open door—Goat, then Portman. Their probing gunlights showed the room had been trashed, ransacked. There was still some furniture standing.

And something leapt, thumped down onto a desk, to their right. A dark shape. They swung their weapons, and opened fire. The shape leapt over their gunlight beams, past the two soldiers—and out the door as Portman yelled in wordless reaction. Had he hit the thing?

"Contact!" Goat shouted, into the comm. "Contact. Moving east from the gene lab—fast!"

It was heading Sarge's way . . .

In the corridor near the Weapons Lab, Sarge saw the dark shape whip past at an intersection of hall-ways, just thirty feet from him. He fired at it—nowhere near hitting it, it had gone by way too quickly—as Duke caught up with him.

"Certify contact," Sarge said into his comm, "closing fast from the south corridor. Pinky, get a visual."

"What is it?" Duke asked.

Sarge shook his head. No clue.

The Kid saw it next—glimpsed it, anyway, racing around a dark corner.

Younger and more agile, he sprinted ahead of Destroyer, hunting lust pumping in him, and opened fire, snapping off a half dozen rounds at the thing. Thing—or person. It was human-shaped, so far as he could tell from the glimpse he'd had—but its movements were inhuman.

"Hold your fire!" Reaper yelled, coming around a corner behind the Kid.

The Kid held back, gritting his teeth, waiting for orders. Reaper pushed past him, pushing the boy's gun down as he went. Saw the thing—maybe a man—run around another corner . . .

Reaper ran around the same corner and stopped short, finding himself in a dead end. No lights here. Dark.

Something was breathing in the darkness.

He threw his light on it—a face he'd seen on a video. Sarge caught up with Reaper and stared.

"Dr. Carmack?"

SIX

Dr. Todd Carmack was half-naked, shivering, bab-bling, anorexic—and cradling someone else's rotting arm. He held a woman's severed limb clutched against his chest. The dead hand's manicured, painted finger-nails were touching his face. Unconsciously, Carmack began to nibble one of the red-painted fingernails on the stiff blue-white hand. Not like a cannibal, but like someone nervously chewing their nails.

"If you have a weapon, drop it!" Reaper yelled, aware of the Kid and Destroyer coming up behind him. Reaper felt kind of foolish making the de-mand—probably the only "weapon" Carmack had was that detached limb.

Carmack only muttered gibberish in response, blinking in the gunlights, as Goat and Portman ar-rived, adding theirs. A fresh cut bled copiously from Carmack's lower neck. He looked at the decaying, severed arm. A wedding ring on one of the fingers. And let it fall to the floor.

Sam came rushing up, beside Reaper. "Oh my God. Dr. Carmack . . . ?"

"Sam," Reaper said tersely, "get back!"

"He *knows* me!" she pointed out. "Dr. Carmack—it's me, Samantha . . . I'm not going to hurt you . . ."

She started toward him—startled, he shrieked and shied backward, into the corner, one hand reaching up *to rip his own ear from his head*. He flung it at them, reminding Reaper of a monkey flinging offal. Sam stared at the torn-off ear, oozing blood on the floor at her feet. She seemed on the verge of throwing up—but Reaper could see her swallow, get a grip on herself.

Tough kid, he thought admiringly. *My sister.*

"Jesus Christ," Portman muttered.

"Anyone got a field medical pouch?" Sam demanded. "Gimme quickclot!" Reaper tossed her his medikit.

Carmack whimpered, cringing, but let her get closer. She dug in the pouch, found the quickclot packet, tore it open with her teeth and poured it on his wounds. "Where are the others, Doctor?" she asked, her voice soothing.

Carmack twitched but said nothing.

"Steve—Hillary . . . ?" She prompted. "Dr. Olsen? Dr. Thurman, Dr. Norris—Dr. Clay?"

Carmack only rolled his eyes, again and again, shaking fingers exploring the wound where his ear had been, mouth crumpling, as if he was confused as to who'd done it to him . . .

Sarge pushed Portman and the Kid out of the way. "Duke, get him out to the infirmary with Dr.

Grimm. Reaper and Goat, clear the genetics labs, work back this way, LOE junction with the west corridor . . ." As he spoke to the squadron, Sarge never took his eyes, or his gun, off Carmack. "Destroyer and I'll swing around from here to meet you. Portman, Kid, you two dig in at the air lock, anybody trying to run away from us will get driven to you."

Sarge shouldered his weapon. Nudged the severed arm on the floor with the tip of his boot. "Let's see if we can find the body that goes with this."

Sam emerged from the lab air lock, into the atrium area. Duke was close behind her, carrying Carmack in his arms. The scientist was still babbling, almost seeming to take comfort at being carried; he veered between an infantile state and an atavistic madness.

Base personnel gaped at them as they came, murmuring Carmack's name, exchanging looks of horror, fear.

"Dr. Willits!" Sam called.

Jenny Willits, brisk and crisp and bespectacled, hurried up to examine Carmack, still in Duke's arms. "Oh my God. What's happening in there?"

Duke wondered, too. What had happened to Carmack—and what were his own buddies facing while he was babysitting this lunatic?

Hunegs saw the panicked look on the faces of the base personnel. "There is no cause for alarm—UAC has assured me that the situation is entirely under control . . ."

They absorbed this remark, then looked at Carmack. Their faces registered a familiar cynicism. They were used to the disconnect between UAC's public reality . . . and reality.

It was quiet. The only sound was water dripping somewhere.

Moving with Goat down the corridor between the animal experimentation room and the genetics lab, slipping carefully from pool of shadow to pool of light and back into shadow, Reaper felt a strange disquiet flutter its leathery wings at the back of his mind.

Nothing surprising in Reaper feeling worried, right now. He was on an alien planet where his parents had died; there were unknown antagonists making cool, rational scientists crazed enough to rip off their own ears and throw them, and that severed arm hadn't been terribly reassuring.

But he was used to risk, uncertainty. Unseen killers hunting him.

It took him a while to figure out what that particular odd nagging at the back of his head was . . . then it hit him:

He was worried about Sam. Carmack was dangerous—hell, this whole place was dangerous. He wasn't there to protect her. For years, he'd blocked all thought of her well-being from his mind . . .

But now that he'd seen her again, it was hard to

go off on a mission and just assume that his sister was going to be safe here.

Stay professional, he warned himself. *She'll be okay. Duke's with her. He's a good man. Better behave himself though, or I'll . . .*

Goat was moving along the opposite wall, both of them probing ahead with the lights on their guns. Couldn't see what was around that dark corner up ahead. Looked like a flight of stairs going downward.

They inched up to the corner, hesitated—Goat took a step . . .

Bang, clatter, his foot knocked something down the stairs, the sudden noise making them both jump.

"Goddammit," Goat swore.

The object kept bouncing down the steps, clattered onto the hard floor below, rolled into a pool of light. It was just a small cylindrical container, a can of some kind. Trash.

Reaper waited to see if the noise prompted anyone—or anything—to investigate.

Nothing, just a deeper quiet now.

He turned to Goat—and winced to see him pulling a hunting knife. Knowing what that was about. Goat cut into the skin of his arm, cut a deep cross adding to the numerous scars, like crosses in a military cemetery.

Goat noticed Reaper watching. "I took His name in vain."

Beads of sweat stood out on Goat's forehead as he made his penance, pushing the knife in deeper. "In the name of the Father . . . and of the Son . . . and of the Holy Spirit. . . ."

Waiting a short distance beyond the air lock, the Kid heard a footfall behind him. Flicked his pistols off safety, spun on his heel—and nearly pulled the trigger. Second time that day he'd almost shot a friendly.

If you could call Portman a friendly. But he seemed not to have noticed that the Kid had almost shot him. "It's messed up, right?" Portman said, swinging the medical pouch almost jauntily. "A guy like Carmack, trained to put logic before emotion, so freaked he rips off his own ear?" He shook his head. "I tell ya, shit like that . . . gets under your skin."

The Kid nodded—felt his hands twitch on his gun. They were starting to shake. He needed a booster. Shouldn't have gotten started. The first dose, this morning, had been small. But once you started, you kept going so you didn't have to face the crash . . .

"Do you . . ." He licked his lips, lowered his voice. "Do you have any?"

Portman flashed a grin that would make a serial killer shudder. "Do I have any *what*?"

The Kid grimaced. He hated it when Portman made him beg like this. "You . . . you know. I'm just a little shook up. I need something to get my focus, y'know. My game face."

Portman smirked as he fished in a cargo pocket.

Brought out a bottle of pills, waved them teasingly. "Whattya say?"

"Please . . ."

"Please and what?" He waited. The Kid blinked at him in confusion. "*Please and what*, skirt?"

"Thank you?"

Portman handed over the pills. The Kid had the top off and a pill popped in under two seconds. He chewed it up, handed the bottle back—and lifted his head, sniffing.

The Kid was noticing something else. "What's that smell?"

Portman sniffed. Frowned. Sniffed again. "Uh . . . Smells like . . . smells like barbecue."

They followed their noses and the faintly visible curtain of smoke hanging in the air. It led to a lab they hadn't checked yet. The Kid kicked the door in.

Guns ready, they burst through the entrance, tracking the room with the muzzles, looking for a target. Portman found a working light switch and flicked it on. The place was wreathed in smoke.

"Whoa," Portman began, "someone burned the—"

But then he saw the woman's charred body—and he had to break off, retching, just to keep his breakfast down.

"Holy fuck," the Kid said softly. "She fried herself."

They were staring at the body, dead but kneeling, at the back of the room: the blackened corpse of a woman, missing an arm. Still twitching—maybe she'd been twitching like that for a long time—the hand of her remaining outstretched arm was gripping a lab tool, shoved in a humming, sparking power outlet.

Her hair had burned away. Her charred clothes clung to her, a garment of ash, flaking away bit by bit with her twitching. The fluid from her eyeballs, mostly cooked away, was still bubbling in their sockets.

Portman closed his eyes. Forced himself to report. "Sarge . . . we found the body that goes with that arm."

In the corridor to the control-area infirmary, Sam and Dr. Willits and Duke—still carrying Carmack—had just reached a plain gray wall of dull metal. Plain except for the control panel, into which Sam punched a code.

The wall sighed and softened, suddenly looking like it was made of gray clay.

"Oh no no no," Duke said, shuddering. "I don't do nanowalls." Walking through a wall always gave him the creeps. It was like something from a dream—and most of his dreams were bad.

"Quickly," Sam said impatiently. "He may be dying." Sam pushed through the wall, Dr. Willits right after her.

Okay, Duke thought. *I can't be too pussy to do it, now she's done it.*

He took a deep breath, muttering *"Fuck this shit,"* closed his eyes—and stepped through the wall. You

81

had to push, a little, it resisted, flowing around you with a sensation like static electricity and warm mud.

But then he was through, opening his eyes, carrying Carmack to the gurney. Apart from the gurney, the room was all stainless steel and clucking, humming monitors, instruments Duke couldn't identify.

And that nanowall—a high-security device. *What went on in here?* Duke wondered.

Carmack stared at the ceiling with dilated eyes as the doctor began her examination. Sam and Dr. Willits put on some gloves.

"Did they find the others?" Dr. Willits asked, looking into Carmack's pupils with an instrument that looked to Duke more like it was for poking eyes out than examining them.

Sam tried to keep her voice even and confident. "Not yet. I'm sure Steve's fine."

"I told him they needed to get some rest," Dr. Willits murmured worriedly, as she looked at Carmack. "But he said they were close to a breakthrough. And Dr. Carmack wanted to keep going . . ."

Sam tied a rubber tube around Carmack's biceps, jacking the scientist's arm like a pump handle to get a blood pressure reading. Carmack lay there passively as she took the reading . . .

Until he suddenly sat bolt upright, dug his fingers into Sam's hair, pulling her close.

"Oh God," Carmack moaned. "I can feel it!"

"Whoa!" Duke burst out, coming at Carmack— but she'd pulled back somewhat on her own and waved Duke away. She judged this was her chance to get the story out of Carmack.

"It's okay—I'm okay. Dr. Carmack? What happened in there? It's me, Dr. Grimm . . . Samantha Grimm . . ."

"Shut it down!" Jerking her face up to his, spraying spittle as he shouted, nose to nose.

He let her go, sinking back into the cot. His lips were moving, but they couldn't make out what he was saying. Sam leaned closer . . . making Duke nervous. The guy might go psychotic on them again any second.

"It's inside . . ." Carmack whispered. Barely audible.

And then his eyes glazed over.

"Looks like we missed the party," Reaper remarked.

"What happened to all the animals?" Goat asked.

He and Reaper were in the animal experimentation lab, staring at the broken cages. The cages were all opened—the test subjects gone. Some of the cage doors had been bent back, ripped away.

Gurgling and giggling came from near one bank of cages.

Goat and Reaper nodded to each other. Weapons ready, they eased around the pens, poised to shoot—and found a scientist in a white coat, hunkered down, half-turned away over a fallen, open cage.

"Sir?" Reaper asked. "RRTS, we're here to help. You all right?" No telling if this was an enemy or someone he should save, yet. They didn't know who or what the enemy was. He went with friendly until he knew differently. "We're here to help you."

The scientist turned toward them—his eyes were wide, his skin the color and consistency of dough. Blood rimmed his mouth and ran from a wound on his neck. "Sir, are you injured?" Reaper persisted.

Still gaping at them, registering nothing, the scientist thrust both his hands into the cage, pulled something white and squirming out. And shoved two white rats into his mouth at once. Bit down . . . they squealed and writhed, tails lashing.

Goat and Reaper took a step back, shocked. Goat touching the cross at his neck, murmuring a prayer.

"Sir," Reaper said, thinking he should just blow the guy's head off instead, "whatever's happened to you we can get you hel—"

Spitting bits of dead rodents, the man seized a cruel-looking knife from the table and charged them, howling as he came—a rat's head spinning out of his mouth with the last long ululation. He was nearly against the muzzles of their guns before they opened fire, the bullets slamming him backward to crash into the cages, knocking them into a clattering wreckage.

The scientist twitched, moaned, and went limp. His lab coat was on fire from the close proximity of the gun muzzles; smoke wisped from him like his escaping soul.

"Contact report!" came Sarge's voice, on comm.

Reaper cleared his throat. Went to look at the

84

name tag he'd glimpsed on the scientist's coat. "Found one of our missing scientists. Olsen, I guess. He rushed us. Crazy. Just like Carmack."

Reaper wondered if it *was* just like Carmack—who was with his sister now. Suppose he should go off the deep end, like Olsen had? He had shown incredible bursts of speed. Unnatural agility, preternatural energy. He might get at Sam before Duke could stop him . . .

In a corridor on the other side of the lab division, Sarge was talking on the comm to Reaper, with Destroyer just behind him, watching his six.

"He dead?" Sarge asked.

"*Yeah, very . . .*" Reaper said, his voice almost lost in the comm's hiss.

Destroyer was feeling extra nervous. This place made him nervous anyway: it wasn't like the jungle or the desert or some urban-warfare scenario—he knew what to do in those locales. This place seemed to be operating according to rules he didn't quite understand.

But now he felt like something was watching him. He didn't know where it was. He didn't know what it was. But he could feel it watching him.

And then he heard it. Creaking noises from that big ventilator duct that ran along flush with the wall, overhead . . . something deforming the metal with its weight.

"Sarge?" Destroyer pointed his gun at the duct.

Sarge looked, saw the duct was shaking, just slightly, as something moved through it. He nodded and swung his weapon toward the grating high in the wall.

Destroyer went to the grate, reached up, quietly removed the grate, pulled himself up . . . gun in one hand, pulling himself along by his elbows, into the duct. Turning up ahead. He got to the turning, peered around in time to see something rush at him, teeth bared, squealing with hatred as it came—big eyes, muzzle, fangs, fur—

He scrambled backward—firing the gun spasmodically, the muzzle flashes making a strobe light that chopped up his visuals so he didn't know if he hit the thing. He fell backward, out of the duct into the hall, firing the gun as he fell, puncturing the metal of the vent, the chaingun doing a demolition job on the duct, the ceiling.

Found himself sitting on his ass with the chaingun smoking in his hand.

"What the hell was it?" Sarge asked.

"A . . . monkey. Some kind of monkey." Realizing it was probably just an escaped lab animal. Gone a little nuts in here.

But then maybe the animals could've been affected by whatever had affected Carmack . . . presumably the experiments had started with them.

Blood was dripping from the bullet holes in the duct. Sarge went to it—put out his hand. Blood dripped on it. Not ordinary blood. Not the right color.

It was the same as the blood Dr. Willits was just then drawing from Carmack, in the infirmary.

Jet-black.

In the animal experimentation lab, Reaper and Goat were still puzzling over the dead scientist. And the rats on the floor he'd bitten in half.

Reaper shook his head. He wanted to move on. Get to the bottom of this—and get the hell out of the room. He called Sarge on the comm, wondering what they should do, if anything, with Olsen's body. "Sarge—should we bag him and tag him?"

Goat was looking at something different on the floor now. A shadow, lengthening, twisting. Cast by something behind . . .

"Negative," Sarge was saying. *"Continue your search."*

But Reaper wasn't listening anymore. The low, wet rasping sound from behind him had his full attention. He caught Goat's eye, who nodded; their fingers tensed on the triggers of their weapons—

And they spun, firing at something just glimpsed in the dim farther reaches of the cluttered room. It roared in fury, wounded, and retreated, around a row of cages.

Reaper just made out something bigger than a man, rippling with muscles. Dark scaly skin—and a leg iron, its chain broken, locked around its ankle—and then it was gone from their line of sight.

They advanced on the row of cages it'd vanished behind.

"Shoot-pause-enter," Reaper said. A standard tactic. Goat nodded.

They jumped around the corner, firing—nothing. It'd moved on, through the open door into the corridor. They shoved fresh clips into their guns, and Reaper led the way into the hallway—empty. Nothing. Except black blood on the floor.

"Reaper," said Sarge on the comm, *"what've you got?"*

"We're chasing something," Reaper replied. It seemed as if every second light was out in this corridor. The long hall was paced by pools of shadow that were darker than they should naturally be.

"What do you mean, 'something'?" Sarge asked, on the comm.

"Something big! Not human!"

"Godammit, give me a confirmation on what you see!" Sarge hollered over the comm. *"Reaper! . . . Pinky, you get a look at it?"*

"Roger that. Enhancing now."

At the comm center, Pinky was rewinding Reaper's guncam, from the digital record. Mac was watching over his shoulder, a hulking presence that made Pinky nervous. But he didn't know how volatile the Japanese Privine might be, so he didn't tell him to back off.

There—something in that dim image. Pinky froze the frame, rewound a little, put the cursor on a silhouette seen down the corridor. He pressed the keyboard combination for enhance and render. The computer hummed and something began to appear, almost seeming to materialize out of the digital murk. Whatever it was had its back to the camera.

It was bigger than a man, mostly nude—shreds of clothing left around its groin suggesting it had been smaller and had grown, ripping the clothing. Human clothing—had it originally been human-sized?

Its huge head, growing neckless from its hunched, muscle-rippling shoulders, turned just enough so that Pinky could make out small tusks in a wide, snarling, bestial mouth. It seemed eyeless, apparently perceiving from membranes at the front of its head. The whole creature was the color and texture of skin with a second-degree burn. Difficult to see its feet clearly in this cloudy image—but that foot, lifted to take a step. Was that . . . a hoof?

The enhanced figure in the image was most definitely inhuman—and looked like it was designed by nature to be a living kill-machine.

Staring over Pinky's shoulder at the screen, Mac whistled softly to himself.

"Hey, guys," Pinky said, staring at the image. "It ain't a disgruntled employee." Pinky hit a few more keys, distantly aware that his fingers were trembling. "Uploading the image to you now, Sarge . . ."

In his own end of the facility, Sarge projected the uploaded image onto the floor. He stared. "What in the . . ."

* * *

Reaper and Goat heard the thing thumping around a corner. They sprinted, fingers wrapping triggers, around the turn . . . and found themselves in yet another dead end. *Who'd designed this warren of corridors,* Reaper wondered, *the people who designed mazes for rats?*

The thing they'd been chasing was gone. Where the hell did it go *to?* The only door here had a big chained padlock on it. The thing was too big to just vanish . . .

". . . Reaper," Goat said.

Reaper looked at him—Goat was looking down at a big manhole grate in the floor, half-open. "Sarge," Reapter reported, into the comm. "It's in the sewer . . ." They knelt, Reaper pointed his gunlight into the gap. The facility's sewage system and waste-water outflow looked alike. He saw a dead rhesus monkey floating by on a stygian stream.

He heard Sarge requesting data from Pinky. *"Talk to me, Pinky."*

"An outflow tunnel," Pinky said. *"It connects that section of the sewer to the main facility's system."*

An inhuman growl resounded from somewhere down in the sewer.

Goat then looked at Reaper, slightly wide-eyed, pointing his weapon at the manhole grate. "So . . . you wanna go first?" he said, shrugging nervously, cracking a hint of a smile.

Reaper couldn't really tell whether or not Goat was kidding.

"All units, all units" Reaper said into the comm, "request assistance at the southeast corridor, med lab!"

Sarge's voice boomed over the comm in response. *"Copy that, Reaper. Stay put until we get there! All units— converge on Reaper's position. Southeast corridor, med lab. Move!"*

SEVEN

THE RRTS SQUADRON was dropping into the sewer.

"And I thought 'in the shit' was a figure of speech," Portman groused.

"Get in the goddamn hole, Portman," Sarge growled.

Weapon slung over his shoulder, Portman descended the metal ladder to step into the thigh-high sewage runoff. Most of it was just water, but spotlit in the shaft of light from above, Portman could see human wastes swirling by, including bits of toilet paper, and small dead animals from the labs. Animals—or parts of them. A string of entrails twined around Portman's leg as he bent over to fit into the tunnel, but he made himself slosh forward to join the others, choking with the smell as he went. His gagging echoed in the tunnel along with drippings, footfalls, and creaking sounds from unknown sources.

Probably annoyed by Portman's griping, Sarge gestured for him to take point. Still gagging, pointing his gunlight down the low, echoing tunnel, Portman splashed onward.

"Hey, Portman," the Kid said, his voice quavering, "when you were young y'ever picture yourself doing *this*?"

"No," Portman said immediately, "I pictured myself getting laid."

Goat came just behind him, murmuring verses from the Bible: *"Be sober, be vigilant, because your adversary the devil . . . walketh about seeking whom he may devour."*

"That's real comforting, Goat," Portman grumbled. "I mean that's not freaking me out *at all!*" Goat glared at Portman—and as if the look was a biblical curse, as Portman said, "Why don't you shut the—" he *vanished* midstep, plummeting out of sight into the water.

"Portman!" Goat burst out.

Their gunlights shone in a convergence of beams on the water where he'd been. Bubbles and offal floated by. Nothing else visible.

"Portman!" Reaper yelled, easing up to the spot.

No response.

Reaper bent, almost kneeling in the tunnel, wrinkling his nose as his face got all too close to the malodorous stream. "I got his hand. Damn he's heavy. He's too deep." He reached into the sewage, found a hand flailing up under the water.

Reaper grabbed Portman's hand and pulled, grunting. But Portman was stuck. Desperation communicated through his tightening grip. Reaper

93

leaned back, using his weight—something popped loose down below, and he dragged Portman thrashing up into sight.

"Dammit!" Portman gasped. "Shit!"

"Congratulations, Portman, that's your first bath in months," Reaper said.

As Portman swore and muttered, trying to wipe himself off, Reaper felt around for the hole with his toe. Found it, around a big wheel-shaped valve of some kind. Not a passage. The thing they were chasing couldn't have gone down that way—but the valve recess was deep enough for Portman to stumble into.

"Up ahead," Sarge said, pointing with his gunlight.

The beam laid an oval of light over a pale object, reminiscent of a human torso, floating along the tunnel toward them. Sarge fished it out—it was a lacerated and bloody lab coat with a name on it.

DR. STEVE WILLITS was stitched in cursive over the breast pocket.

"We got Willits's lab coat," Sarge said, into his headset. "John, Kid—on point." He looked at Portman's disgusted face, and added, "Watch your step."

They moved on around a curve in the tunnel—everyone stepping carefully around the hole Portman had fallen into—and found it split off into several directions. Sarge gave his orders, punctuating each by pointing at the tunnel he was sending them into. "Goat, straight. We'll go left." Meaning him, Destroyer, and Portman. "John, Kid, on the right. Destroyer, you're on point."

As Reaper passed the Kid, to move into point just ahead of him in the right-hand tunnel, he noticed the Kid was wearing his night-vision goggles in the dark tunnel. And the Kid noticed Reaper wasn't.

"How come you don't wear night-vision?" the Kid asked.

"Don't like NVGs," Reaper replied, sweeping the tunnel ahead with his gunlight. "They limit your peripheral vision."

"Yeah, plus you can't see shit to either side," the Kid said.

Reaper was trying to decide if the Kid was joking when a loud splash came from behind. The Kid spun around, splashing Reaper with the sudden motion, autopistols taut in his hands—but it was a noise of the others moving in the adjacent tunnels.

The Kid was panting with fear. He turned back to face the darkness of the tunnel ahead, bubbling over with nerves. Jabbering.

"Portman told me some stuff about you," the Kid chattered. "Said you lost your parents when you were a kid, right? Small. I lost my parents, too."

"Every time you open your mouth you're giving away our position," Reaper told him.

"Yeah. See, I woke up one morning, everything was gone. Only thing left was me. They wanted the TV more than they wanted me."

The tunnel must be getting to the Kid—connecting him to the primal fear he'd felt, waking up to find his parents had abandoned him. Back in that other dark childhood tunnel, in a way.

Anyhow, it was better that the Kid cowboyed up, and stopped being so personal. This was the time to be professional and nothing but.

And Reaper didn't want to hear about the Kid's parents vanishing on him. His own parents hadn't exactly abandoned him. But one day they were just . . . gone. Dead.

The Kid stared owlishly back at him, mouth moving soundlessly, his eyes . . .

Reaper found a small flashlight in his belt pack, pointed the red-tinted light at the kid's face. "Your pupils," Reaper burst out, furious. "They're *dilated*, Kid! Are you fuckin' high?"

The Kid looked away. Tried out a lie. "I got this condition, Reaper . . ."

"Who's supplying you?" Reaper demanded. "Portman?"

The Kid didn't answer. Which was answer enough.

Great. The Kid and Portman were high on some trashy neurostimmer. In Reaper's experience, guns times drugs equaled fuckups. Stoned people always fucked up big-time, in a tense situation. Meaning somebody would die, as a result . . . and not necessarily the enemy.

"You take any more of that shit, Kid," Reaper said, deliberately making his voice loud enough for Portman and Sarge to hear, too, "and I'll blow holes in you *and* Portman."

"Oh sure, Reaper," the Kid snorted. "Like you're gonna *shoot* me."

Reaper pointed his gun at the Kid's head. Settled in like he was about to follow through on his threat.

The Kid swallowed. "Hey—look—I was just kidding."

There was something moving, something big and bulky, in the side tunnel just beyond the Kid.

"I won't do it again, okay?" the Kid was saying. "I'm sorry."

"Get down," Reaper said.

Something was coming closer . . .

"What?"

"Get down!"

The Kid crouched low into the water. "What is it?"

It slipped past them—swimming now, but unmistakably a bipedal shape, a large, living creature . . . then he lost sight of it.

But as he pressed back against the curved wall, the Kid now against the wall opposite him, Reaper saw a V-shaped ripple moving along the surface of the water, its motion purposeful, sliding between them. Heading back down the tunnel . . .

Heading for the squadron like a submerged alligator.

Reaper followed, came to the place the tunnel divided, saw it turn into Goat's tunnel.

"Goat," Reaper said into the comm, "something's behind you! It's under the surface! It's coming toward you!"

"Oh fuck!" Portman hissed, hearing the report on the comm, pointing his gun at the water. Not sure where to shoot. He might blow someone's kneecap apart before he hit the thing swimming under the water.

"It's under the water!" Reaper repeated, on the comm.

Portman fired a nervous burst into the water—the rounds sent up little geysers of sewage, ricocheted down the tunnel.

"Hold your fire!" Sarge ordered. "It's not in this tunnel!"

In the center tunnel, Goat had turned, was swinging his light from side to side, trying to spot the thing Reaper said was coming for him. Seeing nothing at all but floating crap.

"I don't see it!" Goat reported.

"It's there!" came Reaper's voice, crackling in the headset.

But he still saw nothing but water and spiraling waste. Worse, his light was going out. Getting weaker and weaker . . .

Wait—was there something under the water, over there? It was hard to tell in the weak gunlight.

Should have brought an extra flash or a flare or something, but he liked to carry as little as possible. Stay sleek. So he had no other light on him. No night goggles. Not even a match.

And as Goat peered, eyes aching, into the dimness—his light went out completely.

Total darkness snapped down around him. Perhaps this was a message from God. He remembered a line from the Bible, Matthew 6:23, *If then the light in you is darkness, how great is the darkness!*

God was showing him the darkness of his own soul . . .

But the soldier in him struggled to stay in control. *Don't give in—fight! Let the others know.*

"This is not happening," he muttered into the comm. "My light is down. Think my battery's out. Pinky . . . you see it?"

But the cameras he bore were in darkness, too. *"No, nothing,"* came Pinky's voice on the headset.

Then he heard a splashing sound, and a kind of reptilian chuckle. He remembered the coat they'd found floating down the tunnel.

"Dr. Willits?" he whispered.

Something rose up from the water, quite near him; he could hear liquid dropping from its body, could hear it breathing—close beside him, on his right . . .

Less than a foot away.

He swallowed . . . and turned, could just make out a shape that was a deeper darkness than the background gloom—a misshapen head.

The dark shape opened its eyes. Two luminous eyes . . .

Then the rest of its eyes opened.

A whole cluster of them—glowing against the backdrop of darkness. Goat stumbled backward—

A light flashed on them from down the tunnel: Reaper's gunlight. But he was too far away to shoot the thing without hitting Goat.

There was a flash of spiky teeth, a flicker of something rocketing from its maw—a sickly pink tongue stabbing like a stinger but coming like the tongue of a frog zapping an insect, flying harpoonlike into Goat's throat—and he felt the impact on his neck, stabbing and pumping to gush a fluid into him, a venom or worse.

Goat shrieked and fell, thrashing. Hot pain spread rippling out from his neck, washed over him—and then a terrifying numbness. Not the numbness of blessed relief, but a malevolent dullness. Paralysis started in his lower body, making it go rigid and he slid down into the water. His hands flailed at the barbed tongue embedded in his neck . . .

The creature that'd injected Goat stepped back—and as it did, its tongue *unspooled* from its throat. It reeled out, out . . . longer and longer, an absurd connection of flesh between its drooling maw and Goat's jolting form . . .

Then, as it was supposed to, the tongue snapped free, detaching itself, shortening, becoming about two feet long; pumping its fluid sack furiously into Goat as it writhed around his body, finishing its work. Goat tried to pull the tongue off, but it was no use, he was losing control of his upper body . . .

The creature moved away from its detached tongue. The tongue would follow a homing instinct back to it, in time to be ready for the next anointing.

But then it turned, startled by a flash of light—Reaper was there, splashing up the tunnel toward it. It ducked down in the water.

"Man down!" Reaper shouted, seeing Goat twitching in the water.

He'd seen the thing shoot its tongue into Goat—but where had it gotten to?

There was an eruption from the foul water just two yards from him, then the creature was transfixed for a strobic moment by his gunlight beam: sheathed in sliding water, its semihuman head lifted; a cluster of eyes like a spider's, no nose to speak of, most of its head taken up by vast jaws bristling with teeth, its skin raw-looking, its hands ending in talons, its body rippling in muscle.

And then it charged.

Reaper fired, and the creature let out a long, high-pitched sirening screech as the bullets struck it—black blood fountaining as it clawed at the wounds, dancing in the ripping impact of a whole clip from the light machine gun: a hellstorm of gunfire into the darkness, lighting up the tunnel with flashing chaos, the bullets zipping and ricocheting around the tunnel where the creature had gone, scoring the walls, smashing through pipes, chipping metal. Cloaked in shadow, the thing shrieked as it was hit, the sound otherworldly, quavering, echoing on and on.

Reaper finally ran out of bullets—only the bullets had kept it from falling, the last few rounds: it flopped down with a splash into the muck.

The rest of the team came up from behind. Stopped to stare at the thing floating, slowly turning, faceup, twitching in death.

They gaped at it . . . and saw its tongue detaching from Goat to swim off down the tunnel like a sea snake seeking its den.

Then Reaper splashed over to Goat—only the top half of his head was sticking out the polluted water. His eyes open, unblinking, staring.

Reaper looked at him for a moment, then picked him up in his arms. Sarge led the way back to the ladder.

Sarge and Reaper carried Goat together, almost double-timing it through the atrium; Duke and Destroyer followed, dragging something behind them; the Kid and Portman brought up the rear . . .

Mac grinned when he saw them come in, and ran over to join them—but his smile fell away when he saw Goat. He gave Portman a questioning look.

Short explanations were mumbled at him, but the explanations only baffled Mac more.

Hunegs came hurrying up, giving them a look of white-faced inquiry.

"We gotta move the quarantine zone," Sarge told him. "Evacuate the entire facility. Get all personnel to the Ark immediately."

Hunegs chewed the inside of his cheek as if wondering whether Sarge had the authority to issue that order to the whole facility.

Reaper decided there was no time to play "who's higher on the chain of command."

"Get those people out of here now! Move! Move!"

"What's going on out there?" Hunegs demanded.

Sarge tried keeping it simple. "Everybody through the Ark!"

Hunegs pursed his lips—then nodded, started barking orders to the security men staring at the reeking squadron and their disturbing burdens.

"Move! Everybody out!"

That was it—the milling became running, panic set in, and people, voices high-pitched as they told one another to get out of the way, ran for the Ark.

Though there was pandemonium in the atrium, it was still quiet in the infirmary; the only sounds were the occasional low moan from Dr. Carmack and the humming of the biomonitoring equipment. But Sam was at least as tense as the people running to the

Ark, as she dropped samples of Carmack's blood into a spectrographic analyzer.

"Attention!" Lieutenant Hunegs's voice, coming tinnily over the public address system. *"All personnel, please report to the Ark chamber for immediate evacuation. Attention—all personnel . . ."*

"Dr. Willits," Sam said, as she frowned over the readout, "listen, his condition is stable. You should go."

"I want to stay." She shined a light into Carmack's eyes. She wasn't about to get too close to Carmack, though he was now in restraints.

"Steve'll be okay," Sam said. "The guys looking for him are the best. . . ."

Dr. Willits looked at Sam—and Sam could tell she didn't trust the squadron to find her husband, Steve.

Sam herself doubted that Dr. Willits's husband—one of the genetics researchers in the labs—would be found alive. But you had to reassure people, didn't you? Why obvious lies were supposed to be reassuring was another mystery.

"Jenny—go . . . please."

Dr. Willits looked at Carmack, twitching in the restraints. She wouldn't be sorry to leave—she didn't feel safe with Carmack, whatever she'd pretended.

At last she nodded. "I'll be back as soon as I can." She gathered up a few things, waved good-bye to Sam, and left the infirmary, the nanowall melting back into place behind her, once more going flat and gray and permanent-looking, as if someone hadn't just walked right through it.

Sam turned back to the spectrograph. She squinted at it, trying to comprehend what it was telling her about Carmack's blood. Five words blinked up at her, in luminous green LCD letters.

BLOOD GROUP CANNOT BE IDENTIFIED

"What the hell?" she muttered aloud. As she puzzled over the spectrographic reading, some part of her mind registered an odd noise from the gurney, behind her—a creaking sound.

"Blood group cannot be identified?" Black the blood might be—perhaps from a dysfunctional liver—but it was some kind of human blood. Wasn't it?

Duke came back in and looked over her shoulder. Read the same message from the spectrograph. "No blood match? That can't be good, right?"

Sam shook her head. It simply didn't make sense.

She went to a glass-doored cabinet, found another blood draw kit. She'd just have to test him again . . . she turned back to Carmack . . .

He was gone. Nothing remained on the gurney but broken restraints and a dark, bloody smear across the sheet.

The squadron went down a corridor and through the nanowall, on into the infirmary. Looking up from the spectrograph, Samantha Grimm recoiled a little at the lingering smell of the sewer they brought with them, then stared at the lumpy poncho that

Duke and Destroyer dragged after them into the room, the plastic folded over a hump. Something hard to identify was sticking out in back. Legs? Not human, if legs they were.

They laid Goat on a gurney—and Sam held back a moment before approaching him. He looked dead—but things weren't always the way they looked, anymore.

It had looked like Carmack couldn't have gotten off that gurney, too . . .

"What happened?" Sam asked, looking at the wound on Goat's neck. She'd never seen one like it.

Reaper shook his head. He tried to think of a way to describe what'd happened. *Well, this thing shot its ten-foot-long tongue into him, then the tongue scrolled out, then it unlatched, then the tongue . . .*

Right. He ended up saying nothing. The whole team lifted Goat on the table to work on him, their training kicking in. Duke cut open Goat's uniform. Experienced in battlefield medical dressing, Reaper set up an IV—all the makings were to hand on the infirmary shelves—and the Kid held a bloody bandage pressed against Goat's neck.

They were all helping except for Portman. He was simply staring at Goat in shock.

"He was talking about devils . . ." Portman mumbled.

Sam looked at him, eyebrows raised. "Devils?"

Portman flapped a hand at Goat. ". . . all his Bible

shit . . . angels, good and evil, the devil among us . . ."
Mouth slack, he kept staring at Goat.

Reaper glanced at Portman, decided he needed to be kept busy. "Portman, get a second line in here. I need to hit him with some adrenaline."

Portman snapped out of his fog and started moving around, looking for another IV line and the adrenaline.

"Attention all personnel!" came Hunegs's voice, booming over the PA system. *"Please report to the Ark for immediate evacuation! All personnel, please report for immediate evacuation . . ."*

"Like to hit that exit myself," Portman murmured.

Reaper watched his sister work on Goat. She moved intelligently, efficiently, her hands in rubber gloves but otherwise showing no concern for the blood and gore she was getting on herself. As for Goat . . .

"He's not breathing," Reaper observed. "Fuck."

Sarge was looking around, frowning. "Where's the hell's Carmack?"

"He disappeared," Sam said, stanching the wound on Goat's neck with a compress.

"He what?"

"I said he's gone! He disappeared!"

Duke was looking at the heart monitor. "Lost the pulse!"

Reaper grabbed a couple of defibrillators off a console, slapped them on Goat's chest. "Clear!"

The others stepped back, and he thumbed a switch. Goat's body jerked, and fell back. No response. He tried it again.

"Shit . . ."

Tried it again . . . nothing.

Goat flopped again and the air smelled of burnt skin and ozone—and he still registered a flat line. Goat was staring at the ceiling . . . or past it, Reaper imagined. Through the ceiling, through the roof, through the toxic atmosphere of Mars, into the starry heavens. Like a guy watching for a bus—he was waiting for his ride to show up . . .

The men looked on, helpless, trying to think of some way to help. Goat wasn't the most popular guy in the squadron, but he was still their brother in arms.

There was nothing to be done. You could see that the life had gone out of that body.

So Reaper closed Goat's eyelids. Then he reached under Goat's Kevlar vest, drew out his old Bible, now splattered with blood. He handed it to Portman. Who looked down at it uneasily.

Sarge let out a long slow breath, then turned to Sam. "All right. We need answers. What the fuck is going on up here?"

Sam was taken aback by his bluntness—and maybe the generality of his question. "What do you mean?"

"What do I mean? Come *here!*" Sarge commanded.

He nodded to Destroyer, who threw back the poncho, revealing what they'd dragged in here.

Sam took a quick step back, seeing the creature on the floor.

It was dead, already decaying, and a hellish waft rose as they exposed it, overwhelming the fetor of sewage. The thing was much bigger than a man, with a thick black exoskeleton and a cluster of eight eyes. The head was spiky, mostly jaws.

A kind of hideous imp, Sam thought. *Something from Hell.*

She was afraid to get any closer.

Stop being childish, she told herself. Her brother was here, watching. Was she going to show she was scared in front of him? This was a new species, that was all. She should be excited about the scientific possibilities. She shouldn't be reacting with this visceral repugnance . . .

Sam walked up to the creature—which she fervently hoped was as dead as it looked—and looked it over, trying to understand what it might be, where it had come from. And failed.

"Have you people found anything like this on your archaeological dig?" Sarge asked.

"No," she said.

"Is there any way this thing came from outside, from the surface?"

She shook her head. "The planet is completely dead."

"It came from somewhere, lady!" Portman put in.

"Portman," Sarge said, "shut up!"

"The atmosphere on the surface can't support

life," Sam went on. She was about to explain just how toxic the atmosphere of Mars was when Portman interrupted her.

"You just said you don't know what the fuck it is." He waved his hands in the air. Looking a little crazy, to her—possibly stoned. "Maybe it doesn't *need* air! It could be from another planet or something!"

"An alien?"

"Look at that thing!"

"Portman," Sarge roared, *"shut the fuck up!"*

"That's not what *we* saw," Reaper said, looking at the creature. They all turned toward him, every face showing confusion, and he had to explain: "This isn't exactly what Goat and I shot at in the genetics lab. This is something different."

Portman looked at him in shock. "You're telling me there could be *more* of these fucking things?"

Sarge turned slowly to Sam. "Where are the surface entry points?"

She shrugged. "There's a pressure door at the end of the north corridor . . ."

"Portman, Destroyer, Kid," Sarge barked, "you'll get there on the double, gimme a sit-rep."

"Yes, sir," Destroyer said, for all of them. Seeing Sarge's mood, seemed like a good time for a yes sir.

"Whatever this thing is," Sarge went on, "we can't let it get back through the Ark. Mac, give Pinky a sidearm and some STs, seal the Ark door, and rendezvous at the atrium—now!"

Mac nodded and stalked off through the nanowall.

"There's another door," Sam said, realizing it even as she said it.

"Where?" Sarge asked.

Sam hesitated—and Sarge seemed about to slap her with his impatience.

Reaper knew he'd never allow anybody to raise a hand to his sister, whatever issues he might have with her. But a potential fight with Sarge would probably end badly for Reaper.

John Grimm was good. But Sarge was a killing machine.

Anyway, Reaper had the answer to Sarge's question.

". . . The entrance to the archaeological dig," Reaper said, after a moment.

In the wormhole chamber, the last few scared evacuees were filing through the huge steel chamber door toward the Ark, shepherded by Hunegs. There were flashes at regular intervals as they went through.

"This is the last of them," Hunegs called to Mac, as he came in. Just a few more technicians . . .

Mac nodded, went to Pinky who was sitting at a workstation, puzzling over the digital file of Carmack's research journal.

As Mac walked over to him, Pinky read the second-to-last entry again:

Twined, twined they are, into the DNA sequence. The fingerprints of the satanic, the darkest of darknesses within us. I dare not call it the supernatural, though it also cannot be called part of the natural world as we understand it. But something inhuman and other-dimensional hid the keys to the gates of Hell in our DNA . . . what is its agenda? Who has left this cunning lure for us?

Pinky just shook his head. Carmack had to have been out of his mind.

Mac dropped a gun and three ST grenades on Pinky's console.

Pinky raised his eyebrows. "What's that?"

"ST grenade. Pop the top, hit the button, throw. Don't forget the last part," Mac said.

As if that said it all, he turned and headed for the exit.

"What? Whoa!" Pinky called after him. "What are you doing?"

"I'm going to work."

Mac went through the doorway, pressed the release, and the enormous steel door rolled into place.

"Wait!" Pinky yelled, starting after him. "Wait up! You can't!"

But Mac was locked away on the other side of the door. His voice came cracklingly over the intercom:

"Ark secure."

Heavy bolts clanged into place. Pinky was sealed in.

"Shit," he said.

Behind him, Hunegs and the last evacuee went through. The last tech to pass through was pale, sweating, stumbling as he went through the metal doors into the Ark chamber.

Hunegs helped him up; helped him go through. Never looking at him closely—busily thinking about his own chance to escape.

So Hunegs didn't see the mark on the man's neck; didn't see the wound just visible, low, under his bloody collar.

EIGHT

THEY WERE ALL there but Duke, who'd been assigned to stay with Samantha. *Seemed like Duke hadn't minded that assignment much,* Reaper reflected.

The squad stood nervously in the atrium, waiting for orders.

Portman wanted to make up his own orders. "We're not calling in backup?" Acting shocked, amazed.

Sarge shot him a cold look. "The Ark is sealed. Nothing crosses back here until everything on this planet is dead." He examined his own weapon, adding, "Weapons check. We're going in hot." As if to say that settled the issue.

Portman just stood there, his weapon on the floor beside him, staring at Sarge in disbelief. "You're serious?"

Reaper looked at him. Was this guy really ignoring an order? "Pick up your weapon, Portman."

Destroyer slapped a belt of ammo into his chaingun. "Come on, Portman—move out."

Portman didn't move anywhere. "Didn't you see the way that thing greased Goat?" His voice was getting shrill. "We don't know what we're dealing with!"

Sarge chambered a round, slammed the breach.

"It's SOP," Portman continued, insistently, almost whining, "to call in reinforcements when a situation—"

"We *are* the reinforcements!" Sarge interrupted, his voice like an ax chopping. "Now *shoulder your fucking weapon,* soldier!"

Portman swallowed—and looked at Reaper for support.

Reaper only slammed a fresh clip into his light machine gun. He looked at Sarge, and said, "Pray for war."

"Pray for war!" the others chimed in.

Most of them. This time it was Portman who didn't say it. Sarge's look bored a hole right through him. Finally, Portman picked up his weapon, and said, "Pray for fucking war."

They broke up into two teams, and started out, Destroyer half dragging Portman with him and the Kid.

Sarge, Reaper, and Mac headed toward a tunnel marked D4.

Reaper thought about trying to brief Mac on what they'd seen in tunnel—but you couldn't brief someone about something you didn't understand yourself.

Sam pried open the "imp's" jaws and shined a light in past razored teeth.

Duke stood back—looking at the monster, then at Sam, his eyes lingering on Sam. Nice view of her from behind. Much preferable to looking at that horror on the examining table.

Sam's hand twitched as a particularly noxious smell wafted out of the thing's gullet, and she dropped her penlight down its throat. The light shone from down there like a flashlight from a scarlet, slimy cave.

"Shit," she said. She turned to Duke, "Hold this open."

He hesitated. Didn't want to get near that thing—even dead.

"Don't be a wuss, Duke."

That tore it. A girl calling him a wuss. He had to do it.

He stepped in, gripped the thing's jaws, careful to keep his hands away from the sharpest teeth—a scratch from those, and who knew what unspeakable interworld infections you'd get. He held them open as she reached into the creature's mouth, pushing in half her arm.

"Little tension between you and the Reaper?" Duke asked. Get a girl to confide in you about her problems. Sometimes it worked.

"Why does a talented student throw it all away and join RRTS? Turn himself into a killing machine?" she asked, fishing around. Her arm made squelching sounds in its throat.

"I guess most of us are running from something." Try to sound sensitive with the ladies. That works sometimes, too.

"What about you, Duke?" she asked, still fishing around, grimacing. Making fun of him, probably, as she went on, "What are you running away from?"

"Today," Duke said earnestly, "it's mostly been big ugly-ass demons . . ."

She couldn't help but smile at that. She drew her hand out, clutching the penlight and, relieved, he let go of the monster's jaws.

"What was he like before?" Duke asked.

"As a boy?" What had her brother been like? She thought about it a moment. "Empathetic. Sensitive."

Duke looked at her in surprise. "Hard to think of Reaper as sensitive."

"Well, I knew him before all the drop-down-gimme-fifty woo-ha stuff." She resumed her examination of the imp, peering at its chest now.

Duke laughed. "It's *hoo*-ah."

She tapped its chest. "You have a family?"

"I have Destroyer—grew up together."

"He seems like a good guy."

Duke nodded—a little embarrassed.

She stared at the horror on the table, decided she needed to cut it wide open to see how it ticked.

"You know . . ." She tapped the other side of the imp's broad chest, over its heart. "I bet secretly you've got a big heart, Duke."

Yeah, she was definitely making fun of him. "It ain't the only big secret thing I got," he said. What the hell, a shot in the dark.

She looked at him, raising her eyebrows. "Little rusty, huh?"

Duke sighed. "Lady, you got no idea. I been bunked up with a buncha Marines, none of whom I find remotely attractive, for like, *ever.* Right now, having sex with me is practically your civic duty."

She was careful not to smile at that. Though she wanted to.

She picked up a scalpel, began a Y-incision on the exoskeleton over the chest. And the scalpel snapped in half.

She tapped the broken handle against the imp's thick skin. "I need a power bone saw. There's one in the procedure room."

"Power bone saw? Lady I been waitin' for you my whole life . . ."

Who are you?

I'm you. I always have been. The animal in you. The hungry animal.

No. I'm not you. I . . . I am Carmack. I'm a scientist. An award-winning researcher. I'm not an animal.

You amuse me, giving yourself airs. All embodied beings are animals.

We become more than animals when we become rational.

Your rationality is like the thin coat a man wears when he's expecting a light rain. And then comes a blizzard and he freezes to death.

No! Reason built our civilization. Reason is power. It builds weapons to destroy such as you. I know who you are—you're a part of my mind altered by the infection!

What of it? Can you destroy me, Carmack, without destroying yourself? We are becoming indistinguishable.

Oh it's dark here, it's so dark. You—you're just a nasty little voice in the dark. At least tell me—where am I?

In a safe place. As for the darkness—you are blinded with the rigors of transformation. Hiding from them while your body completes its revolution. That which has so long been hidden away in you will now come to light. The façade of civilization will tear away—underneath is the face of the beast. That is who you really are: me. The hidden part of you released by the genetic infection.

So dark . . . so dark here . . . I hurt, my limbs burn . . . what is happening to me? I feel as if I am pregnant with a child, bursting with new life, but I am male—I feel like that insect that is injected with offspring by its mate, so that when they hatch out they eat their own father from within. I feel like my legs are wriggling with a life of their own, breaking free of the body; I feel like my heart and liver and guts are writhing inside me, fighting one another for space, tearing their way from my skin . . . Oh God the pain . . .

We are growing, changing . . .

Liar! We are not one thing! You're just some psychological fracture of my own mind. You're the result of the pressure, the horror of what I've gone through . . .

What you've gone through? You mean when you locked the door on your friends and colleagues? When you shut the door on that poor woman's arm, cut it off so you could be safe? When you let them all die so the important Dr. Carmack could live? What is your ordeal to theirs?

I had to do it—so that I could survive, and warn the others! I had to warn the world!

How you justify your negligent homicide, Professor Carmack! It is most amusing!

You're a figment of psychological pressure— you're not real enough to be amused. You're a nothing—just a nothing that can talk! Go away and leave me in the darkness with my companion: my pain . . .

But I am that darkness; I am your pain. That is exactly what I am. Who do you think you have been conversing with?

No!

Oh yes. Your eyes are blinded with the substance of my being; your nerves sing with the vitality of my growing life. I am growing within you. I am taking you over. The phenomenon you experimented with so cheerfully is infectious— didn't you know that?

It can be stopped. It can be . . .

It cannot be stopped. You are proof.

No. Not me.

Don't you remember what happened, in that lab, after you called for help—after you summoned fresh meat for us?

I can't remember . . . It's all so dark . . . I don't want to remember . . .

You have been infected. I am that infection—and the infection is even now becoming you. You are in a conversation with that which is slowly eating you! I eat you! I eat you! I steadily eat you even as I speak to you. I am eating you and digesting you and making you into me. Whatever is in you that I have no use for—like your rationality—will become my waste product.

No, I will break free! I will break out! I will . . .

You will . . . ?

I will . . . I am . . .

No: I am . . .

I am . . . darkness and pain.

Yes. I am darkness and pain. And I will spread it to all that lives.

I am darkness and pain.

"Mac, secure our line of retreat," Sarge told him. Mac used the RRTS hand signal for assent and took up a post just outside the door of the "mudroom"— the prep room on the edge of the Olduvaian archaeological dig.

Sarge and Reaper made their way, very warily, into the mudroom. Tinted the color of rust by the strange sky outside, light angled through an observation window looking out on the windswept surface of Mars. Most of the place was taken up by worktables.

It had the look of having been abandoned in miduse, like the labs. There were tables crowded with hand tools: big power drills, small shovels and trowels, a hundred kinds of fine-work digging implements. And on one table lay a long row of heavy-duty chain saws.

Reaper thought: *In a pinch, if a guy ran out of ammo, those chain saws could be used as weapons.* A strange thought, bringing with it a chill of recognition.

On a debris-removal table was a clutter of half-cleaned artifacts, each surrounded by a ring of scraped-away soil. Some of the artifacts were clearly vases, bowls, small metal cabinets; others were unidentifiable: cryptic, but teetering right on the edge of familiarity . . .

My parents were here, working at these tables, once, then my sister, Reaper thought. *I was supposed to be working here, too . . .*

His own memory of his childhood on Olduvai was dim, an uneasy fog shot through with red lights, flickering with half-seen faces. He had worked hard since, trying to forget this place.

But one memory came back to him vividly—the day, with his father, he had visited Dig Twenty-three. Young John Grimm had seen something watching him from the shadows. A monstrous face, with a vast toothy mouth. Only it wasn't quite there physically. It blinked in and out of existence . . .

Your imagination, his father reassured him. *This is a spooky-looking place. Your mind is finding patterns in the chaos.*

But after that young John had refused to visit the digs. He'd just wanted to leave Olduvai.

Not long afterward, his parents had died—in that same part of the digs. Number Twenty-three. Just an accident . . .

Reaper noticed his sister looking at him from the walls.

He walked over to the photos taped up there. Here was his sister, smiling from a photo taken in a dig. And there were his parents, in a group photo. Their names underneath: Prof. A. Grimm; Prof. D. Grimm.

Reaper felt a twisting wrench of loss inside—and he turned away from the photos, going hurriedly to the observation window, wanting to look beyond the claustrophobic confines of the facility.

Once, millennia ago, Reaper knew, there had been plants, trees, animals, lakes, and rivers here. The archaeological and paleontological record indicated as much. But now it was a desert with poisonous air: the stony landscape inhabited only by the shadows of lowering, lividly colored clouds. Dusk lay thickly on bouldered hills, misshapen buttes, and, nearer, the digs themselves—terraces cut into soil and rock; crumbling archways and doors into darkness. Heavy mining equipment, abandoned midjob, was lit up by standing arc lights.

This was the foreign landscape in which his parents had given their lives, where they'd been sacrificial lambs to the meaningless pursuit of knowledge. Or so Reaper felt in his worst moments.

"That where it happened?" Sarge asked.

Reaper didn't answer. But he thought: *Dig Twenty-three . . .*

"You find the door?" Reaper asked, after a moment.

Sarge moved away. Reaper stared through the window at the starkly shadowed, terraced dig, till Sarge called, "John . . ."

He found Sarge standing by the air lock hatch. The locked exit glistened with a fairly fresh spatter of blood. On the floor under the hatch were two bodies in overalls and lab coats. One face down, and the other was facedown, but his head was turned 180 degrees around, faceup.

Sarge bent down and read off the name tags. "Thurman and Clay. Look at 'em. They weren't trying to stop something from getting in. Something stopped them getting out."

Destroyer's voice crackled over the comm. *"Sarge—we reached the north air lock. It's secure."*

Reaper grunted to himself. *Things pop out of the ceiling and run off into the floor here. How could anything be secure?*

He shook his head. No reason to say it aloud. The team was spooked enough.

He hunkered to look at the two bodies in front of the air lock. Seeing they had no respirators, he said, "What could make you want to escape into . . . nothing?"

*   *   *

"Sarge," came Destroyer's voice on the headset. *"Reached the north air lock."*

Mac stopped pacing, cocked his head to listen, as Destroyer went on, *"It's secure. Console indicates nothing's come in or out for twenty-six hours."*

Mac nodded to himself. Maybe there weren't a whole swarm of those things out there after all. Destroyer would've seen something, for sure.

Mac was fingering his weapon and watching the corridor leading to the "mudroom"; thinking about home, Tokyo; thinking about how his uncle had asked him to come into the synthetic saki factory. Wondering what natural saki had been made out of him. Rice, wasn't it? Or was it water chestnuts? Should have gone into business with Uncle. Anything could happen here . . .

His uncle, though, kept trying to get him to marry that second cousin of his, Inki. Pain in the ass, that girl. Following him around, looking at him mooneyed, her hands clasped in front of her. Geisha complex. Not many of those left. Most of the girls from his own neighborhood had been in the Yakuza Lady's Auxiliary. Not the geisha type.

But then there was something touching about Inki, too. Maybe he should've given her a whirl. Be comforting to come home to an old-fashioned girl. Get a massage. Back rub. Never tell you she's got a headache that day . . . and after all—

Something move down there, in the dark end of the corridor?

The lights were only on in half of the corridor; the farther end was pitch-black. Something big shifting down there? No. Nerves, Mac.

He scratched his nuts and turned, prompted by a noise behind, and a sudden strange vinegary smell, and . . .

He had half a second to see the great reddish thing that hulked over him, snarling, before it slashed out with its scythelike talons.

And with one razoring slice, it cut Mac's head off his shoulders.

He'd always wondered if a human head remained conscious, for a few seconds maybe, after being severed from the body.

Now he knew.

Because from where his head lay on the floor he was able to watch his own headless, blood-spouting body stagger and fall . . . into the swelling sea of shadows.

NINE

SOMETHING INHUMAN ROARED in triumph, from back where they'd left Mac.

Sarge and Reaper looked at one another and ran back toward the corridor. "Mac!" Reaper called. "Mac?" No answer,

They dodged between tables, to the corridor—and saw Mac's body, headless, in a growing pool of blood.

Whatever had killed him was retreating into the shadow at the far end of the hallway. There was just a glimpse . . .

"What *was* that?" Reaper asked. Not really expecting an answer. They were left standing in the open, under the corridor light, with the body of their long-time buddy gushing blood at their feet. His severed head was near Reaper's boots; Mac's face, going blue, staring in wonder at nothing.

Instinctively, Sarge and Reaper went back-to-back, half-crouching. Both of them felt it: more than one thing was watching them from the shadows.

Whatever had killed Mac was just out of sight—and was very aware of them.

"What you got?" Reaper asked, hoping Sarge had a fix on a definite, solid target . . . he almost ached for it.

"Nothing. You?"

"Nothing," Reaper said hoarsely. He glanced again at Mac's decapitated body. "Shit." It had to have happened in the space of a second. The body was so fresh—still pouring blood, the puddle spreading out around their feet.

"Still glad you came?" Sarge asked.

Reaper didn't answer.

Something was moving down there, in the darkness at the end of the corridor. A flash of yellow eyes.

"I got something," Reaper said. "In the shadows— on my three."

"Ten degrees cross fire on either side," Sarge said softly. "Sweep through the shadow."

"I'll take the left side."

"I've got the right."

Then they turned and opened up, Sarge firing *thud-thud-thud-thud* with his big autorifle, Reaper thundering with his light machine gun, the weapon jumping in his hands till his fingers ached from keeping it leveled.

Sarge yelled into the comm: "We're in pursuit! Everyone meet at the air lock!"

Reaper's machine gun hit it: the thing shrieked and rushed into view for a moment, chewed by bullets, spewing black blood before it stampeded howling down a side corridor.

Reaper and Sarge, grateful for something definite to shoot at, sprinted after it.

"So like which one of you's the oldest?" Duke called to Sam, casting about for sane conversation as he returned with the bone saw.

"Me," Sam replied, not looking up from her work. "By two minutes."

He was coming down the corridor toward the nanowall—she'd directed it to remain open for him, knowing he hated pushing his body through its glutinous-metal mass, and he could see her in the infirmary, looking at the creature on the table through an instrument he'd never seen before.

"You two are . . . twins? Shit. Nonidentical, right? Because that would be weird."

"What would be weird?" she asked innocently. Pretending she didn't know he meant having sex with Reaper's identical twin would be too much like having sex with Reaper.

"Nothing," Duke said, clearing his throat as he hesitated outside the door. Was this nanowall going to close on him as he was going through it?

Maybe that wasn't the only reason he was hesitating out here. Sure, Sam was a fine-looking woman; her smarts and poise were attractive, too, maybe even more than her looks. But still . . .

He wondered why he felt so drawn to her.

Oh come on, man, you've been a long time without a woman. You'd be drawn to a hundred-year-old grand-mother buying incontinence diapers, about now.

It wasn't that, though. Since he'd lost Janet—since she'd blown him off for a guy she could count on being there at night, a guy with a square job who would probably die in bed and not in some jungle clearing half a world away—he'd made up his mind it was going to be all work and party, all the time. Just the job, and the party afterward. No attachments. From here on, he'd told himself, it'd be whores or women who might as well have been whores. The kind of airheads who went on viddy shows gassing about trying to get a rich bachelor to marry them. Slick sluts.

My star guide said I was going to meet someone hot tonight but I thought he'd be, like, someone into stock-breaking—is that what you call it, when you, like, buy and sell stocks?—and not a Marine but, whatever, because I've always been into muscles? Even when I was a little girl I liked to look at those Mr. Bodybig shows, and, I'm all, whoa, a Marine, oh wow do you have, like, a Humvee we could ride around in and maybe cruise my homegirls, be-cause, I'm, like, all into a guy who's got a big ride, with, like, big wheels, and . . .

Verbatim from his last date.

And here he was drawn to a scientist. A woman with a clinical glint in her eyes; a woman who was eagerly looking forward to using a bone saw, for God's sake.

But there was something about her—behind that shell of complete independence, skepticism, there was a smart woman who needed someone to make the world mean something again.

Oh, get over yourself, he thought. *She'll never go for you. She . . .*

Something was growling, on the other side of that table, in the shadowy farther reaches of the infirmary.

Sam turned to Duke—she hadn't noticed the sound, but something about the way he'd just froze there at the door, listening, had drawn her attention.

"What?" she asked.

A beast not much higher than his knee was stepping into view. He stared. Was that *a dog*? A large, snarling, drooling, red-eyed dog—coming around the corner of that cabinet?

It was. One of the escaped lab animals, probably. It lowered its head, muzzle wrinkling, baring teeth as it prepared to lunge toward him—its eyes crazed with fear—and Duke raised his automag, ready to shoot it down.

Sam, seeing the dog, opened her mouth to speak, probably to tell him not to shoot it, which was going to be a problem because this animal was ready to kill—though he didn't blame it, considering what it'd probably been through—

But she never had a chance to say it. Because just then he realized that the dog wasn't growling at him at all, but at something behind him. The dog backed away . . .

Duke spun, but it was too late, the creature in the corridor behind him slashed out, its talons ripping into his arm. Duke floundered away from it, fell onto his back.

"Duke—!" Sam called, running for the nanowall.

The imp loomed over him—a lean thing with clusters of eyes, its skin looking raw; drooling, almost sneering down at him now, a sound like a rattlesnake's warning issuing from deep inside it.

He fired—the gun was set on semiauto, and he squeezed off three rounds, stitching the thing across the middle, making it stagger back screaming.

He got his feet under him, was aware of Sam poised at the opening nanowall, waiting for him.

"Sam—get back inside!"

The imp turned to glare at Sam—Duke backed away from it and fired again, so it'd come at him and not her—it came slashing the air, a few steps from ripping him into chunks.

"Come on!" Sam yelled, ready to close the nanowall. *"Come on!"*

Duke turned, lunged for the doorway, the imp close behind him. Duke shouting as he passed through, "Now—do it now!"

He leapt—and the imp came after him. Duke kept going—

Sam hit the nanowall's manual controls and the

gray wall solidified around the imp, head and torso caught partway through. It shrieked, and Duke could hear its bones cracking.

Its tongue shot out of its mouth—unspooling, stabbing out to its full length—just shy of Duke's neck.

The tongue reeled back into its mouth and it shuddered—and fell limp, jaws clacking and spewing black blood . . .

Reaper and Sarge tracked their wounded quarry down corridor after corridor—all the way back to the D4 tunnel, through it and up into the atrium, then to the air lock that led into the corridors outside Carmack's lab.

The creature was big, but they'd practically shot it to pieces—hadn't they? How did the damn thing keep going?

"Nothing could have survived that!" Reaper insisted—trying to convince himself more than Sarge, as they rushed out of the atrium.

They were following a trail of blood that led from the atrium, across the floor, and right through the air lock.

Reaper shook his head in wonder. The thing knew how to open an air lock? What exactly did that imply?

They passed through the air lock, not bothering with a reseal. That horse was out of the barn. The things could get into the atrium another way. The air lock was set to seal automatically if there was a break in the facility's walls or windows interfacing the planet's surface.

Reaper and Sarge now stood in the corridors a short distance from Carmack's lab.

"It's back in the lab," Sarge muttered.

Do these things have an agenda? Reaper wondered. *Are they after something in the lab? Are they intelligent enough to use the equipment? They managed to get the airlock open . . . what else can they use?*

Or do they move about randomly, driven by the afflatus of rage or fear or hunger? That seems more likely.

Reaper and Sarge moved on, searching through light and shadow, getting closer and closer to the lab.

"Clear," Reaper said, as they reached the end of the corridor. Redundant to say it, since it was obviously clear, but they stuck with procedure. That was the RRTS way.

"Clear," Sarge confirmed. "Damn it's fast."

Running footsteps drummed a short way behind them. Something was coming at them from down the corridor—Reaper turned, finger tightening on the trigger, and came a hairbreadth from blowing the Kid's head off his shoulders.

The Kid, Portman, and Destroyer were rushing up to them, weapons at ready, panting. "Did you get it?" the Kid asked, looking around, his mouth hanging open, eyes more dilated than ever.

Reaper shrugged. Useless to brief the Kid. The

young soldier's brain was frying on drugs, he'd lose anything you tried to tell him.

Sarge called Pinky on the comm. "Pinky, anything comes through that door, use an ST grenade."

Pinky replied with a nervous affirmative. Sounding like he wanted to say a lot more and was afraid to come out with it.

Portman shook his head, gaping at Sarge. "He uses an ST in there, he'll blow the Ark!"

Sarge acted like he hadn't heard. "Reaper, Kid—pairs, cover formation, sweep the corridors."

Reaper nodded and led the Kid to the next cross hallway. It was dark down there. He switched on his gunlight and plunged into the corridor leading away from the squadron. Knowing what he was leaving behind.

He was going away from back-up. Away from the Ark—the only means of getting off the planet. Away from his sister.

Away from hope.

Outside Carmack's lab, Sarge was still giving orders. "Destroyer, you and Portman maintain a perimeter here."

"He blows the Ark," Portman pointed out again, "how the hell we supposed to get the fuck home?"

Sarge didn't answer him directly. But he made himself clear: "Destroyer, that prick"—meaning

Portman—"gives you any trouble, shoot him in the knee, we'll leave him here to starve."

"Roger that," Destroyer said, calmly. Both of them ignoring the look of shock on Portman's face. "Where you going?"

"Armory," Sarge said. "I think we're going to need something with a little extra kick."

Sarge jogged down the corridor, rifle ready, finger poised near the trigger—not quite on it. He passed blood blotches on the walls, wires leaking sparks, swaying ends of hoses like mechanical boas, finally skidded to a stop near the darkened dead end he'd been looking for. Panting, he pointed his gunlight into the gloom. Was he lost? He searched the floor . . . the damn thing was here somewhere . . .

There it was. The woman's severed, rotting arm, oozing yellow stuff onto the floor tiles.

This was a weird assignment all right: he was feeling good that he'd found a woman's severed rotting arm on the floor. Hot damn.

But he needed it to get through the door.

He picked it up, wincing a little as some of the skin sloughed off under his fingers. He set off again, wishing he'd brought along some gloves as he carried the severed limb—holding it awkwardly, to keep it from falling apart in his hands—off down the corridor. Not liking the feeling or the smell of the thing in his hands. But there was no getting away from stench on Olduvai—it seemed like this job was all about being up to your neck in decay. It was always that way—the closer you got to the UAC's secrets, the more rot you found. He'd long ago stopped caring. He'd learned to isolate all feelings of empathy; compassion. They got in the way of the job.

Probably it was that time on the island. Beautiful, gemlike little place, just far enough north of the equator it didn't get too hot. No big problem with insects, no sea wasps concealed in the coral. White sand beaches, emerald trees, women the color of honey. Should've been paradise.

But the local people hadn't liked the UAC transmitter base on the island. The base gathered energy from solar receptors and transmitted it in microwave beams into orbit, where it was soaked up to power the UAC's orbital labs and missile platforms. Only, the thing leaked microwaves, so that people around the transmitter—even passing too close—had a tendency to get brain tumors; children were born with birth defects.

Sarge, shipped to the island to help keep order, had seen all those children with missing jaws; with shriveled limbs.

Some of the local men had formed a militia, surrounded the transmitter base, demanded it be shut down. To keep peace, UAC had temporarily complied—just until the arrival of UAC's Special Implementation Squadron, led by Lieutenant Brevary and Sarge.

Don't call it a death squad. Sarge didn't like that

term. Just because they were sent out to locate the leaders of the militia and march them off for execution, sent to shoot anyone who tried to escape into the rain forest, sent to set rebel villages on fire . . . did that make them a death squad? No. They were trained professionals. They got the mission done, that was all. In short order, the native militia was disbanded—most of it, actually, was buried—and the UAC transmitter was back online. Peace again. And UAC provided free pain meds and euthanasia to the sick inhabitants of that lovely little island. Most of them eventually took the euthanasia. On a routine return to the island, they found hardly anyone still living there. But walking past the mass grave on the south side, Sarge had smelled all those bodies, the militia he'd helped execute, all at once, shallowly buried under the pretty white sand. Animals had dug some of the corpses out. Gulls were getting at them, snipping off pieces of rotting flesh, tossing their heads back to gulp it down.

That's what a UAC project was like. Pristine on the outside. Even glamorous. Just don't get too close. Or you'd find out where the bodies were buried . . .

Maybe even end up carrying a woman's severed arm down a corridor on Olduvai.

He went through another series of hallways . . . thinking that this woman'd had no idea a part of her was going to end up being carried by a soldier as just another field tool.

Was this the turn? Yeah. He was starting to get to know this hellhole. There was the sign:

SPECIAL WEAPONS LABORATORY

He went to the door panel, opened the hand print pressure pad.

"Please provide DNA verification." A friendly woman's voice, robotic but sounding like a real person anyway. One more in a stacked deck of ironies.

Sarge slapped the hand of the mangled limb against the pressure pad.

No response. Maybe the tissue was too decayed to provide an accurate DNA reading.

But then the invisible nonlady chirped her welcome: *"DNA verification confirmed."*

The security door to the weapons lab slid open, and Sarge dropped the decaying limb, wiped his hand on his pants, and went in to find some of that seriously scary balls-out ordnance. He smiled and his fingers twitched; he could almost feel that kill power in his hands already.

He went into the innermost chamber.

Some religions had their holy of holies. This was Sarge's.

The gun was hanging in a luminous high-intensity electromagnetic cushion, floating in midair— rotating there, as part of the display. A bioforce gun. He'd heard a rumor about the new weapons being developed out here, based on technology discovered on Olduvai—some gabby lab tech returning from this hell planet had shot off his mouth about them. And if the size of that gun was any indication, it was more than enough bioforce to kill an elephant.

That thing could kill a small herd of them.

The question was—would it kill Sarge, too?

Portman and Destroyer were standing guard outside Carmack's lab. Portman was wondering just what the hell they were guarding. Sometimes Sarge gave them arbitrary assignments just to keep them busy. Maybe that was for morale. But Portman's own morale was in the dumpster, right about now.

"This is bullshit," he told Destroyer. "I enlisted to serve my country, not to protect some corporation's goddamn science project."

Destroyer ignored him. As per orders.

Portman fidgeted, thinking that if they didn't get some backup out here, they were all going to die. He'd heard chatter on the comm about what had become of Mac. His head gone, swish, just like that. One second he's there, thinking about pussy no doubt, next moment he's a bowling ball. And Mac had been the closest thing Portman had had to a real buddy in this group. Hell he knew these bastards didn't like him. He tried to prove himself, tried plenty, but that only seemed to make it worse.

Mac had invited him along to chase tail on furlough, one time. They'd ended up alone in a *saki* bar, only Mac's .45 keeping the bartender from closing, but it was okay, they were drunk enough they didn't care—Mac teaching him drinking songs from the homeland. Mac was okay. Now the only guy who'd been anything like friendly was smoked—and his team was pretending it didn't matter.

Not me, Portman thought. *I'm not gonna be the next one to die—and be forgotten in the time it takes to take a short piss. Uh-uh.*

Portman made up his mind. But he needed some way to get off by himself . . .

"I gotta take a dump," he announced.

Destroyer looked at him. His eyes like chips of flint. "Now?"

"Unless you want me shitting in my pants right here."

Destroyer snorted and nodded toward the lab door. They'd seen a bathroom off Carmack's main lab room.

Portman stepped into the lab, pointing his gun-light into the dark corners. Nasty things in here . . .

But nothing was moving now. Could be, though, that something was waiting in that bathroom.

Come on, he told himself. *This is your shot. You won't get another . . . Sarge'll be watching you too close . . .*

He took a deep breath and hurried across the room to the bathroom door. Licked his lips—then stepped through, swinging his gun this way and that, half-expecting an attack. Nothing. Seemed empty.

141

He kicked open a stall, gun ready—nothing to shoot in there but the toilet.

He went in, closed the booth door, sat down. He put his gun on the tiled floor.

"Portman," came Pinky's voice, crackling out almost immediately on the comm. *"I got floor and wall on your vid . . ."*

"Gimme thirty goddamn seconds," Portman snarled back, "I'm taking a shit!" Though he wasn't.

Pinky started to say something else, but Portman twiddled the frequency knobs on his comm and chestcam, cutting him off. He pulled out the little input, keyed in a code. Then spoke quietly into the comm:

"This is Subcorporal Dean Portman with RRTS 6 Special Ops on Olduvai, 0310 hours. We have encountered hostile activity, require immediate RRTS reinforcements . . ."

TEN

DESTROYER WAS GETTING tired of waiting for Portman. But he didn't feel like going in there and inhaling the gaseous residue of Portman's meals, either. Portman was a fuckup—but he had a point. This mission had the feel of being a one-way ticket.

Not that Destroyer was going to tell him that.

He hoped the Kid would get out of it all right. Portman was screwing the youngster over by giving him dope—another thing the asshole had to answer for.

Destroyer had come to feel a kind of responsibility for the Kid—he'd taken on the young soldier's secondary field training himself. The Kid wasn't particularly good, but he was eager to please. Making Destroyer think of himself at age seventeen . . .

He was an up-and-coming gangster in the East Side ghetto, sure of himself, feeling immortal, invulnerable—which was of course when he got shot by the cops while robbing a liquor store.

Superficial wound, but it had put him out of the fight, then a grinning white cop had busted his head with a nightstick.

He'd awakened in a hospital, to find himself staring up at a RRTS Field Recruitment Agent standing with arms crossed, at the foot of his bed. This Privatized Marine was all spit and polish, standing there, looking flatly down at the boy known on the street, then, as Steppin' Razor. The agent was a man blacker than Destroyer, about forty-five. His broad shoulders straining at the material of his dress blues.

"So they call you Razor?" the guy was asking. His nameplate said CANNER.

"Steppin' Razor," the teen had corrected him. "Who the fuck are you, and what the fuck you want?"

"I'm here to offer you a choice. Jail or RRTS Field Recruitment. We've got a deal with the courts, boy. Word is you're good with weapons. Got nerve. But you're using it all wrong." Canner's eyes had glinted; other than for that, no expression. Just . . . waiting. Watching and waiting. Never taking his eyes off the boy—who would someday be a man called Destroyer.

"That right? Fuck you."

"That's it—that's the all-wrong part. That 'fuck you' bullshit. Man doesn't get far that way. Serve your country, you serve yourself."

"My country? You motherfuckers, what I heard, serve UAC more than the country. You're Privatized. You ain't no real soldiers for the country."

"Country uses us and UAC does, too—UAC's interests are the same as the country's. You want to go to jail?"

144

"I ain't afraid of jail."

"I didn't ask you if you were afraid. I know you ain't. That's why we want you. I asked you if you wanted to go there, dumb-ass."

"Fuck no. 'Course I don't want to go."

"Then get up out of bed. You sign these papers I got with me"—he waved a manila folder—"and you're in my custody. We can tell that cop outside the door to go to hell. Then me and the MPs escort you to Training Center Thirty-two. Sign the paper, 'Steppin', and get up—you don't let a little wound like that slow you down. Then you join my cadre."

"Training center. Cadre. Yeah right. You mean boot camp. Pure hell, that's what I heard."

"You can't take a little hell? No, that's wrong—it's a lotta hell. So what? It's a challenge, boy."

The challenge was there, in Canner's eyes. But there was something more . . .

Understanding. This guy had grown up without a father, too—"Steppin' Razor" knew it intuitively.

But he didn't trust easily. "Why's your 'gang' better than mine, man? 'Cause it's *all* gangs. Some are big, and they got uniforms made in a factory. Some are small and they make their own uniforms. But it's all gang soldiers. We call our country the 'hood, that's all. I can be a 'general' in this army, man. I'd never make no general in yours. And I get myself killed in yours as easily as in mine—maybe more easy. Why I want to do that? For medals? I'd rather have a hot car. And bitches."

He had the satisfaction of seeing some surprise in Canner's eyes, then. Most of his recruits probably didn't think much.

Finally Canner nodded. "Something in what you say. But there's . . . levels of being a warrior, son. I can give you a kind of training you'll never get down here. Achievement of a kind you'll never get anywhere else. And I'll be there for you. I'll make it hell for you in boot camp—but afterward, we'll go on a training mission together. I'll be there, too. Anytime you want advice—you come to me. And that's a guarantee, son."

Ten long seconds. Then the young man who would one day become "Destroyer" said, "You got a pen?"

"A pen?"

"How else I going to sign?"

That was a long time ago . . .

He wondered where Canner was now. And what he'd think of this mission. Of Olduvai. Probably he'd shake his head, and say, "That's a UAC mission for you. Just do it and get your black ass home."

Only, home is a long way from here, Destroyer thought bitterly.

Destroyer looked at his watch, then at the door to the lab. Where the hell was Portman? He waited a few moments longer, then yelled into the semidarkness of the lab: "Portman!"

No response. He sighed, went into the lab, scanning the room as best he could with limited visibility. Found the bathroom door and knocked. Hammering on the door with his fist, shouting:

"Portman, how long does it take for a goddamn—"

He broke off, aware of a smell like rancid vinegar and something coming at him—he didn't have time to level his gun before being jerked off his feet, yanked him violently into the darkness.

Destroyer found himself on his back, the wind knocked out of him, staring up at a gaping, salivating mouth big enough to swallow his whole head in one easy snap. Big the thing was, bipedal, every muscle outlined in unhealthy pink-and-blue tissue; bulky, without eyes—but with plenty of teeth and claws. A manacle on the thing's leg with a broken chain trailing from it . . .

All these impressions came to Destroyer in the fraction of a second it took him to see his enemy and roll aside, trying to get his chaingun.

He tried for his knife, but the hulking mutant swatted it away—the blade skittered across the floor, fell with a *clink* into the holding pit.

The creature's slashing claws just missed him as he rolled, leaving a row of gouge troughs in the floor, torn-up tiles flying like tossed playing cards as Destroyer slammed a kick into the creature's inside right thigh, toppling the beast—even as it batted his chaingun from his hand, the heavy-duty machine gun crashing against the wall.

The monster scrambled to its feet as Destroyer sucked air into his tortured lungs.

. . . and kept the roll going, got his feet under him and at the same time grabbed the chain attached to its leg, putting his weight, his motion, and his muscle into it as he jerked the monster off its clawed feet. The chain wrapped around Destroyer's wrist.

The chaingun was almost in reach—Destroyer grabbed for it, missed—then yelped as the beast leapt up and wrenched the chain on its leg with tremendous force. He felt himself being flung, pitched through the air, tumbling, skidding, rolling, feeling the beast bounding over him, the two of them falling . . .

Into the holding pit. Falling, he grabbed at the gurney hoist—it snapped in his hands as he fell but broke his fall so he was able to land on his feet. Winded, half-stunned, he straightened up, confirming he was in the pit with the steel sides that Goat and Portman had found. Dark in here, just a little light coming from above.

Something was in the pit with him.

He could hear it breathing liquidly, growling deep within itself. It shuffled forward, and he saw that the hulking creature had fallen in with him.

Destroyer looked at the walls. Twenty feet or more up to the rim. No way he was getting out of here anytime soon. Not alive.

So this was it. He was going to finish his life fighting in a steel pit with a thing that was pure aggression . . .

Kind of fitting, really. He was just sorry that Canner, that cold-blooded son of a bitch, wasn't here to see how well one of his men could die, when the time came.

Anytime you want advice—you come to me. And that's a guarantee, son.

He knew what advice Canner would give him now. *Sell your life dearly, son. If you can, take the miserable bastard down with you . . . and the gods of war will be waiting to give you the gang handshake in the next world . . .*

The beast came closer, an enormous, fevercolored scabrous presence in the gloom; almost magnificent, monstrously Herculean, snarling, raising its claws as it prepared to meet its enemy headon. It growled again—and, intuitively, Destroyer understood that growl:

One of us will die now.

"I see we speak the same language," Destroyer said.

Pinky, at the secondary comm. console in the wormhole chamber, was staring at the screen trying to work out where Destroyer was. But Destroyer had evidently dropped his gun—the guncam was sending only a nondescript wall. Was that a little blood on the wall? That could be anywhere in the facility.

"Destroyer?" came Sarge's voice, filtered, over the comm from the corridor near the special weapons lab. *"Portman? Come in . . ."*

Pinky wanted to be able to give Sarge some sense of where his men were—but Destroyer's tracking blip was going in and out. Maybe . . . Carmack's lab?

But maybe not. Hard to say for sure. The transmitter had been damaged. Chances were, Destroyer was dead. And Portman, too.

"Lost Portman," Pinky said, into the comm, "and all I've got from Destroyer is some kind of wall . . ."

In a steel-lined pit . . .

The big mutant charged and whipped out with a clawed fist, hammered Destroyer's uplifted left arm hard—faster than he'd have thought so big a creature could be—and Destroyer staggered and fell, rolled, got his feet under him again, and lunged at his enemy, all his strength going into that assault, slamming his shoulder into the thing's lower torso, making it stagger back into the wall.

Crack! High-voltage electricity making the thing howl, the pit strobing with the fat sparks, the monster lit up for a moment, roaring, quivering with the voltage, smoke rising from where its flesh fried on the metal wall. It shook, its jaws spastically opening and shutting, clacking—then it tore itself free, whimpered just once, lowered its head like a bull and came at him like a locomotive—

Destroyer laughed and ran at his enemy, screaming, *"Pray for war, motherfucker!"*

They met in the middle, the creature with more sheer bulk coming harder, lifting Destroyer off his feet, even as he dug his fingers deeply into the wet places where its eyes should be, sank his teeth into the place that should've been its neck so that he tasted its tarry blood, and head-butted it so hard his scalp split open like that orange Mac had pitched to him . . .

Until the two of them crashed into the wall, the electricity searing through both of them now, as they tore flesh from each other's bones in the death throes of shared electrocution.

Crashing white light, all consuming darkness, infinite journey to nowhere . . . and then . . .

Good job, son. Welcome to Valhalla.

Duke was sitting on a chair as Sam sewed up his wound. He was pretending it didn't hurt as much as it did.

He was staring at the "imp" trapped in the nanowall. It'd gotten some of its strength back, was thrashing around, jet blood streaming between its teeth, foam dripping from the corners of its jaws, blood leaking from the edges of its eyes . . .

The creature thrashed and moaned.

"That's why I don't do nanowalls," Duke said. He

looked at the wound. Good, neat sewing. "Now that I'm dying," he said gravely, "I want you to know I will accept mercy sex."

"Sorry," she said, bending to bite through a suture thread. "I'm afraid it missed the brachial artery. You'll live."

"Just my fuckin' luck."

Half a smile from her, then. Almost.

The lights flickered—off. On. Off and on. Duke and Sam looked up at the ceiling lights as they fluttered another time . . . and finally, almost reluctantly, decided to stay on for a while.

"Good," Duke said dryly. "Because it's not as if it wasn't scary enough in here already."

Sam grunted in agreement, and went over to the exam table, looked at the incisions she'd sawed into the dead imp's chest.

Duke looked at the other imp trapped in the door. Almost felt sorry for it. Almost.

"Give me a hand here," Sam said.

Duke turned to see Sam bent over the monster's corpse on the gurney. She had a crowbar in her hand, was working on the thing's chest. He sighed and went to help her pry it open. She used the crowbar, he used muscle, grabbing the two halves of the thing's chest-exoskeleton, pulling them apart. Repugnant smells and fluid gushed and sputtered out, runneling over his hands, down his forearms.

This was not Duke's ideal of a good first date.

They got the chest wide open—and Sam stared into it, mystified.

Duke didn't look too close, himself. Sure he was tough—but he was a little squeamish about *some* things. "Jesus . . . you ever seen anything like it before?"

Sam nodded numbly. "Yes."

ELEVEN

IN THE INFIRMARY'S observation room, a zipped-up body bag on a gurney was stirring. Whatever was inside was getting restless. The bag was squirming like a chrysalis just before the moth breaks out.

The body bag settled into stillness . . .

Then it suddenly lurched, the motion carrying it off the gurney, onto the floor with an ugly thump.

It lay still for another few moments—until an arm punched through the vinyl, at a place where the seams met in a corner; another arm ripped free.

And Goat, who'd been dead for some time, thrust his head out through the break. The whites of his eyes had gone red; the pupils were the color of dead flesh. His skin was like the imp's—as if outer layers had been stripped away.

But it *was* Goat. Wriggling, ripping, climbing out of the body bag—insect from cocoon—getting to his feet, swaying, staggering to the glass wall between him and the two human beings who had no notion that he was there, that he was staring at them, that he wanted to shred their throats with his teeth . . .

Sam and Duke were staring into the imp's pried-open chest.

"Look," Sam was saying, her voice hoarse, "there's a heart, lungs, liver, kidneys . . ."

"But . . ." Duke was trying to think his way out from under the conclusion that was threatening to settle on them both. "But like, dogs got kidneys, right? Pigs . . . pigs got kidneys . . ."

Sam shook her head. "See this scar? On the lower right side abdomen here . . . and this ligature, and stitching . . ." She swallowed, and looked at him. "It's . . . had its appendix removed."

He stared. "What are you saying? Are you saying . . ."

She nodded. Looked back at the imp, having difficulty accepting it herself. "It's human."

When she looked back at Duke again she saw him staring, suddenly pale, at the observation room behind her.

She turned to see Goat glowering balefully at them from the other side of the glass wall. Goat tilted his head and bared his teeth. His eyes were two embers glowing from the hollows of his skull.

Then he raised a hand to his forehead and made the sign of the cross.

"Oh my God," she breathed.

Goat turned away . . . walked a few steps . . . Then

turned and sprinted toward the window and rammed it with his head—the audible crunch of bone reached them and black blood ran down the glass.

Duke saw it then—a look in Goat's eyes. Horror. Recognition. Despair. A mute entreaty . . .

And again Goat slammed his head on the glass. And again. Duke and Sam watching helplessly as Goat pounded his head on the glass, over and over until bone fragments flew and gray matter clumped on the transparent wall beside the blood, to ooze slowly down the glass. And at last—Goat collapsed. He shuddered and twitched, then lay still.

A second death. A final death.

It was a long moment before either Duke or Sam could speak. "He knew," she said at last, softly. "He knew he was turning . . ."

Sam looked at the imp on the gurney as the realization struck her. "That thing didn't butcher Willits—it *is* Willits."

She turned to the imp in the nanowall. Walked toward it, suddenly on a mission. "We've got to keep it alive . . ."

Duke looked at her. Keep it alive? As far as Duke was concerned, that sentiment was totally baffling.

Once, in a faraway desert place, they'd been driving half the night in a big, six-wheeled armored vehicle, Sarge and Destroyer, Duke and Reaper and three other men. Sarge was driving—all three of those other guys were now dead. Red Morrison, Rolf Gestetburg, Lee Zhang. They had the bad luck to be in the rear of the ATV when the RPG hit just above the right rear fender.

One moment they were ribbing each other about flatulence and snoring, the next they were screaming as shrapnel cut them to pieces. Blown clear, Zhang lived about ten minutes and then blew out his own brains with his sidearm when he realized he was missing most of his lower half.

Upfront, Duke had been wounded, but got out in one piece. Sarge had been stunned by a spinning chunk of steel fender, was slumped over the steering wheel of the burning vehicle, vaguely aware of what was going on but unable to move. Reaper was out on the road, firing at the enemy—the insurgents cresting the dune on the east side of the road. They were skidding down the dune to kill any RRTS who'd survived the blast. Maybe torture them a while before they killed them, knowing these desert guerillas.

Destroyer grabbed Sarge under the arms, pulled him from the ATV just before it went up in a fireball.

All of them—even the enemy—were knocked flat by the secondary explosion. Reaper's jacket caught fire; Duke had been stunned; Destroyer's eyebrows had been burned off. He must have been a terrifying sight as he got to his feet, smoke rising from his brows as he stood over Sarge, firing his chaingun, mowing down the surprised insurgents. The guerillas had expected to find these outlander 'Privines' without any fight left in them. Duke and Reaper opened up on the enemy on one side, Destroyer on the other.

Sarge had gotten movement back, some of the mist cleared—and looked up to see Destroyer towering over him like a giant statue, an ancient wonder of the world. Sarge was flat on his back and Destroyer was standing over him, boots planted to either side of his chest, ready to go down protecting his NCO.

When he'd run through the last bullet on that chaingun, he'd run through all the guerillas, too. Twelve of them were lying sprawled on the face of the dune, blood seeping into the yellow sand. Dead or dying.

Then Destroyer had tossed the gun aside, stepped back, and hunkered down, helped Sarge up. Sarge had tried to walk—and had collapsed. He'd sustained a pretty serious concussion.

Destroyer shrugged and picked Sarge up, only grunting once with effort, slung him over his shoulder, and carried him—a man who weighed as much as Destroyer himself—off down the road, toward the Marine outpost, seven miles away.

Now that, Sarge thought, *was a real set of balls. Destroyer was a helluva damn soldier.*

He remembered all this, thought all this, as he stared down into the holding pit, his gunlight picking out the two bodies on the floor, wrecked cadavers still smoking and bloody, barely recognizable: Destroyer and the monster he'd killed, locked in lethal, terminal embrace.

Sarge let out one long low rumble, deep in his chest, which is as close as he ever got to expressing grief, and went to find a ladder.

In the wormhole chamber, Pinky was thinking about Sam. He'd always liked and respected her. He hoped she was going to get through this. He suspected few would.

A sudden motion from the monitor drew his attention back to the crisis at hand. He checked the squadron thumbnails. Sarge was now jogging down a corridor where the lights flickered on and off. Duke was looking at Sam—

Pinky scowled. Duke's cam was squarely pointed toward Sam's rear, as she worked over a table. Though the cam was on Duke's chest, you could tell by the centeredness of the image that he was staring at her ass.

"What a dog," Pinky muttered.

He looked at the other thumbnails—Portman's guncam was pointing under the door of the bathroom stall . . .

And something was moving toward Portman's stall. Moving toward that camera angle . . . something big. Moving slowly, in a careful way. The way an animal does—when it's stalking prey.

Pinky stared—then found his voice, hitting the comm button. *"Portman!"* Pinky was yelling. *"Holy shit, Portman, get out of the bathroom. Sarge! Portman! Can you hear me!"*

No response. Portman had cut off all input from the others. Pinky could see what was going to happen to Portman and had no way to tell him about it.

In the lab bathroom, adjusting the equipment, Portman was feeling nervous about Destroyer. He'd heard him shouting to come out. Easy enough to ignore that. Then there was another noise from out there—something crashing around maybe. But he'd been listening to his headset, not really paying attention.

But finally it occurred to him that maybe Destroyer had been jumped by one of those things . . .

Fuck it. He was going to finish what he'd started, then he'd check on Destroyer. What he was trying to do here might well save Destroyer's life.

Another moment's adjustment, and he got the quantum-send connection he was looking for. He let out a relieved breath and hit SEND, transmitting his digitally recorded message home. He hoped.

The comm screen announced:

**Transmission sent. Time until reception
2:56:18 . . . 17 . . . 6 . . .**

Fucking hell. Almost three hours before the message arrived through the Ark transfer.

Okay, so he'd get in trouble later, when the reinforcements showed up. Sarge might haul him up on charges for disobeying orders—but most likely he'd take care of it himself: beat the crap out of him. Maybe kick him out of the unit. So fucking what. He'd never belonged there anyway. They'd never really accepted him. Especially Sarge—who'd had to let him into the unit only because Portman's uncle, in Marines Op, had pulled some strings. Fuck 'em. Let 'em punish him.

It was better than being dead.

Anyway, he had to get out of here and find Destroyer—even that stone-cold killer might need some backup . . .

Portman plugged his guncam cable back in, retuned his comm, immediately hearing Sarge calling to him:

"Portman—what's your position . . . get out of the bathroom, repeat, get out of the bathroom!"

Portman swallowed. He dropped the earpiece from his ear.

"Portman, we're tracking something—!" came Reaper's voice, distant and staticky from the fallen earpiece.

He reached down and switched the comm off, not wanting whatever was hunting him to hear it jabbering.

Silence. And then a snuffling sound. A scrape, from outside the cubicle . . .

He opened his mouth to call out, to ask if it was Destroyer—and then thought better of it.

He knew damned well it wasn't Destroyer.

Slowly, feeling the sweat start popping out on his forehead, holding his breath, Portman bent down and laid hold of his rifle, very slowly picked it up, trying to make no noise at all . . . but the strap scraped on the concrete floor.

Portman winced and looked into the breech—the weapon was unloaded. He fumbled in his pocket for a clip.

Something was definitely breathing out there. There was a sharp smell, and the sound of claws on the floor . . .

Portman tried to load the gun—and the clip fell from his shaking hands. It skidded with a rattle under the cubicle to his right.

Immediately, something large snorted in reaction, on the other side of the cubicle wall.

Trembling, Portman knelt and looked under the divider—there's the clip. He couldn't see anything else over there. Just the toilet and his ammo. He reached for the clip . . . couldn't quite get it. He got down lower, the floor cold under his fingers, and squeezed partway under the divider, swiping at the clip . . . almost had it . . . But . . . he was stuck under the divider. Christ!

Grimacing with discomfort he forced himself a little farther—almost laughing at the ludicrousness of his position.

Don't you fucking laugh, he told himself. *You're on the edge of hysteria. Stay fucking frosty. Almost got the damn thing.*

Then he heard the creature again. *Snort.* The *click-click* of claws . . .

Where was that clip? There! Got it. He writhed back into his stall, sat up, pressed the clip in place as quietly as possible, and stood. He took a breath, dizzy from holding it, and slowly pressed the door open with the muzzle of his gun, inching out to look into the bathroom, finger on the trigger, ready to blow the thing's head off.

Only, it wasn't there. What the fuck?

Dust sprinkled down, into Portman's hair. He didn't think much of it for a second—then realized . . .

The ceiling overhead was shaking. He looked up . . .

A kind of fatalistic paralysis gripped him. He knew. He just knew, somehow—it was too late. He could run—he stood and prepared to run—but even as he did it, he knew.

And that's when a huge-taloned rawboned hand smashed down through the ceiling from above, making ceiling tiles and insulation tumble down—as it reached for him.

"Aw shit . . ." Portman muttered. His last coherent words in this life.

After that, there was only screaming—as the massive arm encircled him, plucked him up into midair.

163

The comm unit fell, his gun with it—he grabbed at his knife, as the thing hauled him upward, into the shadows of the crawl space, Portman jerking the blade from its scabbard, slashing at the brawny, scabrous arm.

His knife had no effect—and then that big arm pulled him up into the ceiling.

Still at the comm console in the wormhole center, Pinky slammed a fist against his wheelchair in frustration as he watched on the guncam—Portman's weapon was leaning against the toilet, pointing upward—as Portman was yanked into that crawl space, vanishing for a few seconds only to be lowered by the ankles, smashed back and forth in the stall, battered from wall to wall like the clapper in a frantically tolling bell—blood splashing, his screaming was the bell's ringing.

Pinky swore under his breath. It was bad enough being trapped in this cyborgian wheelchair the rest of his life—but watching as other people were torn to pieces, one after the other . . .

Portman's screaming came over the comm in filtered distortion, muffled but somehow all the more awful for it.

Then Portman was jerked bodily upward one more time, vanishing entirely into the darkness of the hole in the ceiling.

The image shuddered with a vibration—then

went dark as Portman's blood rained down on the guncamera's lens.

Reaper and the Kid rushed into the lab's bathroom, firing as they went, the Kid letting go with both autopistols, Reaper chewing the ceiling up with his machine gun. Knowing damn well that Portman was dead—and all they could do was avenge a fellow Marine.

They paused—not sure if they'd had any effect.

And then Sarge pushed in between them, shouldering them aside.

"Step back," he said.

And he let go with the new gun he'd brought from the weapon's lab: the BFG.

They stepped hastily back as Sarge's weapon emitted a multicolored fireball that engulfed the stalls, the ceiling, the bloody remains of Portman, and the creature that'd killed him, all of it merged into a puddle of molten metal and smoking flesh.

Sarge lowered the gun. When the smoke cleared, there was nothing but a crater that encompassed floor, wall, and a big section of the ceiling.

"Did we get him?" the Kid asked, somewhat ridiculously. No one bothered to answer him. "We must have, huh?"

Reaper looked at the barrel-shaped gun in Sarge's hands. "What the hell is *that?*"

"BFG," Sarge responded, calmly, patting the gun affectionately.

"What's a BFG?"

Sarge smiled thinly. "Big Fucking Gun."

Reaper could only nod.

Duke was watching Sam work on the imp trapped in the nanowall, amazed to see her start an IV on the thing. A section of the nanowall opened, to one side of the creature, not disturbing its immuration, and Sarge came in, walking backward, dragging Destroyer's body. Reaper came after him, dragging another of those unsettling lumpy ponchos, this one containing pieces of Portman, mingled with the monster that'd killed him, like ingredients mixed in a casserole.

"Destroyer!" Duke blurted, running to Destroyer's body.

Sarge noticed Duke's emotional reaction. He'd known Duke and Destroyer had grown up together. But he didn't like sentiment getting in the way of focus—Duke had better get frosty, and fast.

"Portman, too," Reaper said.

"What the fuck's that?" Sarge asked, looking at the gore on the observation window.

"Goat," Sam said. "He killed himself."

Sarge gave her a chill, skeptical look. "What do you mean he killed himself? He was already dead."

Duke was standing over Destroyer, wracked with sobs but not shedding any tears—the sobs were

166

silent. He wouldn't let them out. But his body shook with wave after wave of them.

Sam went to Duke, pushed him out of the way, hunkered to check Destroyer's neck—she was looking for the telltale neck wound that seemed to presage infection. But Destroyer's neck was one of the few parts of his body that wasn't lacerated, burned, or broken.

Reaper pointed to the poncho where bits of Portman were mixed up with the thing that had killed him. "That's all that's left of the thing we were chasing. And we found two more dead scientists in the dig. Clay and a balding guy with glasses."

"An imp . . ." Sam said, glancing at the poncho.

"A what?"

"Imps. Just a scientist's urge for classifying—what isn't classifiable." She looked over at the imp on the gurney, muttered, "Dr. Thurman . . ."

Suddenly feeling exhausted, she sat on the floor, knees drawn up, rubbing her eyes. Trying to think. "Did you check their necks?"

Reaper's look said it for him: *Their necks? Why their necks?*

"Were there wounds on their necks?" she persisted, sounding like a weary teacher with a dense student.

"They were dead, all right?" Reaper replied, irritated with her supercilious tone. It was back to the condescending Sister Scientist again. "We were in a firefight; we weren't conducting a goddamn field study."

Sarge ran a hand over his head, struggling, like Sam, to collect his thoughts. There were just too many X factors here to organize into one clear picture. "We came here to find six scientists—anyway, the six big shots in the facility. We got four known dead and Willits is probably KIA down in that sewer. So all we're missing is Carmack."

They all thought about that a moment. Remembering that Carmack had vanished from his gurney—after he'd seemed dead. Then Goat had gone living-dead. Was Carmack where Goat had just managed to keep from going?

Sarge turned to Duke. "Carmack shown up yet?"

Duke pointed at the imp trapped in the door. Drooling, barely alive. "Oh he's shown up all right."

The others stared, not getting it. Maybe not wanting to.

"Look at the left ear," Sam said.

Sarge went over to the trapped creature—close enough for a good look, but not too close.

He stared at its head. It was missing an ear—like it had been crudely carved off. Just the way Carmack had ripped away his own ear in his madness, when they'd caught him in that dead-end corridor . . .

"Son of a bitch," Sarge murmured.

Sam pointed at the imp cadaver she'd been dissecting. "I think that one is Dr. Willits. I'm going to run the DNA, check it against his med records."

Sarge turned to her and voiced what all the men in the room were thinking:

"What the fuck were you people working on up here?"

TWELVE

SAMANTHA DIDN'T ANSWER immediately. She only had suspicions, after all. She couldn't be sure . . .

They waited.

Finally, she said, "In *my* part of the facility, we analyzed bones—and artifacts." She nodded toward the imp. "We weren't doing *anything* like this."

They weren't going to let her off the hook. Sarge gestured toward the thing that had been Carmack. "What the hell is that?"

Sam sighed. "It must be a genetic mutation. Maybe caused by something environmental or viral. I just need time to figure it out, see if there's a way to stop it, reverse the condition . . ."

Sarge shook his head, looking at the other imp struggling in the nanowall. "Carmack's condition is irreversible."

Reaper looked at him. There was a particular flatness in Sarge's eyes. Reaper had seen it in him before. Sarge had made up his mind. When Sarge got like that, the shit came down hard.

Sarge stepped closer to the imp.

"It's not necessarily irreversible," Sam said, watching Sarge closely, "he's still alive. Perhaps we could replicate hyperplasia, create antioncogenes . . ."

"It's irreversible," Sarge repeated, with icy conviction. And he drew a pistol, shoved it under the imp's chin . . .

"No!" Sam said.

The imp's eyes opened, one after the other, three and four and five and six eyes looking at him—then Sarge pulled the trigger.

Blew its brains out. Black blood and gray matter fountained, slopping onto the nanowall, instantly running off—none of it clinging—to puddle on the floor.

Sarge hadn't only killed an "it" Reaper knew—he'd killed Dr. Carmack, too. Whatever was left of Carmack had been trapped in that thing's skull. But Sarge was doing the man a favor, Reaper decided. There just wasn't going to be time to "reverse the process."

". . . Because," Sarge continued, his voice even and casual, "Carmack's condition is that he's dead."

Sam stared, stunned by the summary execution.

"Kid," Sarge said, methodically checking the load on his pistol and turning to what remained of the squadron, "go back to the dig and make sure those other dead scientists are really dead."

The Kid looked at Sarge, at the dead imp, swallowed, then went in a hurry to follow orders.

"I've lost four soldiers," Sarge said, turning to

Sam, advancing on her. "What are you people experimenting with up here?"

Sam merely stood there in stunned silence.

"I'm not going to ask you again," Sarge threatened.

"I told you, this is an archaeological research center."

Reaper watched them closely. Was Sarge going to harm his sister? Wasn't that implied, somehow? If that's what Sarge had in mind, he had figured John Grimm's loyalties all wrong.

"You think I'm lying to you?" she said, looking at Sarge, her face white with shock, her eyes hot with anger, her voice sharp. "You think I'm hiding something. I'm telling the truth." She turned to Reaper. "I'm telling the truth, John."

Reaper was pretty sure she hadn't lied—not exactly. But had she held something back? He looked at her uneasily. "What's on the hard drives?" he asked, at last.

She blinked. "What?"

"What's on the MICDIs, Sam? What were you downloading? What were you sent in to protect?"

She chewed her lower lip. "It's just research data."

Reaper glanced at the imp. What remained of it was slumped like a question mark in the nanowall. "Research into *what?*" he asked.

Exploitation of Mineral Wealth, Water,
Oil, Oxygen, Plant Life, Coal—

The words appeared on the computer screen in Carmack's lab as Reaper and Sam—with Sarge and Duke watching—fast-forwarded through MICDIs.

—Agriculture, Livestock, and other animal assets . . .

Reaper looked at the door to the bathroom—the room Sarge had cratered with the BFG. He had hard-core misgivings about being back in Carmack's lab, especially with Sam along. They shouldn't be here. A few steps away, Portman had been smashed to pieces. And a few yards more was the pit where Destroyer had been killed. The imps, whatever else was scuttling around the facility—the things might be anywhere. But right close to here seemed a good bet . . .

Duke kept an eye on the main door to the corridor; Reaper and Sarge tried to keep a watch on the rest of the room, between checking the computer— but how did you stand sentry against things that could pop out of the ceilings and floors?

He looked at the console as he heard Carmack's voice: *"—test rats have evidenced increased musculature, endurance, ability to—"*

Sam shook her head and Reaper reached over, hit EJECT, scanned for something more recent. There was an image of Carmack, looking a bit older—or more worn-out. Like a guy who hadn't been sleeping for days.

"—skeletal development, stimulation of the rhesus's metabolic systems . . ."

Nope. Reaper ejected the MICDI, they popped in another.

"—subject was injected with study agent at 00.03. DS solution used with 10 micrograms IV bolus—"

"Here we go," Reaper muttered.

The digital video cut to a new image, poorly framed from a fixed camera mount above, maybe on a ceiling. Some poor sap on a gurney. Most prominent in the image was a naked arm, bar code tattooed on the forearm, and part of the man's torso. The video—about as clinically cheap as you could get—was stamped:

SUBJECT: STAHL, CURTIS. 003 HRS

"Vitals normal," came Carmack's voice, over the image. *"Elevated heart rate, attributable to subject anxiety . . ."*

Reaper shook his head. How did researchers working on human beings stay so detached? How could they talk about a man like they were talking about a lab rat? Maybe that was really what had gone wrong here—treating people as something less than human made it easier to turn them into something . . . less than human. But it seemed to Reaper that the inhumanity started within the scientist.

On the screen, Carmack's hand came into the

video shot, carrying a syringe. He drew something from a bottle marked C-24, coolly injected it into the clearly terrified man's IV tube.

"*C-24 successfully grafted to subject's marker cells at 00:09 . . .*"

"What's C-24?" Sarge asked.

Sam tilted her head, as if she wondered herself. She looked at the bottle on the video, then turned to the equipment on the bench next to the VDU. On a solute spinner was an identical bottle—marked C-24.

She picked it up, looking at it with something resembling awe. "Carmack must have managed to synthesize a stable solution of the synthetic chromosome . . ."

When she thought the others weren't looking, she slipped the bottle into her pocket. But Reaper saw her do it.

On the grainy video, the experimental subject, Stahl, was lifted on a winch, gurney and all, across the room . . . and then lowered into the pit. Down into the very holding pit Destroyer had died in.

Reaper was just guessing when he murmured: "He reconstructed chromosome mutation in human subjects . . ."

"*Subject moved to protected observation area,*" Carmack was saying, on the video, "*at 00:17 . . .*"

"What the hell are we looking at?" Sarge demanded.

"Genesis, chapter one," Reaper muttered. And he

thought: *Mary Shelley would've liked this—Carmack playing God.*

Various angles on that grainy video—finally showing Stahl looking from side to side, in a kind of sublime panic, trying to think of some way out of this. He was trapped on a gurney, in unbreakable restraints, in a pit twenty feet deep, in a locked-down research facility, surrounded by coldhearted men who thought no more of him than of a gerbil, men who would not hear him—who would mentally edit it out—if he begged them to let him go. They'd already injected him with some nightmarish agent; he could feel it taking hold inside him.

Still, driven by instinct, Stahl looked this way and that, straining against the restraints, hoping for a way out.

"Who was he?" Reaper asked.

Sam went back to the console, typed in a search: *experimental subject Stahl background.* Text flickered by. The scrolling stopped on the experiment's biographical records.

Stahl, Curtis

She pursed her lips, scanned the data, encapsulated it for them. "Curtis Stahl. He was condemned to be executed. He's a paranoid schizophrenic with convictions for multiple murders and pedophilia."

A hard guy to feel sorry for, Reaper reflected. But

watching him lowered into that pit, seeing the terror in his eyes, his mouth quivering like a two-year-old's, like a child lost in a big city crowd at night, you felt sorry for him anyway.

Sam pointed at the computer screen—as the video jumped to 004 hrs.

The arm and torso began to swell—was that swelling . . . or growing? Their horror grew, too, as they watched. "Oh my God . . ." Sam muttered.

The video record jumped ahead, from stage to stage, like an animation without enough frames per second, showing Stahl's transformation. At 005 hrs Stahl was writhing—and metamorphosing. His skin was growing lumpy, red, his flesh thickening, then forming the exoskeleton, a scaly hardness. His eyes were sinking away, his nose seeming to melt, lips peeling back, melding with the growing skull, teeth baring, extending; his fingers were merging one into the next, bone projecting out—he screamed in agony at this, as bone burst from the flesh to become claws . . . like the talons that had scythed Mac's head from his shoulders. Maybe the very same ones. And Stahl's noseless face, once the transformation was done, seemed strangely familiar to Reaper. Then it hit him . . .

It was the same monstrous face he'd seen staring at him from the shadows, when he was a kid, that day in Dig Twenty-three.

Ghost? Maybe. Precognition? Could well have been. It didn't matter.

Sam was muttering something about laws of conservation of matter, probable quantum induction . . . And *genetic demons* . . . A "Hell Knight," according to a subtitle on the video.

But all Reaper could think about was how it must've felt, at that moment, to be Curtis Stahl. Getting bigger and bigger—a true *Hell Knight,* all right. He reached out and switched off the video. They could see where it was going.

Reaper felt the fury rising in him. What they'd seen on the computer—that was Olduvai. The soul of Olduvai was in that steel-walled holding pit. Just as he'd sensed it as a boy.

He looked hard at his sister. Did she finally understand? "They sent you in here"—he gestured at the lab around them— "to save *this?* They wanted to protect *this?"*

"It doesn't make any sense . . ."

"You trusted them, and they used you. They lied to you, Doctor."

Sam's eyes were narrowing as she worked out a scientific problem in her mind. "If he perfected xenogenesis, he would have also had to—"

"Jesus Christ!" Reaper interrupted. "Don't you see what this place is? It's hell. It always was. This shit ends here. Gimme those drives."

He snatched them up.

"What are you doing?" Sarge asked, his voice and eyes modulated to a deadly chill.

He closed his fist over the disks. "We have to destroy them."

He shook his head. "That's UAC property."

"The fuck are you talking about, Sarge?" Reaper felt mad enough to take Sarge on right this second if he had to. Where had Sarge's leadership got them so far? Mac. Portman. Destroyer. Goat. All dead. "We got the chance to end this . . ."

"We take the data back."

Reaper waved the disks at him. "You want this to survive? Jesus Christ, did you even *see* what I just saw?"

Sarge locked eyes with Reaper. You could feel it like a physical shock when Sarge fixed you with both beams. "I didn't see shit. I ain't paid to see shit. I got my orders. And so do you."

He walked over to Reaper and stood eyeball to eyeball with him. Reaper could feel the heat of Sarge's body, up that close.

He felt Sarge take the disks from his hand. Without breaking eye contact, Sarge said, "Is this everything?" Talking to Sam—but looking at Reaper.

"I . . ."

"I said *is this everything?*" Sarge bellowed, still facing off with Reaper.

All the time Reaper wondering how to take Sarge out if he had to. And if Duke would back him up. Probably not. Duke was all Marines all the time . . . and that meant complete loyalty to his NCO.

"I have one more to download."

"Then do it," Sarge said flatly.

Reaper decided to wait. If he decided to challenge Sarge head-on, there'd be a better time than this.

He nodded, just slightly, and turned away.

Sam went to the computer.

The Kid had never been this scared.

Not that anything was jumping at him right now, as he walked through the mudroom to the surface air lock. Nothing moved here. There was nothing at all but pottery, and crusty old artifacts, and tools. And somewhere in the room were a couple of dead guys—he was supposed to shoot their bodies in the head, when he found them.

He hoped to God they were still dead.

No, nothing moved, nothing threatened him, not out front. But you could feel them watching you. He knew those things were here somewhere, just out of his line of sight.

And every time one of the squadron had gone off alone—Mac, Portman, Destroyer—they'd ended up KIA.

Guess what, the Kid thought. *You're on your own right now just like Destroyer. You more likely to survive than those vets? I don't think so . . .*

This was seriously fucked up. What was Sarge

doing, sending him out alone? Trying to get rid of him? Let the predators get the weak one out of the way?

You're getting paranoid. Just remember who the enemy is . . .

But he was still buzzing on the shit that Portman had given him—though dope fatigue was starting to set in, that feeling of dirt in the gears of your nervous system—and the stuff, instead of helping him, had just made his nerves vibrate till he was teetering on the top of the greased slide of paranoia.

So it was hard to be sure who the enemy was—maybe it was everyone here.

Cut it out. Think back to when you decided to join the Privines . . . Think about the corps spirit you saw that day . . .

He'd been stationed on a ship anchored just off a bombed-out raggedy-ass town on the edges of a sun-washed sea, two thousand miles from his hometown. That day he was on the docks, supervising a bunch of seamen carrying supplies from the boats to the trucks pulled up to where the pier met the breakwater of jagged rocks—the engineers had tumbled broken boulders along the interior shoreline of the harbor, an attempt to protect it against the rising seas of global warming. He'd been warned, before the last three supply runs, that there might be a raid of the local religious fanatics on the supplies. The rebels wanting to keep the provisions from getting to the base on the other side of what remained of the town. But it hadn't happened yet, and there were rumors like that all the time. Still, the Privatized Marines had been assigned by the civilian supply company to protect the materiel. The Kid hadn't taken the "Privines" squadron seriously. He was just thinking about getting this materiel mission over with, getting back to the ship, watching the comedy DVD that was up that night in the rec center: *Hotties in Orbit*. It was supposed to have some good shots of big-titted chicks in free fall. All that sweetly floating flesh . . .

He'd noticed the Privines lolling about on the crates in the shade—guys he would someday come to know as Duke, Reaper, Goat, and Destroyer—watching as he and his Navy boys muscled supplies up from the boats to the half-broken robot freight mover on the dock. Stupid robot couldn't pick up anything itself anymore, you had to load it and tell it where to carry the shit.

Remembered thinking, *What a bunch of lazy Privine pricks. They could help us and they just sit in the shade, weapons on their laps, chewing gum and spitting tobacco and grinning as we sweat this bullshit in the hot sun.*

That's when the attack came. Starting with an explosion.

No, that was wrong, he decided, as he revisited the memory. It really started with a noise, a *shuh-shuh-shuh-shuh,* and Reaper had popped up like a jack-in-the-box, the lolling Privine vanished, all fighting Marine now, on hearing that noise—shouting, *"Get down, incoming!"*

And that'd saved the Kid's crew. They dived for cover, and the surface-to-surface missile struck the robot freight mover, the machine turning to screaming flak and hissing shrapnel, flames licking up, the massive device half-falling through the hole the explosion busted through the dock.

The Kid's mouth had gone all cottony, and he had trouble being loud enough yelling at his men to move back to the boat, get under the dock, as the insurgents' stolen truck came roaring toward them from the shore, a dark face at the wheel, a man with shades and white teeth bared, barreling it at them. That was the real attack, the missile was just a preliminary to shake them up, disorient them, kill a few. That's the way the rebels liked to hit you.

The truck could be a suicide machine itself, totally wired—but Destroyer and Reaper were running toward it, when anybody in their right mind would be running away; their weapons blazed, tearing the truck's engine apart, and the radiator was the only thing on it that exploded. Then it veered, out of control, smashed into a piling and overturned with a thump that shook the whole dock. The rebels got out of the back anyway, yelling their war-cry gabble, something about calling their God to give them strength to smite evil, charging with those cheap rebuilt assault rifles spitting rounds, bullets chewing up the pier, sending splinters and ricochets off metal bolts whipping past Reaper and Destroyer.

Duke and Goat had moved off to the other side of the dock and were doing what they could to flank the rebels in the narrow space, firing their weapons.

The Kid had finally managed to get the safety turned off on his own assault rifle, clicked a round into the chamber, fired at the rebels—running after the Privines as he fired past them at the enemy.

It'd been just thirty, maybe forty-five seconds of firefight, but it'd seemed a lot longer. The Kid watched in wonder as Duke ran at two rebels, screaming his own war cry. One of them was firing back—Duke staggering, but not falling, running through his clip, blowing the head off one of the guerillas and slamming into the other, knocking him flat, smashing down with his boot, crushing the guy's throat. Another one was coming at him from the side and the Kid was trying to get a bead on that rebel—but there was Goat, jumping over a crate, coming down firing, hitting the guy between the eyes.

The Kid was awestruck by the squadron's tautness in action, their unity, their sheer nerve: Duke turning to cover Goat's six, shooting a rebel who was coming at him from behind; Destroyer getting Reaper's back, Reaper turning to cover Destroyer, giving a hand signal the Kid didn't know and suddenly they were running in a phalanx, all four of them, into the remaining six rebels, who were trying to aim but were too panicked to hit anything. Another second and the squadron was among them, cutting them to pieces. The squadron fired astonishingly fast, moving from target to target with split-second exactitude, as fast as a rock drummer pounding unerringly through his drum set.

The Kid was firing, too, when he could get a shot, but he didn't think he had hit any of the enemy, and by the time he got close enough to do it for sure, the rebels were already dead. Shot to pieces.

Reaper had taken a couple of rounds in the chest, but he was still standing—his Kevlar had stopped them. Goat had lost a chunk of his hip, and Duke had taken a round in his right shoulder . . .

But the bodies of dead guerillas were lying about like a crashed load of mannequins strewn over the dock. The Privines had made every round count—and most of the enemy had died from head shots. Instead of panicking, the squadron had worked like a well-oiled machine.

That's what the Privines were about. Readiness. Readiness in unity.

Afterward, the Kid had walked up to them. Watched as they patched one another up. Cleared his throat.

"What?" Destroyer had asked.

"Just wanted to say . . ."

"You're welcome. Now fuck off." He looked down at Duke's wound.

Reaper glanced up at the Kid. "You call a med-chopper?" Reaper had asked.

"On their way."

Destroyer had gone back to bandaging Duke, Reaper to taking care of Goat. Then Destroyer looked up, feeling the Kid watching.

"What?"

"You guys . . . did a great job."

"So? We're supposed to."

"I guess—we were sort of bad-mouthing you . . ."

"You wanted to say sorry?" Duke had said. "We don't need it. We only take sorry from people we respect."

"Actually," Destroyer pointed out, as he squeezed some pain-stopper into Duke, "I turned around, the Kid was coming up with us, firing at the enemy. The only one of that bunch that did. Shows . . . I don't know. Shows something I guess."

The Kid fairly glowed inside at that.

"So, Kid—" Duke said. "You want a medal? Go get us something to drink, if you want to be useful."

"Sure," the Kid said. "I mean—something to drink. Some water. I'll get it . . . the water I mean." The Kid turned away. Then turned back. "Uh . . . how do I . . . ?"

Destroyer looked balefully at him. "How do you get water? You get a canteen and you shake it. If it goes gurgle, gurgle, there's water in it. Then you bring it here to me first—not to these other jar-heads."

"Hey fuck you, Destroyer," Duke said, "who you calling a jarhead, jarhead? Kid, don't listen to him. Bring me the water first."

"But—how do I . . ."

"What?"

He finally just blurted it: "I want in." He licked his lips. "Be . . . you know . . . one of you."

Duke snorted. Destroyer shook his head. "Hard to jump from your service to ours. Special deals got to be made. Besides—the training alone'd kill you. Now, Big Balls, how about that water?"

"I'll get you water. But . . . I want in."

"What, we don't get water unless we say you can join?"

"No, I'm not saying that . . ."

"Then fuck off."

"Huh? Look—I want in."

"Heard you before."

Confused, the Kid opted for simplicity and ran for the canteen, ran puffing back, handed it over. But as they passed the water around, he said, insistently, "I want in. Or . . . uh . . . I don't get you in to see *Hotties in Orbit* tonight."

"*Hotties in Orbit?*" Duke had said, sitting up, suddenly interested. "You can get us in to that?"

"Come on, Duke . . ." Reaper muttered.

"Hey, I wanta see that thing. Yeah . . . and the kid

187

was good. Boy howdy he was good. You see how good he was, backing us up like that, Reaper? I heard they got that blond with the tattoos on her ladyplaces in that thing, man . . . that genius actress with the humongous . . ."

"Oh Christ," Reaper said, laughing, "are you going to saddle us with a . . ."

He had almost changed his mind about joining, though, when he'd seen Goat using that big knife to take "trophies" from the dead rebels.

The Kid laughed softly to himself now, thinking about it.

He had gotten them in to see the weightless hotties, but that wasn't really why they'd helped him get in their squadron. They'd done it partly because he'd done his best to back them up in the firefight, firing at the enemy, charging the rebels when the other sailors had gone to ground . . .

And partly because Destroyer had said he'd take the responsibility. Destroyer had stepped up and taken the Kid under his wing. A minor politician, the Kid's own father had been absentee most of the time—one day a pushy reporter had burst into his office to find him boffing an intern, the two of them standing up at his desk, her underwear down around her ankles. It made a nice photo in the tabloids. Mom divorced Pops faster than an MP chucks a shit-faced soldier in the tank, and that's fast, and after that the Kid saw his father once a year—the old man was just a distracted, irritable presence when he was around, nothing more. No big brothers; teachers all hated the Kid's smart mouth, same with the officers on the ship. He'd barely made bosun. Giving the authority types crap and all the time looking for someone to tell him what the hell to do with his life. Then along comes Destroyer . . .

Now, looking around in this ghostly archaeological workroom on a faraway world, he thought: *Along comes Destroyer—then there goes Destroyer. He's dead . . .*

Tears welled in the Kid's eyes. He was glad he was alone, now. If they saw him crying—even for a combat brother—he'd never hear the end of it.

But Destroyer had been the closest thing to a big brother he'd ever had . . . best combat teacher anyone could want.

He let out one last shuddering sob, wiped his eyes, and decided that Destroyer wouldn't want him bawling like this. So he cussed himself out for a minute, squared his shoulders, and went to check out the dead guys.

Wondering, as he went, if he'd ever see his woman again. Millie—a nurse back home. Nice girl. What would she think of all this?

Crossing the room he walked past a neat row of heavy-duty chain saws, numbered sequentially, "9, 8, 7 . . . 5 . . . 4 . . . 3 . . ."

What'd they needed chain saws here for? Weren't chain saws for wood?

He went to where Sarge had told him, on the

comm, he'd find the bodies of Clay and Thurman. He found the blood, all right, and plenty of it. But there was a problem about the bodies.

He touched the headset transfer. "Sarge? We got a problem . . ."

It was a simple little problem. He'd been sent there to find some bodies.

The bodies were gone. Some other place, you'd think: *They're dead bodies, they couldn't just get up and walk away.*

But here—they could do exactly that.

In the wormhole chamber, Pinky was fumbling with the med-remote on his wristband, trying to adjust the antidepressant and analgesic feed on his cyberchair. He was running short of the pharms— should've checked the implant panel that morning. He needed a little something extra to get through this.

If he could just see Samantha, see her walk through the door and into the Ark. See her get safely home. She was like an adopted sister to him.

He'd never let himself fall for her, of course. He didn't have a lower half. You proved your love, for the most part, with your lower half. Intimacy started in your lower half and traveled upward—he remembered it, from other women, before the accident. Now he'd never feel it again.

Still, it tormented him thinking that Samantha was probably going to die in this interplanetary limbo. Some nightmare from Carmack's lab was likely to get to her. Tear her to pieces. Or worse— from what he'd been gleaning, over the comm—it could make her into a monster.

He almost threw up, at that thought, and tapped the remote again, squeezing another few drops of trank into his system.

The meds weren't working today.

He ached to get out of here, detach from his cyber-chair, hook up into his life-support recliner, go to sleep for a day or two. But he was needed. And any-way, he was afraid of the nightmares that would come if he slept. He knew the nightmares were there, stored up in his head, waiting to spring at him the way the imps were waiting to kill the others.

It bothered him that he was safe here while they were all at risk. He went to the computer console, thinking that it was bad enough being handicapped, trapped the way he was in this machine, without facing the same dangers the others faced . . .

That's when he heard the sound outside the big, locked metal door. Sounded like an engine starting up. Then another sound, a squealing of metal on metal: something grinding against the thick steel of the door.

Okay. So maybe he wasn't safe here after all.

"Sarge?" Pinky said into the comm. "Something's outside the Ark door—is that you guys?"

"Negative," Sarge responded immediately. "We're still in the lab."

If it wasn't them . . . and everyone else was dead . . .

"I was afraid you'd say that," Pinky said, as something on the other side of the door began to cut its way into the wormhole chamber.

THIRTEEN

IN CARMACK'S LAB, nothing was really resolved between Sarge and Reaper—but the new crisis, a possible assault on the Ark itself, superseded everything else.

"Reaper, let's go," Sarge said, slapping a fresh clip into his rifle.

Reaper read him to mean they were going to check out whatever was trying to get at Pinky. Which meant only the squadron was going.

"She's coming with us," Reaper said, nodding toward his sister.

Sarge shook his head, just once. "Negative."

"We're gonna leave her here alone?"

"She's got a job to do, Reaper. Just like you have."

Reaper could tell that Duke clearly didn't like the idea of leaving Sam either. But he only shrugged at Reaper. He wasn't going to argue with Sarge.

Sam was engrossed in a computer file, trying to reach some deeper understanding of the phenomena of the imps and the Hell Knight. "Carmack's happy little elves," Duke had called them.

"Sam . . ." Reaper began. Not sure what he wanted to say.

"I'll be okay, John," she said distractedly. "Go." She was leaning close to the monitor, fascinated by some DNA signature, some nuance of the chromosomes that was all cryptic code to Reaper and an open book to her. Sam had come a long way as a scientist, he thought. And once more he felt a rush of admiration for his sister . . .

Sarge looked at him. Almost expressionless—but it was a warning. Reaper couldn't shake his bad feeling about leaving Sam. But it was hard for him to let his squadron go into a probable firefight situation without him.

He tossed his sister his comm headset. "Keep the door locked," he told her. "Don't open it to anyone. Use this if you need help . . ."

She glanced up, nodding. For a moment their eyes locked. She looked as if she wanted to say something . . . something that bridged the gulf of years, reached back to their childhood together. To the times when they'd made their own action figures out of bits of old cleaning robots; when they'd watched old movies on the digital feed; when they'd toyed with being musicians together, him playing his crude guitar, she banging on a cheap little electric piano, laughing when she hit a sour chord . . .

That laughing little girl. And he was leaving her alone in here.

Sarge was heading for the door. Duke hesitating—

looking between Reaper and his sister. Reaper sighed and nodded to Duke.

They followed Sarge into the corridor. Sarge signaled them to double-time it, and they began to run.

Pinky stared in fascination at the rock-saw blade pushing its whirring snout into the wormhole chamber, roaring and squealing as it cut through the door. Sparks rooster-tailed into the room, metal grit accumulated on the floor under the diamond-tipped chain saw as it cut out a good-sized, jagged-edged circle. It was obviously cutting an entry into the room—a doorway, big enough for something large to climb through.

"*Pinky?*" came Sarge's voice, over the comm almost lost in the screech of the chain saw gnawing at the metal. "*Do you have a visual?*"

"Oh, I got a visual all right," Pinky said, in chilling understatement.

He had a pistol already on the computer table beside him. Doubted it would be of much use.

Staring at the growing, smoking breach in the door, Pinky reached down to the bag of ST grenades Mac had given him, having to strain to reach it from the cyberchair. Picturing himself popping from the chair like a cork from a bottle if he went too far . . . just caught the edge of the bag with two fingers, worked it up to a better grip, pulled the sack of grenades onto his synthetic lap.

He pulled one out, and got it ready in his right hand, held the pistol in his left . . .

Heard Sarge shouting in the comm as he and Reaper and Duke ran down the corridors to the atrium:

"Don't let it get into the Ark!"

Amen to that, Pinky thought. *But it's just about too late for that, too . . . probably too late for all of us . . .*

The saw finished its circular cut. The metal from the hole vibrated like a dull gong, then fell into the chamber, clattering. The rough edges of the hole smoked.

Pinky waited, staring at the hole, sweat making the grip of the gun slippery in his hands.

Then the thing showed itself.

Pinky screamed—and fired.

"Use the grenade!" Sarge shouted into the comm as he and Reaper and Duke ran into the atrium. The Kid came running from the dig tunnel as Sarge again urged Pinky, "Use the goddamn grenade!"

Ahead was the door into the Ark chamber. There was a hole cut in the enormous metal door—from the look of it, Reaper figured they'd used a diamond-frosted chain saw. The chain saws were used by archaeological engineers to saw through the metal walls of some of the ancient Olduvaian structures, and to free things trapped in stone, Reaper remembered. He'd noticed them in the mudroom. Hadn't thought for a moment they'd ever be applied here.

If those things had gotten to the Ark—to the wormhole that leapt through space, to Earth—then they'd gotten to the UAC compound at Papoose Lake.

And there was a whole planetful of people to infect, to transform, waiting there. Most of them without a clue that they were about to be invaded by a kind of vicious genetic aberration, a thinking infection from a distant world.

Only—the horror didn't come from an alien world, not entirely. It had been created by a fusion of human science and the lore of the long-dead savants of Olduvai.

Pistol fire cracked from beyond the hole cut in the metal door. Then two flashes of color-challenged light . . . the weird light, all colors and none, that they remembered from the Ark.

Sarge got there first, fairly diving through the hole. The other three followed—and found the wormhole chamber deserted.

No Pinky, no chain saw, no crazed scientists, no imps, no Hell Knight. Just a grenade, twirling slowly on the floor, where it'd been dropped—unused.

They stared . . . Duke was the one who said it for all of them. "Jesus. It's home. It got through."

Sarge took a deep breath. His voice was almost a monotone. "We gotta stop it before it gets out of the home-side compound." He looked at Duke and Reaper and the Kid, one after the other. "Are we ready?"

But Reaper was thinking about his sister. "Sam?" he called into the headset comm. "Sam—do you read me? Over." Nothing. Just static in his ears. He felt a wave of desperation. A sinking feeling of defeat. First this planet had gotten his parents . . . now maybe his sister. *"Sam? Do you read me? Over!"*

Sarge was reloading his gun. Acting like he didn't hear Reaper, like it was not his concern.

Reaper licked his lips, watching Sarge as he waited for a reply on the comm. Was he going to have to choose between protecting his world—and his sister? "She's not answering . . . *Sam? Do you read me? Sam!"*

Sarge started for the Ark. "Lock and load."

Reaper knew what that meant. It was Sarge's succinct way of saying that Sam was a lost cause. They had a bigger mission to think about, responsibilities that went way beyond the personal.

Reaper knew he should go along with that decision. But he wasn't sure he was capable of it. Maybe she was dead—but maybe not. He just couldn't leave her behind, no matter what the stakes. It just wasn't in him to do that.

That's when the lights around the wormhole went dim. Flickered. Came back on . . .

And then switched off. They were left in near-complete darkness.

"What the fuck is that?" Duke demanded. As if anyone there had the answer.

A soothing female voice issued from the PA system:

"System reboot . . ."

And the lights came back on.

"Quarantine is breached," Sarge declared. "This mission is no longer containment. Double in, gather up all the weapons and ammo you can find."

"Sam!" Reaper yelled into the comm. "Do you read me? Over!"

Only static replied.

The soothing digital lady intoned, *". . . Time required to begin renewed operation. Five minutes . . ."*

Reaper looked at Sarge, waiting.

Sarge said, "You got three."

Reaper thought about arguing, but there would be none with Sarge. He had three minutes to find Sam and get her back to the Ark.

He ran to the door, climbed through, and sprinted across the empty atrium—half-expecting, in this wide open, shadowy space, that something was going to rush him, rip at him with claws of razor-sharp hardened bone, pierce his throat with a lancing barbed tongue.

But he made it to the air lock, sprinted through it, found himself in the corridor leading to Carmack's lab.

Seemed to take a lot longer to get there than he remembered—and he was running full tilt, his

199

weapon heavy in his hands, breath burning in his lungs, heart pounding in his ears. Long time since he ran track as a kid.

He remembered when he was a boy, before they'd gone to Mars, he and Samantha had been back home, without their parents, staying with an older cousin. He'd won a ribbon in track. He'd hoped his dad would hear of it, say something. Transmit his pride to his son. Nothing. He'd been pretty bummed out—hadn't heard from Mom or Dad in a while. Hadn't said anything about it to anyone, but his sister had watched him, and saw how he felt.

Then he'd gotten an interworld e-mail from Dad. *"Heard about your triumph in track. Doesn't surprise me when you do well at anything—always been proud of you. Congratulations. Love, Dad . . ."*

He felt better. It was several years before he realized that his sister—clever with computers—had faked it up, managed to send it to him as if from Dad.

Christ. Sam . . .

And the worst thing was what had happened to their relationship when their parents had died. He had retreated into himself, going morose and silent. He hadn't been much comfort to her. She'd buried herself in science—as if to reclaim her parents that way—and he'd run from science into the military. First the Army, then the Privatized Marines . . .

"Sam!" he shouted, running into Carmack's genetics laboratory, gasping for breath. He skidded to a stop, again expecting an attack as he swept the room with his gunlight, ready to fire—aware that he was on edge and hair-trigger right now, and if he wasn't careful, he'd shoot his sister, thinking it was one of them, in the dimness. No attack came—and no Sam, either.

He searched the room, sweat stinging his eyes, even looking in the wrecked bathroom.

She was nowhere to be found. Not her and not her body.

They might have gotten her—dragged her up into the crawl spaces, chewing on her as they went. Tearing her to pieces.

No. He had a strong feeling Sam was still alive. But where?

The seconds were passing. *Think . . .*

If she'd finished here in the lab, where would she have gone?

Of course! The infirmary. Finish the research there. Should have gone there first, he was wasting precious time . . .

"I'm an idiot," he muttered, turning to run back the way he'd come.

He ran back through the corridor, into the air lock, racing across the atrium . . . down the hall, pressed through the nanowall . . . there were several corpses and pieces of corpses on tables and gurneys. And Sam . . .

She was there, bending over a cadaver. Sam's

face was rapt with concentration, her hands operating a scanner as she ran it slowly over the battered chest.

That was Destroyer's body, some part of his mind noted, and veered immediately away—he didn't want to deal with Destroyer's death yet. He had to put all grieving off till the mission was over. His pain over losing his buddies was like a child weeping in a detention cell—it wasn't time for that child to be let out yet.

"What the fuck are you doing, Sam?" he rasped, between gasps for air, as he stalked up to her. "Didn't you hear me over the radio?"

The question didn't register. She kept frowning into that scanner—and asked a question of her own. "Why did they take Goat but not Destroyer? Why Carmack but not Dr. Thurman?"

He slapped the butt of his machine gun with impatience. "Sam—you've got to come with me. Now! We got, like, a minute to evacuate—"

She was still caught up in her stream of thought—seemed about to be swept over some inward verge. "Lucy had the twenty-fourth chromosome . . . but she wasn't a monster—she died protecting her child, not devouring it. Why did the same chromosome that made her superhuman turn Stahl into a monster? Just give me one minute to show—"

He glanced at the door. Were the others already going through the Ark? He had to be with them when they went through. They could be facing the enemy instantly, on getting home. He couldn't let the squadron down—they'd need all the help they could get. The whole world would need it.

She bit at the tip of her tongue, looking again at Destroyer, that detached scientist's state of mind, narrowing her eyes again. "John—give me just one minute to show you . . ."

"We don't have one minute!"

"Then give me ten seconds!"

He looked at her. There was something in her expression.

It was as if she were saying, *You didn't trust me when our parents died. You wouldn't talk to me. To anyone. And you sealed yourself off, inside, from people. This time . . . trust me.*

He looked away—a kind of acquiescence.

But he turned back to watch as she snatched up a biopsy needle, sank it into the base of Destroyer's skull—sucked out the gray matter with a practiced motion of her thumb.

Reaper grimaced and looked away again.

She moved to a table where—he hadn't noticed it before—Portman's head, still in its helmet, lay in a grisly lump.

He found himself watching her again—and regretted watching her when she found a swab, collected matter from the head by the simple expedient of sticking the swab through a hole in the skull, dipping it into the brain like a candymaker stirring caramel in a pot.

She leaned over the remains of Carmack's torso, separated the lungs, revealing another strange organ where none should be.

"This is its tongue . . ."

A tongue inside a chest? But that long, long tongue had to start somewhere.

She held the swab up and looked at it critically—it was lathered with brain matter from Portman, looking like moldy cottage cheese. Then she held it over the tongue hidden in the Carmack imp's chest.

The tongue suddenly churned and wriggled, spattering them both with black blood.

"Brain matter from Portman . . ." she said, as if thinking aloud.

Then she took the biopsy needle, squeezed some of the red-gray sludge onto a swab.

"This is from Destroyer . . ."

She held the sample from Destroyer's brain over the tongue—and the tongue just lay there. It didn't react.

She passed Portman's brain matter over it again—and the tongue jerked in instant reaction.

Reaper stared. Worried about the Ark but fascinated despite himself.

Sam ran through her impromptu theory as she worked. "There are genetic markers for aggression, violent behavior. The marker could be a specific neurotransmitter it's picking up on, a ganglion. It's *choosing*, John. It's choosing who it infects."

He shrugged helplessly. "Choosing? Choosing how?"

She considered. "Latching on to numbers in the DNA code linked to . . ."

"Sam . . ."

He looked at her skeptically. She was getting fanciful. "Linked to what, Sam? To 'evil'?"

It'd been well over the ten seconds she'd asked. But he intuitively felt this could matter—if the creatures had gotten to the other side, knowing how the things decided to do what they did could help stop them.

She spoke rapid-fire. "Ten percent of the human genome is still unmapped. Some think it's the genetic blueprint for the soul. Maybe C-24 is what destroyed the Olduvaians. It would be why some of them had to build the Ark—to escape to a new beginning. It made some superhuman. Others—monsters."

It felt right to Reaper. He looked at the imp. "Goat was right. Said we are all angels or devils . . . we become one or the other."

They looked at each other. *Which are you?*

Then an implication hit him. "Oh my God . . ."

"What?"

He started toward the door. "The people quarantined on the other side of the Ark—"

"What about them?"

Reaper hadn't heard what'd happened to the people who'd been evacuated—but it made sense there'd be a quarantine, for a time, back home; they'd be contained in the compound where they couldn't spread any of this genetic infection . . . contained where they'd also be sitting ducks.

"He's going to kill them!" Reaper went on. "But they won't all be infected!"

FOURTEEN

THREE MINUTES HAD been used up seven minutes ago.

Sarge was done waiting for Reaper and Sam. As far as Sarge was concerned, Corporal John Grimm was AWOL.

The Marines were stripping off everything they didn't need and loading up with all the extra ammo they could carry from the crates of munitions that'd been stacked in the wormhole chamber during evacuation.

As he took off his extraneous equipment, Sarge decided he'd made a mistake: he shouldn't have let Reaper go after his sister. Only reason he'd done it at all was he figured the girl might've found out something handy—something they could use against the enemy. She could've been a resource.

But, of course, she was either dead, by now—or she *was* one of the enemy. Same probably went for Reaper. Too bad. Reaper was a good soldier.

Sarge felt nothing much, as he contemplated Reaper's probable death. Maybe Destroyer's dying had used up the last of his caring. It'd been a long time since he'd been able to feel much. Except satisfaction in destroying the enemy.

"*System on line,*" said the soothing mechanical voice.

"Get ready," Sarge said, looking at the mercurial droplet, defying gravity in the midst of the Ark chamber. He charged up the BFG with the flick of a switch. It throbbed inwardly, as if eager to discharge its bioenergy . . . as if it were eager to begin killing.

He looked at Duke and the Kid. "Here are your orders. Uphold the quarantine. Nothing leaves the compound. If it breathes, kill it. Pray for war!"

Trained to the marrow, Duke and the Kid cocked their weapons. And as one they intoned in turn: "*Pray for war!*"

Sarge shouldered the BFG, took a deep breath, and stepped into the Ark . . .

On the other side, the steel door into the compound was wide-open.

That's the first thing Duke noticed when they came through the Ark—that and the waves of nausea he was experiencing.

After the door and the sickness, the next thing he, Sarge, and the Kid noticed were the bloodied bodies of UAC employees, sprawled randomly across the floor. Some familiar faces were among them.

And at just that moment, Portman's message came through from Olduvai, Mars. Since it came over an emergency channel the central computer piped it over the public address system:

"... *Portman with RRTS 6 Special Ops on Olduvai 0310 hours* ..."

Jumping over the dead, Sarge jogged to the wall comm. Its small screen blinked with:

RRTS ENCRYPTED

On its monitor was Portman's grainy videocam image from the bathroom of Carmack's lab on Olduvai. The message Portman had sent some hours ago, only just arriving:

"... *we have encountered hostile activity, require immediate RRTS reinforcements* ..."

"No shit," the Kid muttered.

Duke went to the control panel of the compound, at a computer terminal near the wall comm. The monitor there read out:

Quarantine Lockdown Time Remaining
... 59 min ... 58 min ...

"We've got 58 minutes," Duke said, shrugging resignedly, "before the auto lockdown is lifted ..."

Sarge grunted. Thought about it a moment, then said, "Reset it for another six hours."

Portman's transmission was repeating again, on an emergency band loop: "... *Portman with RRTS 6 Special Ops on Olduvai 0310 hours* ..."

Visibly annoyed—here was a recording of Portman disobeying his orders—Sarge hit the control for the PA and turned Portman's voice off.

"I can't reset it," Duke said, after tinkering with the computer. "It's been disabled. Same with the topside comm link."

Meaning, Duke thought, *there was no way to get a message out for reinforcements*. The reinforcements they needed after all—Portman had been right.

"They're disabling the computers now?" the Kid said, sounding confused.

"They're rocket scientists," Duke said, "remember?"

"They may be rocket scientists . . ." Sarge said, cocking his sidearm. ". . . but they're still dumb enough to try to fuck with me."

He slung the BFG over his shoulder, and walked over to the nearest corpse. He shot it in the head.

He went to another corpse. He shot that one in the head.

Duke and the Kid grimaced—but followed suit. Over and over again, black blood fountained and bits of bone sprayed.

Sarge had broken into a weapon's locker, armed himself with a light machine gun. Gave the Kid an assault rifle. Dangerous in close quarters, the BFG was slung over his shoulder on a strap, like a sinister scuba tank.

Then they split up into the two corridors forking off from the main Ark chamber in the compound.

Sarge took the Kid with him, gestured for Duke to head down the right-hand corridor. Duke gave Sarge a haunted look, just before he went—he didn't want to set off on his own, but he wasn't about to say anything about it, and Sarge never rescinded an order.

Guns at ready, Sarge and the Kid moved carefully into the hallway. It got darker as they went, as if the lights were getting scared to stay lit the closer they got to whatever was waiting for them in the depths of the compound.

There was a peculiar sound, coming from around the corner, at the end of the hall. Hard to make out exactly what it was. A sloppy, wet sound, with cracking, gulping noises mixed in, and low snorts.

Instinctively crouching, they turned the corner, turning their gunlights toward the source of the noise.

Demonic semihuman things crouched over human bodies. Feeding.

Interrupted, the creatures looked up, snarling, blood and tissue dripping from their fanged jaws, glaring at the source of the irritating lights. As if they resented being exposed in their feasting.

There were bits of clothing still clinging to these things. Looked to Sarge like they weren't through transforming yet: You could see they'd once been people, UAC employees from Olduvai or the compound. Their foreheads were swollen in angry red folds, like some aquatic being's, and their eyes were sunken, barely visible, receding into the mutated opticals of the new, murderous configuration; bone ends had thrust out through the tips of their fingers, burst raw from the flesh, dripping mucus and blood; their heads were sunken into broadened shoulders, their feet had become something quite inhuman . . . as they growled, their tongues flickered like separate creatures with a sentience of their own.

At their stubby, disfigured feet were what were barely recognizable as human bodies, like sides of beef gone over by amphetamine-crazed butchers. Only, one of those flayed human beings was still alive. Impossible to tell, in what was left of it, if it was a man or a woman. But a set of human eyes, missing the eyelids, looked back at them in quivering, agonized madness from the wreckage of flesh.

The Kid made a soft sound of terror in his throat. But he didn't run. That was good. Sarge was almost proud of him.

There was that stretched-out instant, when they and the creatures, blinking in the gunlights and ruminating on human flesh, regarded one another.

And then as one the demonic things emitted high-pitched screams of pure fury and rushed at Sarge and the Kid. One of them swinging an emergency ax . . .

Two steps back—but the Kid wasn't going to run, not with Sarge standing there. He and Sarge opened up at the same time, assault rifle and light machine gun blazing, filling the corridor with a hail of metal-jacketed death. The Kid didn't neglect to put a couple of rounds between those staring eyes on the floor. That light had to be shut off.

The half-humans kept coming at them, the snarling mutant in the lead raising the ax over his head, despite being ripped by the bullets, seeming to push upstream against the automatic-weapons fire, as bits of flesh and bone and droplets of blood flew from him.

The Kid was glad Sarge couldn't hear him whimpering when he ran through his clip, the gun out of ammo.

The creatures were almost within reach . . . and then all but one of them fell facedown with a sickening squelch.

That one obstinate horror was still reaching for them—it was on its knees, one of its arms hanging by a shred, pouring black blood, its right arm reaching out twitchily to rake at them with its claws— Sarge had run through his clip, too, so he drew a knife and simply stuck it to the hilt in the thing's right eye, then twisted to slash its brain up from within.

Sarge had been clear enough.

Here are your orders. Uphold the quarantine. Nothing leaves the compound. If it breathes, kill it. Pray for war!

"Pray for war," Duke muttered now. Wishing it were war.

But this wasn't war. War was with *people*. This was some other category of butchery.

The corridor Duke had taken went straight, zigged to the right, went straight again—and then dead-ended. The door at the end was open: a rectangle of night. Duke wasn't eager to go through it.

But he made himself push ahead, probing the room with his gunlight.

The room was piled with corpses—they were literally piled up, as if someone had tried to use them as a sort of impromptu barrier, a fortress of dead human flesh.

"Christ . . ." Duke murmured.

Some of the bodies were trembling a little—weren't they? Or was that an illusion caused by his hands shaking the gunlight?

He wasn't taking any chances. They could be transforming . . .

He moved into the room, and started firing, putting a round into the head of each corpse. The bodies flinched as he fired into them—just flesh reacting to impact, but in the dimness his imagination made it seem they were trying to crawl away from his gun muzzle. His stomach lurched, and he almost threw up—probably would have except it had been so long since he'd eaten. He had a nutrition bar in his pocket—but the thought of eating made his stomach contort again. He kept firing, firing . . . blood runneled around his feet—red blood, not black . . .

He paused to put in a fresh clip, coughing from his own gun smoke.

There was another sound, besides his coughing.

Something moving, and maybe a moan, coming from the far side of the room.

He swung his weapon around, fired in that direction, toward another heap of bodies—which was twitching ever so slightly.

"Jesus Christ, stop shooting!"

Duke knew that voice, didn't he? "Who the hell's in there?"

Two arms popped up from the pile of human corpses. Duke almost fired at them, out of sheer tension, but he managed to hold back. A face came after the arms. Bloodied but human. It was Pinky.

Pinky glared at him. "Don't just stand there, you dumb son of a bitch, get me outta here!"

FIFTEEN

"YOU WILL NOT hesitate, and you sure as hell won't turn back," Reaper was telling his sister. "Research here is *over*."

They were standing in the wormhole chamber, close to the tank where the silvery droplet spun and pulsed.

"When I go through the Ark," he went on, "you count to three and come after me. I'd send you through first, but I don't know what's waiting over there . . ."

"I'm afraid we do know," she said softly. "I just don't know if those things are the only enemy—"

"You understand what I'm telling you, Sam? You don't get a sudden inspiration and go back to the goddamn lab. You don't go looking for souvenirs or clean underwear. You follow me through. One . . ."

". . . two, three. And I go through. I think I kinda get it, John." But Sam was smiling sadly at him—he was just trying to protect her. She looked at the Ark. "You hate going through that thing . . . Maybe you're the one who's stalling here."

"How do you know I hate . . . well yeah. Everyone does. Okay, I'm going. Remember—"

"I know, I know, one-two-three."

He turned, took a breath, and stepped into the Ark's field of sensitivity—as always getting the eerie feeling he was stepping into the embrace of something alive and sentient.

He shuddered, feeling again that he was diving into cold water that was instantly warm water, then icy again . . .

The mercurial droplet leapt at his eyes, and he was falling into infinity. Living seas swirled around him in impossible colors, improbable smells.

But suddenly he was somewhere familiar . . . familiar tropical colors, familiar tropical smells . . .

He was no longer falling—there was solid ground under his feet. He was back in that rain forest where Jumper had died. Back in the steaming jungle, with all his men. Even the ones who had died there. They were alive now . . . or anyway they were standing up and looking at him.

Mac was there, too. Destroyer. Goat in the background. And Portman. All standing around him, staring at him—Mac had to gaze at him from waist height, because Mac's body was carrying his own head in his hands, holding it at the level of his navel.

"Good to see you, Corporal," said Portman. Sneering it. He was pretty mashed up, but his body seemed to be more or less hanging together, in a raw-meat kind of way, as if the butcher had sliced him up, then strung him back together with what-ever was at hand.

"Good to see you . . ." Reaper said vaguely. Though it wasn't good to see Portman or the other dead men—not like this. Walking, talking ruins.

Reaper shook his head. *Where am I? Wasn't I going through the Ark? Where's Sam?*

"We got some memories, huh?" said Mac's de-tached head, chuckling. How was it talking without a voice box? "Remember that time we all went on fur-lough together—the whole bunch of us drunk in the same whorehouse, shouting at each other through the wall. 'How's yours?' 'She's great—but small!' 'Hey yo, mine's big enough to kick my ass!'"

Reaper dutifully chuckled at that. "Yeah. We had some times . . ." His lips felt rubbery.

"We did," Duke said.

Duke was quite intact. Wasn't dead yet. So why was he here with the dead guys? *For that matter,* Reaper wondered, *why am I here?*

"Don't know," Duke went on, "if we'll have any more good times, way things have been going, Corporal . . ."

"Yeah well . . . talk to . . . to Sarge . . ."

It was hard to think, hard to talk here. This was all wrong.

"Talk to Sarge?" the Kid shook his head. "I don't know about that. I just hope I live to see twenty-one, man. That's all. Just get to twenty-one . . ."

"Remember . . . remember," Portman said, "you

218

guys were going to a ball game. Didn't want to take me along . . . But then you said, Hey, come on, Portman. I remember that. You're not so bad, Corporal . . ."

"Thanks, I uh . . . why . . . why are we . . ."

"But then again, pretty soon Duke and the Kid here are going to be looking for their head like Mac or their arms like me . . . And that's all about you fucking up, isn't it . . . Corporal?"

"I'm doing the best I can. Trying to get somewhere now . . . I'm trying to get to the compound . . . to get Sarge's six . . ."

"Are you? Then you're fucking up again," Portman said. "'Cause here you are. Loafing in the jungle with us . . . You remember this jungle. Where your ol' pal Jumper bought it . . . thanks to you."

"You were our corporal," Mac said. "You should've done a better job. We'd be alive now. You should've kept me in line of sight. Sarge was busy—you were responsible. You let that thing whack my head off. You let me die, Reaper. You should've covered my six . . ."

Reaper felt wet on the outside, with the humidity and his sweat, and bone dry inside. His lips stuck together, and it was painful to pull them apart and talk. His voice came out in a desiccated rattle, "Look, Mac—I just didn't know what we were dealing with."

"What about me?" Jumper asked, pushing to the front of the group, grinning at Reaper with this wrecked, bloody mouth. The top of Jumper's head was missing, just the way it'd been when he'd been shot in the rain forest, but it didn't seem to bother him. He had one eye left, hanging down on his cheek, and it swiveled to look at Reaper as he chuckled. "Did you know what you were dealing with when you let 'em kill me, Reaper? Jungle fighting? Like you never had done that before . . ." He plucked his eyeball, rubbed it against his flak jacket as if he were polishing a marble. "Can't see for shit through this thing . . ." He put the eye back in place. "That's better."

"I . . . I was stuck with those bunk guns, Jumper—Listen, bro, I'd have given my life—"

"Bullshit. And you're making excuses—you could have refused that ordnance," Goat said, stepping into view. "Even if it meant pissing off the major. But you chose sinfully—your sin was not putting your men ahead of your career. You are the accursed of God . . ."

"The major was hot on those guns—"

"Sarge would have stuck by you," Jumper said. "You knew it was a mistake. Then you let them decoy you with that dumb teenager you blew to pieces . . ."

"Nobody can help any of us," Portman said, "except Corporal John Grimm here. He can help us by blowing out his brains. That'd make us feel better anyway. Maybe we'd rest then. Because we counted on him, and he blew it . . . even the stupid guerilla kid, you coulda figured he didn't know what he was doing, maybe captured him . . . but you had to end his miserable little life . . ."

Reaper could bear it no more and burst into roaring, sobbing rage, and he wrenched himself out of the Ark-induced vision, closed his eyes and felt himself falling, falling through the essence of corruption, into oily blackness, to emerge in a spinning tube of liquid colored with colors that weren't colors and suddenly he was staggering out into the Ark chamber in the compound . . . back home. But in another way, they were still a long way from home.

Twenty seconds later the room stopped shifting, and Reaper's gut quieted enough so that he was fairly confident he wouldn't throw up. At almost the same instant, Sam materialized in the Ark chamber, stepped out of the cylinder into the main room.

She took two steps and stumbled, groaning—he caught her as she fell. Held her in his arms. Her eyes were rolled up in her head and she shuddered, went limp—and again shuddered, went limp, over and over . . . as she muttered, "Dad . . . he's . . . John's all . . ."

"Sam!"

She squeezed her eyes shut, then opened them, looked at him. She swallowed. "I hate that thing . . . Seeing things in there . . ."

He nodded, helping Sam steady on her feet. "Me too . . ." But then he thought: *Maybe what I saw was*

221

just the truth. Sometimes dreams show you the truth . . .

He looked around; the UAC promo screens had gone quiet, with all but the barest auxiliary power cut off, and it was nearly dark here, only a few of the lights working. It was like a big catacomb to him then, just waiting for the skulls to stack up.

"So what now?" she asked, running a shaking hand over her hair.

He was checking his gun, adjusting the strap—anything to occupy his mind so he didn't have to think about what he'd just seen, in the Ark . . . his conversation with the dead.

"Nobody can help any of us," Portman had said, *"except Corporal John Grimm here. He can help us blowing out his brains. That'd make us feel better anyway . . ."*

Reaper closed his eyes. Oh God. Jumper. Let his only friend down . . . he'd let him die . . .

Maybe he should just end it now. Kill Sam—do her a favor, keep those things from getting at her. Then he'd kill himself. So that Jumper and the others would have some rest.

It would be the work of a moment. Turn and shoot his sister, then stick the muzzle of the weapon in his mouth, suck metal, pull the trigger . . .

"John? You okay?"

His fingers tightened on the weapon. *". . . That'd make us feel better anyway . . ."*

"John?"

He had a lot of combat experience behind him. He knew, on some level, that he was as posttraumatic as they came, right now. Partly because of what'd happened in the rain forest. Not being there for Jumper. Letting him die.

Then—Olduvai. The pressure of worrying about his sister there. Losing Mac, Portman, Goat, Destroyer.

Theoretically it was all on Sarge's account sheet, it was his responsibility. But Reaper kept thinking maybe he could've saved them . . . After all, what he'd seen in the Ark had been contrived by his mind. He'd superimposed his own nightmares, his own guilt on the quantum field shifting within the Ark . . .

The feeling of remorse and hopelessness was so strong—hopelessness like the weight of ten miles of ocean over his head . . . tons of dark cold sea about to crush him. He'd failed, and failure was death in his profession. He was surrounded by horrors. The world was doomed. Doom was like a dark icy cloak settling over his shoulders . . . it was all so hopeless, they couldn't possibly . . .

"John!"

Sam shook him now. Because he was just standing there, fingering his gun, staring.

"I need you, John!"

He'd just let her down. Better if they both died here and now, a flash of pain and it'd be over . . .

"John—please! Hey—brother, yo!"

Brother. That seemed to call him back. He looked into her eyes—and saw life there, and determination. Intelligence, a range of possibilities . . . and hope.

He took a deep breath and shook himself.

"Fuck you, Portman," he muttered. Seeing them in his mind's eye.

"What?" she said.

"You too, Mac. Yeah—even you, Jumper. The whole fucking bunch of you. I did all I could. Some days, things just go sour . . ."

She waited, sensing he was working through something.

He wasn't through with it. But he'd put it back into the dark corners of his skull—he was ready to move into some other dark corners now.

"I'm sorry," he said huskily, squeezing his sister's shoulder. "I guess I lost it for a minute . . . Let's do this thing."

SIXTEEN

"SARGE," REAPER SAID into his comm, "what's your position?" No answer. He tried again. "Sarge—do you read?"

A burst of static in his headset. And maybe, from far off in the compound, the distant sound of gunfire, abruptly cutting off.

Then: *"I copy, Reaper . . ."*

But Sarge was a little occupied, right now. He and the Kid had just finished killing a full-blown imp. And now he saw someone crawling toward him, from a heap of wreckage—the wreckage of fallen rafters and fallen human beings.

The individual crawling toward him was not *obviously* turned as yet. He wore the tatters of a uniform; one of his legs was twisted the wrong way.

"Sarge," Reaper's voice said, over the comm, *"we don't have to kill everyone. Transmission of the condition is self-selecting."*

Sarge watched the man crawling toward him across the bloody floor of the corridor.

"Help me," the man begged. His tears made the dried blood on his face run once more. "Help me please . . ."

The Kid lowered his gun, obviously intent on lending aid. Sarge pulled the Kid back, shook his head.

Sarge leveled his weapon . . .

"Please . . ."

. . . and fired, at close range, so that the man who'd pleaded with him was hurled back into the shadows, his head shattered.

The Kid gaped at that, put up a hand to cover his mouth.

"Roger that, Reaper," Sarge said calmly. "I'm on my way toward you . . ." He turned to the Kid—who took a nervous step back from him. Sarge pretended not to notice that. "Clear the rest of this sector," he ordered the Kid. "Meet me back at the Ark chamber."

Sarge dropped the exhausted chaingun and went off in his own direction.

The Kid watched for a moment, then turned and hurried off on his mission—only looking back over his shoulder at Sarge once.

At first, the Kid had felt glad to get away from Sarge. But a short ten minutes later, in the echoing gloom—in a corridor that was all too much like the ones on Olduvai—the Kid was wishing Sarge was still with him.

Because this corridor was mostly blacked out . . . and because it seemed so empty and quiet. And that just made it fairly creak with imminence, as if the silence were an arranged prelude to an attack.

I'm going from paranoid to having crazy thoughts. The amphetamines turning to crap in my bloodstream.

There was a noise from a door, to his left. He turned the gunlight on the door. STORAGE, it said. A cough from in there. A noise that might've been a sob. Something or someone was definitely in there.

He could go and get Sarge . . . but Sarge was on the other side of the compound—and judging by the bursts of gunfire coming from that way, the Kid figured Sarge's hunt was yielding up some game. He was busy.

And if he went back for Sarge, he'd look like a pussy. Was Sarge calling for backup every time he ran into the enemy?

As if replying in the negative, another burst of gunfire echoed down the hallways to him . . .

Okay. So he was going to check out this storage room on his own. The door was narrow. If they came through it, they'd come one at a time. The Kid would be ready.

Aim for the head, he reminded himself.

The Kid held his weapon at ready, held his breath, too—and kicked the door in.

There was a squeal and a gasp from inside—but nothing else. No imp, no half human launched itself out at him. It was dark in there.

He took a step closer and shined his light into the small, dark storage area—but the center of the room was crowded with people, scared but otherwise ordinary-looking people, all staring back at him, blinking in the light.

Startled, the Kid raised his gun to fire—and the humans in the room cried out in fear, some of them covering their eyes.

He lowered his weapon and found the light switch on the wall. It lit up about twenty people in various stages of damage and desperation, crammed in with shelves packed with food and supplies. Some of them clutched chair legs, pieces of metal, as makeshift weapons.

"Holy shit," the Kid said.

Jenna Willits came out from the crowd—the Kid recognized her. She'd been working with Samantha Grimm in the infirmary.

Her eyes were haunted, as if she were staring in disbelief at something she'd seen, something that stayed before her eyes no matter what she looked at.

"My baby . . ." She licked her lips. "They took my baby . . ." She said it as if she still couldn't believe it was true. "They took the baby . . . please help us."

She'd lost her husband, the Kid remembered—now it seemed like she'd lost a child, too. This thing was tough—but in the Navy he'd seen refugees, running from war and revolution, carrying dead children in their arms so they could find a proper place for a burial; he'd seen old people left lying in ditches to die, to save on food supplies, so the younger ones could have a chance to live. That was life for a lot of the world. But for the upscale people at the facility and the compound, this kind of desperation was a new experience.

One of the older men in the crowd looked at the Kid with a mixture of expectation and mistrust. *"Are you here to help us?"*

The Kid licked his lips. "Uhhh . . ."

"Please," another woman sobbed, breaking down. She'd held herself together for a long time now, huddled in the darkness, running from hellthings who'd once been friends and colleagues, and she just couldn't cope anymore. ". . . Please . . ." The words almost indistinguishable from moans. ". . . save us . . ."

The others took up the chorus. "Help us!"

"For God's sake . . ."

The Kid was backing out the door.

"Somebody's got to do something—"

"—we have no weapons—"

"—you have to protect us!"

The Kid slammed the door on their pleading. And ran to find Sarge.

"Sarge?" Reaper called, on the headset comm.

"Yeah . . ." Sarge's voice crackled.

"We're in the compound infirmary, looking over the medical supplies—thought we could all meet up here."

"I'm not far away . . . Hold on . . . I'll get back to you . . ."

"Sarge?"

No reply. But distantly, they heard gunshots. A lot of them.

Sam looked up from the wound-spray kits she was sorting. They figured there'd be a lot of patching up to do here. "He is shooting who he's *supposed* to be shooting . . . Isn't he, John?"

"Yeah well—he got the message. I told him that not everyone gets infected. He said roger that."

"But suppose . . ." She looked back at the kits, but her mind was clearly elsewhere. "Suppose he isn't discriminating?"

Reaper shrugged wearily, suddenly sitting heavily in a chair. "I'll try to convince him."

"But suppose—"

"I said I'll try to convince him!"

Instead of reacting to his anger with anger, she looked at him with concern. "You look tired . . ."

"So I'm tired . . ."

"Here . . . just sit still . . ."

She went to a cabinet, got out an inst-infuse nutrition kit, brought it over to him. She sponged his arm with alcohol, then pressed the cylindrical inst-infuser against his bare shoulder. There was a flash of pain, then the processed nutrients rushed into him—bringing strength, and a little clarity.

But he still didn't know what to do about Sarge.

She opened another medikit, found a nutrition

230

bar, and tossed it to him. He tore it open and began to eat, not tasting it much. "Sarge'll do exactly what he thinks he's supposed to, as he interprets his orders, and not one iota different."

"You said you were willing to convince him . . ." She hesitated. Maybe amazed at herself, at what she was about to suggest.

He looked at her. Then made sure his comm was turned off, before he said, "You suggesting I might have to 'convince' him—by killing him?"

"I don't know. But—it's not unthinkable, to save a lot of other lives. If he's killing innocent people. But maybe there's another way. A tranquilizer shot, or . . ."

Reaper shook his head. "He's wary. He knows you're not on his side. He's not going to turn his back on you for a second, Sam. Anyway, you're jumping the . . . jumping to conclusions. He might be all right with it . . ."

"Who might be all right with what?" Sarge asked, abruptly coming in.

How much of the exchange had he heard? Reaper wondered. "I heard gunshots, just a minute ago, Sarge . . ."

"Yeah," Sarge said, picking up a nutrition bar, tearing its wrapper open with a practiced motion of the same hand. He bit off half of it, and, chewing, went on, "Ran into some of our little genetically fucked-up buddies."

"You're sure they were . . ." Sam began.

Sarge glanced at her—his expression conveyed his

231

supreme indifference to her opinion. "Close enough for rock 'n' roll."

She shook her head slowly. "Close enough—isn't close enough. We need to know. If they're obviously changed or changing . . . fine. But if they're not . . . we have to wait. Find a way to make sure. Work up a test."

He finished the nutrition bar with his second bite. He swallowed, and said, "We don't have time for that. I don't have time to eat this, and I don't have time to talk to you. While the compound is sealed, we've got to make sure nothing that could've been infected can get out."

"I'm the only doctor here," Sam said flintily. "That puts me in charge of the quarantine. And I'm not going to allow—"

"You're not in charge of anything. Neither is your brother. This is now a military lockdown. It's martial law, Doctor. And for that matter—how do I know for sure you two didn't get infected somehow?"

Sam and Reaper looked at him. Sarge just waited.

Reaper decided, for now, to put his outrage away and answer the question rationally. "We don't have the marks. You can see for yourself. And we're not behaving that way."

"I only have your word for it that the thing infects its victims through the neck and nowhere else. Maybe—maybe not. And there might be stages of behavior in people who're infected, Corporal Grimm . . ."

So now Sarge was calling him Corporal Grimm instead of Reaper—as if creating a little personal distance between them, for what had to come.

Reaper had just about had enough. "Sarge—you make a threat against my sister, or me, even a theoretical one, I'm going to do have to take it seriously. And act accordingly."

Sarge looked narrowly at him, head tilted. At last he said, "I guess you're the same guy—so far. But I can't have you questioning my orders. Not the ones I've gotten and not the ones I give."

"You got any new orders from anyone lately?"

"No."

"Maybe we should call out and get some, Sarge."

Sarge shook his head. "I got mine for this kind of situation. I just didn't tell you every last part of it. They didn't specify what might go wrong. But before we went to Olduvai I was told that if things go sour . . ." He shrugged. "We have orders to contain this facility by any means necessary."

"But I don't think everyone is infected!" Sam insisted. "Or even capable of being infected!"

"We have orders to contain the threat," Sarge said, "by any means necessary."

"We evac the uninfected survivors," Reaper suggested, "and we blow this place back to hell."

". . . And orders to protect this facility," Sarge said.

"We don't have orders to kill innocent people," Reaper persisted.

233

Sarge smiled thinly. " 'By any means necessary.' "

Reaper's hand tightened on his weapon. Maybe, he thought, this was the moment, if Sarge was going to start deciding that anyone but him was infected . . .

He almost jumped when the door banged open. Duke came in, smiling ironically. "Look who I found under a pile of dead bodies . . ."

Pinky rolled in, behind him. He looked haggard, pale, scared. But also looking relieved to see Sam. "Boy, am I glad to see you guys. That thing cut through the door. I tried to use the ST grenade, but it malfunctioned. It followed right behind me through the Ark. Started killing everybody . . ." He swallowed. His voice became husky as he said, "It was horrible . . ."

Sam walked over and examined him, frowning over his neck. Nodded to herself. "He doesn't have the wound on his neck. He's clean."

Sarge took ammo from his belt, began to reload his pistol. "I say who's clean and who's not clean."

Pinky stared at the gun in Sarge's hand. Those bullets going in. Did he really intend one of those—for him? "What are you doing? You shouldn't have left me there. It wasn't my fault . . ."

Sarge cocked the pistol.

Reaper looked at Pinky, then at Sarge. Was Sarge really going to shoot him? Right here and now?

"I'm not a soldier," Pinky was saying, a hysterical edge to his voice, his hands scrabbling at his cyberchair, "you shouldn't have left me . . ."

The Kid burst in then, breathing hard.

Sarge, Duke, and Reaper—all three of them nearly shot the Kid in reaction.

"There's a storeroom to the south!" the Kid blurted. "Got like twenty people holed up in it!"

"Weren't your orders to clear that sector?" Sarge asked him. That flatness in his voice; in his eyes . . . "Is it cleared?"

"I told them to stay put. They're okay; they're just scared shitless—"

Sarge shook his head. "We kill 'em all—let God sort 'em out."

SEVENTEEN

THE KID LOOKED desperately from face to face.

"Okay—" he said at last. "—I think this is wrong." Having a hard time saying it. Wanting badly to please Sarge. But there were limits.

"Son," Sarge said, "you don't have to think—because you've been given a fucking *order.*"

The Kid seemed frozen with indecision.

"We are in the field, soldier," Sarge reminded him.

Reaper said, "Sarge, if nothing's found them yet—"

"We are in the field!" Sarge interrupted, speaking only to the Kid. "You will obey the direct order of your commanding officer!"

The Kid licked his lips. "No."

"Now, soldier!" Sarge said. It was more than just insistence. In those two words was a warning and a guarantee:

Obey the order or you're going to pay the ultimate price for defying a superior in combat.

The Kid was being offered a choice. He could still say *Yes sir,* and lead Sarge to that storage room and stand side by side with him as they cut all those people down together. All those scared, perfectly ordinary people . . .

He thought about those desperate faces in that room. Jenna Willits losing her husband, her baby. He seemed to see the face of his girlfriend Millie, who was a nurse—it seemed like a million years since the Kid had seen Millie, and now he imagined what she'd think if she could see him as he mowed down all those scared people. He imagined Millie looking at him—at *him!*—with disgust. And, worse yet, with fear.

The Kid shook his head at Sarge. He looked him in the eye. And he said it as clearly as he knew how.

"Go to hell," the Kid said.

In one swift motion, Sarge swung his arm around toward the Kid, leveled the pistol, and fired. He shot the Kid through the neck.

The Kid spun, hit the wall, and slumped to the floor.

There was a moment of sickened silence. The Kid choked, fumbled at his ruined neck . . . then his whole body began to spasm.

Duke said it for all of them: "Holy shit."

Sarge's tone was all reason. Just . . . reason. "Mutinous insurrection in the field is punishable by death."

Sam broke from her shocked paralysis and rushed to the Kid. "Oh God—someone get me a medikit!"

"It's his first mission!" Reaper burst out.

Sarge turned toward Reaper—who realized he'd let his surprise rob him of a chance to take the initiative.

"And it's not gonna be my last. I need soldiers, I don't need anybody else."

"Fuck!" Reaper swore. He and Sarge stared at each other.

The Kid's eyes were glazing; blood was bubbling from his mouth. Duke grimaced, looked away.

Sarge swung the gun toward Reaper—

Reaper was about to fire in response—

"Drop the weapons," Pinky said, suddenly.

They turned to see him pointing a pistol at them.

Pinky was wondering if he was a fool to give in to survival instinct this way. He didn't like his life much, and no one seemed to really care if Sarge killed him—though maybe they hadn't much chance to react to the threat—and they were probably all going to be killed or converted into subhumans by Carmack's little playthings within minutes, anyway.

Maybe he should've let Sarge execute him. Get it over with.

But he was a survivor. "Do it," Pinky went on. "I didn't come all this way to be killed . . . drop 'em now!"

They stared . . . and Pinky realized it wasn't at him. They were looking past him now. At something looming behind him . . . he could feel it back there, breathing, the heat of its body. Hear its knuckles cracking, claws clicking in its talons . . .

"Oh no," he said, in a small voice. "Is . . . something behind me?"

No need to answer—the creature standing behind Pinky closed its taloned paws around his neck and jerked him, wheelchair and all, into the air. The gun went flying as the genetic demon slammed Pinky from side to side, up and down, on walls and ceiling, Pinky screaming as he went—the thing was using the wheelchair as a bludgeoning tool, so that Sarge and the others had to hit the floor, but not before Reaper was struck glancingly in the face, sending him spinning backward.

Sarge and Duke fired at the imp, and Reaper— though stunned, firing through a blur—fired, too, trying not to hit Pinky. The hulking genetic demon retreated . . .

As Reaper's eyes cleared, it appeared to him that rather than retreating, exactly, the imp was carrying off its prize . . . Pinky.

"On me!" Sarge yelled. "Let's move!"

Despite having come close to a gunfight with Sarge a minute or two earlier, Reaper only hesitated an instant when Sarge gave the order. Training and situational urgency took over and he obeyed, running after Duke and Sarge, into the corridor, around a corner.

They got there in time to see the genetic demon

239

drag the bleeding, moaning Pinky through an open nanowall—and into darkness beyond.

Sarge raised his hand for a halt as he assessed the situation . . . It was darker, around this corner. Dim here—with only the auxiliary lighting, faint and getting fainter. Up ahead, through the nanowall, it was dark as a cavern.

Pinky and his abductor were nowhere to be seen.

There was a smell coming toward him from that impenetrable darkness: rank, vinegary.

"Listen," Duke said.

Many mouths breathing. Many hundreds of claws clicking on the floor, faster and faster . . .

And then another sound: a kind of chattering; a furious discussion but without a language. An angry discourse in grunts and clicks and sounds you might hear from a monkey in the last stages of rabies.

And then the throng came sprinting out of the darkness. A throng of genetic demons, half-formed and misbegotten. All of them coming right at the squadron, with their jaws salivating in anticipation.

"What the . . ." Reaper muttered.

Sarge cocked his weapon. "You with me here, Reaper?"

Reaper cocked his light machine gun and fixed Sarge with a look. "I don't know who's more dangerous—you or them."

Sarge gave out one of his rare smiles. "Sure you do, Reaper. It's me."

The sounds were louder now; they could make out a great moving mass in the shadows up ahead . . . coming toward them.

"Withdraw," Sarge said calmly.

They moved back to the wider corridor they'd come through . . . and moved to the corridor the enemy was going to come from.

"On my command," Sarge said softly, raising his weapon.

An instant later, the demonic undead were upon them—as if the imps had sent the half-turned as the first wave of attack.

"Okay motherfuckers," Sarge yelled. "Let's play!"

Sarge and Reaper and Duke were rushed by at least a dozen walking dead men, their eyes uniformly red, their mouths streaming black blood, their clothes tattered, their faces contorted with the hunger to kill—there was not the faintest remnant of their former humanity in their expressions—some of them with overgrown foreheads, the beginnings of talons.

Hoping to disorient the enemy, Sarge sent a burst of fire into the ceiling lights, plunging the room into semidarkness illuminated by bursts of automatic weapons fire: a deadly strobe-light show.

The living-dead seemed to dance in the "strobe lights" as the thudding gunfire rocked them, making them spin and jump. But they kept coming, forcing the men to step back and back and back, hurling furniture about as they came.

An imp came hulking in the doorway, then, an unusually big one having to bend to get its head through, slashing the air with its talons, knocking some of the undead out of the way—the blows splashing the creatures bloodily against the wall—as if they were minor irritants between it and its prey.

Reaper could spare only a glance for his sister—saw her huddled against the wall behind them, her fist crammed into her mouth.

Should have armed her, he thought. *We'll need every last weapon we can get working.*

Another imp rushed at Reaper, slashing at him, raking his right arm—Reaper shoved his gun into the imp's mouth and pulled the trigger. The top of its head joined the ceiling and its body met the floor.

"Field of fire!" Sarge bellowed.

The men emptied their clips with a deafening barrage of concerted automatic-weapons fire, chewing the living-dead up, spraying the walls and floor behind the creatures with blood and bone fragments—but only opening the way for the big imp.

Sarge had led the attempt to drive off the enemy, and now he led the retreat, turning and bolting to find another, more defensible position. Reaper's gun emptied and he went to follow Sarge, both of them slapping fresh clips into their weapons as they ran, Reaper shouting for Sam to go on ahead of them—his warning unheard over the roaring of their pursuers.

Duke ran out of bullets a half second after the other two, and was last to run—trying to cover their retreat—turning, taking one step, only to be caught by a great shadowy paw, the dark bulk of the big imp grabbing him the way a grizzly would, pulling him close—

"Duke!" Sam shouted, seeing him caught up and hurled at the wall like a toy hurled by an agitated child—he struck an overturned table and screamed as the splintered table leg went through him, back to front.

Reaper turned in time to see his sister running to Duke.

Damn her—she should be getting out of here!

Reaper turned and fired almost point-blank at the imp—it raked its forepaws in front of its face as if warding off a swarm of bees. Reaper used its momentary distraction to get to Sam, skidding as he went in a pool of black blood, having to leap over a feebly clutching, dying half-turned.

"Go," Duke was telling her, his voice barely audible. Blood running from the corners of his mouth. "Get out of here . . ."

Sam grabbed Duke's gun—Reaper thought she was going to put Duke out of his misery and Duke thought so, too, closing his eyes—

Just then, Reaper had to turn away and fire at an imp and one of the undead, keeping them back—the bigger imp stalking back and forth, roaring and slashing frenziedly at the undead who'd gotten in its

243

way—and turned back to see his sister pulling Duke to his feet, as he wailed in pain. She helped him stagger toward the door.

"John—help!" she shouted, as the creatures came at her and Duke.

Sarge had turned, and he and Reaper laid down a withering cover fire—as all four of them retreated through the infirmary's nanowall. Sam helped Duke into the room.

On the other side, Sarge smacked the nanowall control panel, just as the first of the half-turned started through it—three of the living-dead screamed as the wall solidified around them. An arm and leg jutted out of the metallic gray nanowall, writhing and kicking.

A dead end—the demons had raged through here and the way out was blocked by fallen debris.

Reaper and Sam had escaped—into a trap.

Reaper turned to see that Sam had gotten the big splinter out of Duke, stopped his bleeding with a medikit spray. Duke might live—the wound was low on his chest, looked like maybe below the lungs, above the liver.

A massive *thud* from the nanowall—the creatures were hurling themselves against it—made them all step back, reflexively pointing their weapons at the thumping gray rectangle.

Sparks and arcs of electricity spurted from the nanowall. It undulated, as if struggling to keep itself defined as a rectangle, and the arm that was reaching through was able to push a little farther in, clutching at the air.

The wall began to disfigure, then, showing the outlines of other demons trying to force their way through, like impressions coming through a sheet of clay, howling and roaring and chattering as they struggled with the nano material.

"There's too many," Reaper said.

Sarge nodded in grim acknowledgment. Too many of the half-men, the transfigured, forcing through at once would break the nanowall's interior organization down, interfere with intercommunication between the microscopic machines that composed it. The wall would reach a certain level of entropy and collapse. The creatures roared in triumph as they sensed they were breaking through . . .

Sarge laid the machine gun aside, and swung the BFG around, got a good hold on its grips, aiming it at the wall. This was the place for the Big Fucking Gun—where he could see where to focus it, and the others were safely behind him.

The nanowall was bulging in toward them now, rippling, more and more of the demonic forms pushing through, clawed hands, taloned paws . . . half a snarling face, a fierce rolling eye.

"It's not holding!" Sam blurted, seeing more nightmare faces pressing through. It was seconds from breaking down.

"Here they come," Sarge said, matter-of-factly.

"Oh man," Duke said, disgusted—Reaper could

tell he was reacting to something besides the wall's breaking down.

They turned to see that Duke was standing on a grate in the floor—and raw, skinless, ropy arms had bent the grate's bars and reached through to grasp Duke firmly by the ankles.

There was a moment of shock as the implications came home to them.

"Duke," Sam said, trying to aim her gun at the arms gripping his ankles. "Hold still!"

Duke smiled sadly—all resignation, and then the creature jerked one of his feet through the grate, something down there chattering with wordless glee. Duke quivered with pain—trying to pull free but too weak from his wound to do so.

In two seconds, before they could try to help him, the rest of Duke was pulled sickeningly down, his mouth working soundlessly to express a pain that was beyond screaming as his body was forced through the grate with a repellent sound of flesh bursting wetly, sliced into segments as it went. Stopping briefly at his chest—Duke giving everyone a last, long, imploring look . . .

Until with a final vicious tug he was pulled the rest of the way through the grate—he exploded into bloody fragments and Sam, watching in horror, bit down so hard on her fist that her own blood flowed.

Sam was wracked with silent sobs. Reaper went to her, pulled her away from the grate—which was mucky with torn flesh, bone splinters, and part of a face, still trembling—and pushed her into a corner, hugging her as he brought her there, giving her shoulder a commiserating squeeze as he forced her back into the closest thing he could find to safety in the room. It was all he could do for her, just then.

Sarge's expression was inscrutable except for a bitter determination in his eyes as he turned to the weakening nanowall, raising the BFG.

"Bring it on," he growled, stepping close to the nanowall to give the powerful weapon full play. Electrical arcs crackled the air around him, as if expressing his checked fury, and more limbs flailed through the barrier.

Then he looked down to see a monstrous arm sweeping from the nanowall, its taloned paw getting a vise grip on Sarge's leg—and yanking him violently back into the weakening wall.

"No!" Sarge yelled, dropping the BFG as he was jerked off his feet, twisting his whole body so he was spun about as he fell, slamming him onto his face.

Instinctively—despite the fact that he'd been thinking he might have to kill Sarge—Reaper ran to him, hunkering to grab his body armor. He pulled with all his strength, trying to drag Sarge back from the wall. But the genetic demon, pulling from the other side, was far stronger than Reaper. Sarge slipped farther into the wall.

They needed Sarge to fight these things—even if it was only putting the conflict with him off—and now they were losing him.

Sam ran up and joined Reaper, helping him pull. They strained, groaning with the effort, feeling like their joints were going to pull apart. Sarge helped with his elbows, but they only managed to slow him a bit—he was still being inexorably pulled through the wall, into a room filled with demonic creatures who lived only to kill him—or make him one of their own.

Sarge grabbed at the BFG, managed to get hold of its strap—as he was pulled another fourteen inches into the wall.

"Ahhhhh! Mother*fucker!*" he roared, as he felt himself losing ground—his voice mingling almost indistinguishably from the roars of the man-beasts on the other side of the wall.

Another violent tug and Sarge was in the wall up to his waist. Sarge got a better grip on the BFG as Reaper and Sam strained to pull him back, sweat running down his face, down his neck, sticking his clothing to his skin . . .

Reaper could feel it then—he was losing his grip on Sarge, and the thing on the other side was giving one last mighty heave. Sarge was about to go.

"I'm not supposed to die yet . . ." Sarge said, between gritted teeth.

And then he vanished, pulled entirely through the nanowall.

Reaper and Sam backpedaled, falling in reaction, panting for air.

Sarge was . . . just gone. So were the shapes of the

genetic demons, for the moment—the wall had quieted, a mysterious silence reigned, and the penetrating limbs had withdrawn.

Maybe they were all busy tearing pieces off of Sarge. Reaper was sorry he'd let Sarge hold on to the BFG once the genetic demons had grabbed him.

"Are you okay?" Sam asked, hoarsely.

Reaper looked at his sister, propped on an elbow beside him—she looked lost, haggard. But her eyes focused as she noticed his raked arm.

"We have to go now . . ." Reaper said.

"You're hurt," she said.

". . . we have to go now . . ." he repeated, helping her up, guiding her away from the wall. He bent to scoop up a satchel Sarge had brought in—it clanked with various kinds of ammo—and headed toward the accidental barricade blocking the way out.

It seemed to him that they could get through the debris if they just pulled some stuff out of the way. And if they could do it without making the ceiling collapse in on them, then . . .

Reaper got wearily up, began dismantling the barricade, working alone, letting Sam rest. Now and then glancing at the nanowall, half-expecting it to be breached again.

Sam glanced at the place where Duke had been dragged down to his death—then looked away. But it was still there: she was staring into space, eyes wide, as if seeing his death over and over in her mind . . .

Reaper kept working on the barricade.

After a while, seeing him work on the debris, she started to help him. The effort, however short-term its value, seemed to give her hope and she worked with concentration.

In a few minutes they were through—only to find themselves trapped, yet again, in a farther room.

EIGHTEEN

REAPER AND SAM were hiding out in another infirmary room. Sitting on the floor, knees drawn up, resting. They could hear the genetic demons moving about in the air ducts, roaring and chattering in the corridors beyond this temporary refuge.

How long before they were up to their asses in monsters? Reaper wondered. It sounded like they were getting closer and closer.

Reflexively brushing her hair back into some semblance of order with a shaking hand, Sam asked it out loud. "How long?"

Reaper shrugged. "Minutes."

They didn't have many options. But he knew he couldn't let these monsters get out of the compound. They'd spread their sickness to the whole world . . .

The infection happened so fast. What had Carmack been *thinking?* How much of the experiment had UAC known about? Had they been working on a bioweapon—in the form of a transformed human being?

Reaper's country was in many ways effectively indistinguishable from the multinationals headed by the United Aerospace Corporation—and the UAC had a great many enemies. Religious fanatics formed into well-armed, secretly trained militias—some of them big enough to be called armies—and factions in hostile nations furious over the UAC's exploitation of their resources; over its willingness to prop up brutal hegemonies just to keep the goods flowing from the oil fields, the uranium mines, the methane fields—like the one where Jumper had died . . .

But how could the UAC use these genetic demons as part of an armed force? The damned things were completely out of control. Could UAC's military branch have been planning to drop an infected creature in amongst an enemy force—to get them all changed and killing one another? They must've had some means to control them . . . or they'd intended to develop controls. But then things had gotten out of hand.

Another possibility was that the whole project had gone sour almost from the start: the imps and the Hell Knight had been an unintended side effect of another effort entirely, hinted at by some of the computer files Samantha had unearthed, to create a kind of superman who remained in control of himself, who retained his former loyalties.

Maybe a repeat of the exact same mistake the scientists of Olduvai had made. Some vast, quick-moving catastrophe had destroyed that civilization.

Pretty obvious now what that cataclysm had been—it was replaying itself, growling and snarling, right now, beyond the door. It had killed Destroyer and Mac and Duke and dozens of others. Instinctively, the genetic demons wanted to spread their fury out into the world, wanted all humanity to share in it.

Whatever had happened on Olduvai was about to happen right here on their own world, culminating with some gigantic act of self-destruction, rendering the surface of the world a desert, the air poisonous.

Still . . . some people injected with C-24 didn't sink to a bestial level—whatever dark thing there was in others that distorted their transformation was lacking in certain individuals. There were other possibilities, for someone like that. There was a chance for real power, simmering in the serum.

Reaper wondered . . . *just suppose* . . .

He shook his head. No—too risky. There was another way to stop these things . . . the only way to be *sure* of stopping them.

But he didn't know if he had the strength to do anything more. He'd had longer missions than this, under worse physical conditions—firefights that lasted hours in temperatures ranging up to one hundred-and-ten, unspeakable humidity. But he was feeling so weak now . . . like the bottom was dropping out of the world.

Sam picked up on his distress, looked at him inquiringly—then stared at the blood running from under his body armor down his hip and leg. "You've been hit." She unsnapped his armor, like pulling the shell from a tortoise, peeled it wetly away. More blood gushed, then, and they saw it was coming from a small hole in Reaper's abdomen.

A bullet hole, from friendly fire? Or something else?

Still simmering with adrenaline, Reaper hardly felt the pain from it—just a kind of pinching throb. But he could feel the strength seeping out of him through that wound. He felt cold . . . colder by the second . . .

"You're losing too much blood," she murmured, bringing her medikit over. She examined the wound gravely, then glanced up at him. He saw it in her eyes—he was in bad shape. Not likely to get very far from here.

He nodded his understanding.

She sprayed the wound on his side and the raked places on his arm with skin sealant to stop the oozing.

What they'd gone through already would have pushed most people over the edge into helpless hysteria. His sister had been deeply shaken, had come close to losing it—and then pulled herself back. And now she was right back to taking charge.

My sister, he thought, smiling. *Scientist, doctor, take-charge broad. She really is something.*

He felt colder yet. Dizzy. A redoubled roaring

echoed from the blocked doorway. The door shuddered as something big tried it. They heard the sound of claws on metal—a long, drawn-out screeching . . . then mindless chattering—and a squeal as one of the genetic demons attacked another; their competing roars as they fought. The tendency the things had to fight one another was one of the few advantages he and Sam had left.

The door started shaking again.

It would hold for a while. But not long. Those things would be in here, in minutes—ripping into them, or shooting those hideous tongue-spears into their throats . . .

Reaper had to act. There were just too many of them now—and he didn't have the BFG to even the odds. He'd soon run out of ammo if he took them on, tried to kill them all one by one.

Somehow he had to stop them from getting up to the surface, spreading out into the world. There was just one way.

Blow the Ark. Blow the compound. Meaning he and Sam would probably have to die, too. But it was that or . . .

He made up his mind.

"You have to listen to me," Reaper said. "This is important . . ."

"You're cold," she observed. "You're shivering . . ."

He bent over the satchel of ammo, started taking out grenades, taping and strapping them together with anything he could find. "These are ST grenades," he told her. He had to work hard to get his fingers to move; they were going numb, feeling rubbery from blood loss. "When they get through . . . Are you listening? You pop the top, hit this button, okay?"

He finished the improvised bomb . . . and sank back, swaying in place. Feeling like he might keel over. The room was spinning, ever so slowly.

"John," she said, urgently, "stay awake, please. Stay with me!"

The room was getting dark. The wound in his side was deep, and patching it on the outside hadn't been enough. Internal bleeding. He could feel it—like his insides were gradually disintegrating. He might be able to med himself up enough to stop another wave of the genetic demons. But he doubted he could take care of them all. And every one of them had to be stopped cold.

He put his hand on her arm. "Listen, Sam—if I can't make it to the elevator to keep them from getting topside, you're going to have to nuke the whole place from here."

She didn't get back to him on that one right away.

He looked at her. "Sam, are you listening?"

She chewed a fingernail. Went determinedly back to the computer, monitoring the upload. But she said, "Yes."

"If the quarantine clock gets to one minute, and you haven't heard from me, or if one of those things gets in here—pop the top, hit the button . . ."

She was just going to have to deal with it the best she could. But at the back of his mind he did wonder if he were becoming a little too much like Sarge. She looked at him. Waiting.

". . . and throw it in the Ark," he said.

She nodded numbly. They both knew what that would mean—the Ark was unspeakably volatile. The explosion would set off a chain reaction, a blast that would multiply itself exponentially. The compound and a great deal more would be destroyed and both of them with it.

With any luck, though—the planet would be saved.

He stood up—and nearly fell over. Did they have a vitamin shot of some kind? Drugs? He didn't see anything like that in here.

Sam nodded to herself. Coming to her own hard decision. She took something out of her medical bag. A syringe.

"What's that?" he asked.

"C-24," she said. Looking at him meaningfully.

His mouth went dry. "No."

"I took it from Carmack's lab . . ."

"No, forget it."

"You're bleeding to death," she said flatly. "It might save you."

He looked at her. How could he tell her? He had to be as evil inside as anyone here. She just didn't know what he'd been forced to do, in the RRTS. He flashed to that teenager he'd blown in half, the day they'd lost Jumper . . .

"I've done things," he told her. "You don't know. Places I've been—dark places . . ."

"I know you," she said.

"No you don't. You don't know me."

"You're my brother. I *know* you," she insisted. And there were two big tears rolling down her cheeks.

Another wave of weakness shivered through him. He almost fell right then. A black gulf was opening up in front of him.

She was right. He was dying. This was his only chance.

Increasing clamor from the blocked entrance to the room. The door gave out a jarring thud and shivered. They were trying to break through—and in a concerted way, now.

Let us in! the monsters roared—in the language that preceded language.

Breathing hard, Sam turned to look at the door. Now it was bending inward, shaking; she heard the redoubled roaring. There was no more time for theories or arguments.

Reaper unholstered his sidearm, cocked it, and handed it to her. "One in my heart," he said crisply. "And one in my head, *the second . . .*"

"I won't need to!"

"Don't hesitate! If I start to turn into one of those things . . . don't wait. Do you hear me?"

She bit her lip. Then nodded.

He rolled up his sleeve, and Sam prepped his arm

with alcohol. She intertwined the fingers of her free hand with his, clasping hard as if she could keep him alive, keep him here in the world with the strength of her grip.

"I've missed you," she said. And she gave him the shot, injecting him with the stuff that made men supermen—or into monsters.

The serum was coursing through him and . . . he felt nothing.

It wasn't going to work. Maybe the label had been wrong, or the serum not yet complete . . .

And then—he felt everything, all at once: every nerve, every cell of his body howling in outrage as it was invaded.

He was no longer cold. A wave of inconceivable heat rolled through him, and another, more and more. His back arched, his fingers fisted, his eyes started, his mouth went into a kind of rictus and his throat seized up and he couldn't even scream as the C-24 roared through him, setting up a chain of cause and effect that reached beyond the biological, somehow resonating in the quantum realm: sucking energy from the world around him, forming it into matter, infusing it into him.

His body slowly began to swell, his bones creaking; his clothing tearing at the seams. He wasn't growing like an imp—just firming, thickening, rippling with an energy that the physics of his own world didn't even have a name for, as yet . . .

But it was too much—the sudden complete change

of it all. The pain was unimaginable, a cosmos filled with nothing but agony. His body and brain couldn't take it.

He wasn't going to live through this. Nothing could. It was unbearable. He didn't even *want* to live any longer. Feelings like this—of every last cell of his body interpenetrated and redesigned, made into something alien, in just a few seconds—were beyond comprehension.

And then the pain stopped—and so did his heart. He was falling—

And *bang,* he hit the floor. The world dissolved into a murky blur. Darker, darker yet.

He blew out a long slow breath—and was unable to draw another in. That breath—had been his last one.

NINETEEN

SAMANTHA GRIMM MADE up her mind to shoot her brother in the head.

John had begun convulsing, his face a rigid mask of pain, and she could see the change taking place in him, the C-24 transmuting him before her eyes: his muscles, already firm, were bulking; there was a certain trace of heaviness in the bones of his face, indicating they were becoming more dense . . .

And the eyes. They seemed animalistic—two fires in his skull.

She was almost exhausted. And she was seeing everything through a glass, darkly: she'd liked Duke, despite his clumsy moves on her—maybe because of them—and she'd seen him sliced and diced. She'd seen Pinky, whom she'd worked with for so long, backed into a corner, then abducted by a monster. She'd seen Carmack *become* a monster. She'd seen heaps of bodies. She'd seen Sarge murder that nice Kid for having a conscience. She'd been told it was her responsibility to blow herself and her brother to kingdom come.

She was seeing *doom* everywhere she looked. Everything seemed hopeless. How could she believe, in this moment, that C-24 wouldn't do to her brother what it had done to Curtis Stahl?

And as John fell onto his back, shaking, going into the last stages of the transformation, Sam raised the pistol, to shoot him in the head.

Then the door behind her burst open, and she turned to see an imp rushing at her, drooling mouth agape, squealing with hatred. She fired the pistol at it almost point-blank—wounding it in the right shoulder but not stopping it, not even slowing it. It struck the gun aside, then backhanded her, knocking her sprawling.

"John!" She managed, as she fell.

Head spinning, she felt something grab her by the right wrist and drag her across the floor, toward the shattered door. She struggled feebly, but the blow to her head had left her badly stunned, almost paralyzed.

She shouted her brother's name one last time as she was dragged through the door, into the hallway, into reeking gloom, then it was all too much, and she lost consciousness.

Sam woke to a warped ringing sound—it was in her own ears, as if her head were a cracked bell, still ringing from the blow to the face the imp had given her. And there was a choking smell of rot and vinegar and blood.

Her eyes slowly cleared, and she saw she was in the bottom of a large air shaft, forty feet across: the central station for pumping and purifying oxygen throughout the compound. She'd seen down into it one time, on her first and only tour of the place: a vertical shaft with three gigantic fan blades whirling in it.

A little rusty light filtered down from a skylight, at the top of the shaft about four stories up, flickering with the slow turning of the fan blades. On the other side of the shaft, its back to her, the imp crouched over the body of a woman . . . using its talons to rip pieces of thigh meat from the woman's leg, stuff them in its maw.

Watching it feed, Sam controlled the impulse to vomit—and to scream.

If you want to live, control yourself. This is your chance—when it's not watching . . .

She wondered vaguely why she was still alive at all. Obviously it wanted to infect her, or it would've killed her already. She touched her neck, wondering if the thing had already pierced her with its tongue-barb. She could feel no wound there.

Maybe they needed to do the deed while you were conscious. Maybe it was saving her for later—if it was, it wouldn't be for long.

Slowly, Sam sat up and looked around for an egress. There was a tunnel, the way they'd probably come in—but it was on the other side of the imp. She couldn't get to it without being noticed.

263

She spotted a metal maintenance ladder, rungs built into the wall, running all the way up the air shaft, passing through narrow crawl apertures beside the fan blades. Better than nothing.

Moving slowly, trying not to make a sound, she got her feet under her and stood. Wincing at the pain in her head, the bruises in her limbs, she edged carefully toward the ladder.

Sam reached the ladder and began to climb. She was several steps up when her foot slipped, the toe of her boot clanking on a lower rung. She froze—but the imp lifted its head as if listening. It turned with a roar and saw its prey trying to get away.

She started up the ladder again, forgetting her throbbing head and aching muscles, clambering as fast as she could. She reached the opening, and just managed to squeeze through the narrow aperture beside the fan blades' framework when the imp closed its talons around her ankle and nearly jerked her back down.

No. She wasn't going to let it end like this.

Sam kicked downward, going with the motion of the imp's tugging, and slammed the genetic demon hard in the face with her bootheel, grinding into its optical membranes. It squealed in pain and its grip loosened. She wrenched free and pulled herself up onto the little platform, next to the slowly whirling fan blades. The imp was reaching through the aperture, raking its claws at her, but she was well out of reach. It couldn't fit its wide shoulders through the opening to this level—it'd grown past human proportions.

"That's right, you bastard, I'm getting away from you!" she yelled. Releasing pent-up fear and fury. *"Fuck you!"*

She continued up the ladder, then paused about halfway to the next set of blades when she heard the imp chattering, making a sound close to laughter. She looked down to see it had taken hold of the fan blade, was being spun around, not particularly rapidly, like a child on a playground toy. It slung its legs up over the blade, and began to climb onto it, still spinning around as it climbed. The blades were going so slowly that they weren't much obstacle.

"Shit," she muttered, and resumed climbing, trying to urge her aching limbs into greater speed.

But moments later Sam heard the imp chittering in triumph and looked down to see it leaping from the top of the big fan blade to the lower rungs of the ladder she was on. It leered up at her and began to climb, moving much more rapidly than she could.

"Oh fuck . . ." Riding a surge of terror-charged adrenaline, she redoubled her speed, and reached the next aperture, pulled herself through just ahead of the imp. It raked at her leg, slashing a bit of her left calf away, but she managed to slip through ahead of it.

She turned to see it leap at the fan blade, catching the slowly spinning metal with the agility of a giant chimp, chattering to itself as it spun around and around, doubling up to wrap its feet around the blade.

Despite the pain, she started climbing again. Trying to see what was above that last whirling blade . . . air ducts, going off in three directions. Big enough to move through, hunkered down. But the imp could fit into them, too. It would follow her and catch her before she got fifty paces.

She spotted something else, next to the platform beside the air ducts, above the topmost fan blade . . .

She was panting for air in her effort to keep ahead of the imp, sweat running down her back and pasting her hair to her forehead, blood flowing from her injured leg. Sweat on her hands threatened to make her lose her purchase on the rungs—she almost fell into the imp's arms, and it roared in anticipation, snapping at her heels with its jaws.

"No!" she shouted, reaching the final aperture. She reached up and did a pull-up—something normally she hadn't strength to do—and wormed her way through, banging elbows and knees in her haste.

The imp was already poised to leap at the fan blades.

Sam stood up and opened the metal box on the wall, the controller for the fans she'd spotted from below. There it was—the setting she had hoped for.

FULL POWER

She looked to see the imp just about six feet away, clambering up onto a blade, halfway up, legs dangling down below the fan. In another second it would be up—and upon her.

She turned the control knob and the fan blades responded immediately—although the lights dimmed a bit as it drained more of the emergency power—turning faster, faster, becoming a blur like helicopter blades, humming . . .

And slicing the imp in two.

It shrieked, and its upper half tumbled atop the blades, dancing about like a chunk of meat when first popped into a blender, before being chopped to pieces. Black blood splashed the walls, pieces of talon and teeth and bone flew everywhere . . . The increased turbulence from the fan made her stagger, bouncing her back against the wall so that she nearly rebounded to fall into the blades. Blood from the imp became a horrific rain caught in hurricane winds, bitter as it struck her mouth . . .

She caught a stanchion and held on, caught in an artificial windstorm, her hair streaming, eyes drying in the roaring wind. She reached out and fumbled at the knob, switched it back to normal speed. The fan blades slowed, the gale abated, and she got her balance again.

Sam sat on the platform for a few moments, back against the wall and knees drawn up, resting, cleaning demon's blood from her face and hair as best she could. Then she caught a distant chattering, clicking sound—coming from the tunnel opposite her. She stood up, listening breathlessly. Yeah, there it was again. And it was getting louder.

A genetic demon was coming down the tunnel toward her—she couldn't see it but she knew it was coming, hunting her.

She turned and darted into the round air duct to her right—maybe it wouldn't take this one when it got to the air shaft.

But less than a minute later, as she made her way hunkered over in the narrow, dark metal tunnel of the duct, she heard a low chattering growl echoing from behind her. She could smell the imp; she heard its urgent, clicking footsteps . . .

She turned and looked down the circular tunnel, saw the silhouette of an imp, against the light, its quivering shadow stretching ahead of it, as if reaching out for her in anticipation. It was closing in on her.

Sam turned, hurrying on—then heard a hissing sound and instinctively threw herself flat. The imp's tongue flashed over her, susurrating as it passed close over the back of her head, unrolling out of its mouth—just missing her before reeling back into its toothy maw.

She was up and scrambling down the tunnel, then—and came to a grating, for a vent down into a room under the duct. She could see through the slats, into the room below—a bit. There was a desk and a chair down there; she couldn't make out anything else. The rest of the room might be filled with monsters. But the imp in the duct was almost upon her again, and there was no time to worry about what was below.

She slammed her elbow into the grating, hard enough to make blood flow, and the grating popped out, clattering down. She felt the demon's breath on the back of her neck . . .

It was too big to get through the vent opening. It was her only chance.

Sam dropped through headfirst, trying to break her fall on the desk with her hands—but she never struck it, though it was directly below.

The imp had gripped her lower legs, just above the ankles. She was dangling there, head down. It was running its long, long tongue down her right leg, spiraling it around her ankle, down her calf, wet and raspy, probing toward her crotch. She could feel the barb on it, dragging across her skin, looking for the right spot to strike, like a cobra aiming its fangs.

Sam's hands were dangling over the desk . . . and on the desk—a nice big pair of scissors. She couldn't quite reach them.

She strained for the makeshift weapon. The tongue was slinking along her, stretching . . . leaving a trail of drool on her skin.

She caught the edge of the scissors with the tip of her index fingers, managed to tease them toward her, scooped them up, bent at the waist, reached up and—working her fingers with all the strength she could get into them—severed the tongue where it issued from the thing's mouth.

It screeched as she dropped heavily onto the desk, striking it painfully with her left shoulder, rolling, clawing at herself to get the tongue off—it slithered away, like a frantic snake, thrashing.

She kicked at it, backing away, stumbled over a wastepaper basket, got to her feet, threw the metal can at the rippling, bleeding tongue.

Sam still had the scissors in her other hand, but she was afraid to get close to the severed tongue—it seemed to have a life of its own.

Overhead, the imp was *really* pissed off. It was shaking the duct, ripping at it, tearing it free from its supports, bits of ceiling coming down.

Sam looked around, saw she was in an unoccupied, dimly lit administrative room, with cubicles and desks. She started off between the cubicles—stiff, in pain and bone-tired but urging herself on. The imp would break out of the duct in seconds.

She got to the corridor, stepped out, turned—and saw another big imp standing just forty feet from her, a massive burly figure barely fitting into the hall, seeming to suck the light into itself.

The big imp had its back to Sam, was looking down an intersecting passage, sniffing the air, growling low in its chest. She could feel the growl resonating in the walls, the floors, in her bones . . .

She backed away down the hall—and the imp was staring off in another direction, leaving her. But she could hear the other imp breaking loose in the room she'd left, the thump when it dropped down on the desk.

Sam realized she still had the scissors in her hands.

She had reached another doorway, open into a storage room that connected two hallways. The big imp was going—and she threw the scissors at its back.

Then she ducked into the storage room.

Sam heard a roar—the shears had struck the big imp, not hurting it but getting its attention. It turned—

Which was exactly when the smaller imp came out of the other door, looking for Sam.

The big imp knew that someone had struck it and, as Sam had hoped, it decided it was the smaller imp, the only other individual it could see.

Sam peeked around the corner of the door and saw the imp she'd provoked rush the smaller one, roaring—the smaller imp turned to defend itself, leaping on its assailant's chest, like a panther onto a wild bull, sinking its jaws into the bigger demon's chest.

That ought to keep them busy for a while.

Sam turned, slipped through the storage room to the next hallway. Where was she now? How was she going to find John?

Sam had to get downstairs. She had a vague memory of where the elevators were. They were frozen but the stairway was nearby. She hurried down the corridors, wishing she had a weapon of some kind.

She heard more chattering, something rumbling, not far ahead—the direction of the elevators. She slowed, heart pounding, when she got to the cross hall and looked cautiously around the left-hand corner, trying not to show any more of herself than she had to.

Three half-turned genetic demons were crouched, about fifty feet down the hall, over a heap of torn meat. Feeding.

Sam stared, thinking they'd torn some poor bastard to pieces, until she realized that an overturned cafeteria refrigerator lay beyond them. They'd dragged it out here and pulled the deli meats out—she could see all the wrappers now. Almost reassuring to know they ate something besides human flesh. But it wouldn't stop them from killing her.

One of the half-turned was wearing a uniform. It could almost be identical to her brother's. Only it wasn't—was it? She tried to remember what his uniform had been like.

Could that be John? Could he be one of them?

She stared . . . and though the light was dim, she could see that this man had red hair. Not John.

272

Still . . . John could be one of them right now, somewhere. Her brother hunting through the corridors like an animal . . . hunting Sam.

She wouldn't believe it. She would believe, until she saw him, that he was all right. He wasn't one of them. He was alive. He was trying to find her . . .

But he'd never look up here. She had to find her way back to him.

She looked to the right, saw the elevator about a hundred fifty feet down the hall. It was open—there was a naked, bloody man's body lying in the way of the door, which kept trying to close on it. The door would close against the body's shoulder, then triggered by the blockage, would open, then pause, closing again—breaking the body more, and more, and more with each closing. Beyond was an empty elevator shaft. Where was the elevator? Stuck somewhere below? Then how had the door gotten open? Probably the man had pried it open, trying to find a way to escape—and then the half-turned had caught him. She could see that most of his right leg was torn away . . .

"Hold the door for me," Sam muttered.

She was going to have to go that way—the stairs were down there. But then, she'd never make it down before the half-turned caught up with her. They could be fast.

A rumbling snort from the half-turned—she turned to see one of them looking right at her. The others looked up one by one—and they all stood and bounded toward her.

"Oh fuck . . ."

She had no choice now. It was the stairs or . . .

There was another possibility. Only, it was crazy and she'd probably die in the attempt.

But Sam was already running toward the elevators, going full tilt, hearing the howling half-turned harrying after her. She glanced over her shoulder, saw that two of them were down on all fours, like unfinished werewolves, loping toward her—all of them had their mouths open, ululating with bloodlust as they came.

Up ahead was the elevator, and on the left, the door to the stairs. The door was closed. It might even be locked, or blocked from the other side.

The elevator shaft, though, she knew was open.

The half-turned pursuing her were close, close, very close behind. She could hear them panting almost on her heels, catching up: a second or two more and they'd bear her down. One of them reached to grab the hair streaming behind her and yanked, tore some of it out by the roots, trying to stop her. But she kept going, a few strides more, just a little more—

The elevator shaft was looming . . . the body . . . the doors closing, opening, closing . . . *opening!*

Sam leapt over the body and out into the elevator shaft.

The cables she'd glimpsed were there—and seemed a bit farther than she'd anticipated. But her hands closed over them, lower than she'd planned, her breastbone smacked into them, she closed her legs around them . . . and began to slide down—

Even as the three half-turned, unable to stop in time kept going, floundering over the body in the doorway, falling headlong, tumbling past her, down the shaft, shrieking in fury and fear as they plummeted—to smack messily into the top of the frozen elevator four stories below.

Their howling abruptly stopped.

Sam was sliding down the cables, her hands burning, skin ripping away from her palms, gritting her teeth in pain. She was pressing as hard as she could with her feet and knees to slow her descent . . . and after a few more seconds of hand-scouring agony her slide eased almost to a stop.

Not quite within reach, beyond the cable, was a ladder, built into the farther wall of the elevator shaft. She worked her way around to the other side of the cable, grimacing with the agony in her hands, clamped herself in place as well as she could, and leaned back, grabbing for a rung.

She caught one—and then thought: *I'm an idiot. I can't let go of the cables, my weight will pull me off the rung. I can't go back, I'm leaning too far, I'll fall . . .*

She was stuck, spavined over the void.

She decided on the ladder. She'd just have to hold

on. And she was losing her hold on the cable . . . sliding down . . .

Sam let go of the cable and—feeling absurdly like a primate in a tree—she swung over to the ladder, kicking a foot toward a lower rung, trying to get a hold.

She missed, and fell to the end of her right arm, and shouted in blinding pain—almost losing her grip, nearly dislocating her arm from her shoulder. Sam whimpered, and felt with her toe, looking for a rung, found one, got a foothold and what a blessed relief it was to take the weight off her arm . . .

She clung to the ladder, gasping, for ten long seconds, feeling sweat dry on the back of her neck, her forearms. Then she made herself start down. Her right arm ached at the shoulder, but it seemed intact.

She was almost to the bottom of the ladder when she heard the genetic demon snarling, and she turned to see it crouching beside its dead fellows, preparing to leap at her. Its left arm was broken, turned crazily wrong in the socket, bone ends sticking out. Blood coursed from the corners of its mouth . . .

She moaned in frustration and started back up the ladder—and then the thing leapt and grabbed her by the neck, jerked her off the rungs. She fell shouting wordlessly, falling on her back at its feet. She looked up—seeing it upside down, dripping blood and saliva on her face as it ducked toward her, opening its mouth to tear into her throat . . .

A thud and it staggered—and fell across her, the back of its head shot away.

With a yelp of revulsion she pushed it off her, rolled and got her feet under her—looked up to see Sarge standing there, gun in hand.

"Hello, Sam," he said.

TWENTY

REAPER WAS IN darkness—but behind its cloak was a powerful humming sound . . . like a great dynamo thrumming somewhere . . . What was it? The sound of the universe going on without him?

So this is dying, Reaper thought. *I don't think I like it much. But I always thought it'd be worse than this . . . But then again, my dying ain't over . . . Maybe it gets worse— maybe Hell's coming next . . .*

No, wait a minute. I just came from there.

Hold on: if I'm still thinking, can I really be dead? So maybe . . . Maybe I'm not going to die yet. Maybe I'll survive this thing. The pain is gone. Strength coming back . . . but almost too much. Like I might explode with it . . .

I feel—kind of good. Like in combat when I know I can kill the guy in front of me, even though he's trying with all his might to kill me: I know he's more scared than I am. Somehow I know that he'll die . . .

And I'm going to live.

That humming . . . like a generator going full blast . . . that's the sound of my blood running through my veins . . . But I'm still in the dark . . . Except . . .

Except for the shape of the iris of a single eye. A little light came through that distant aperture, nothing more.

He had thought he heard Sam screaming his name, from somewhere. Her voice falling away as she screamed it, as if she were falling down a deep shaft.

"Johhhhhhhnnnnnnnnnnnnnnnnnnnnnnnnnnn . . . !"

That's how it had sounded. But hadn't that been a while ago?

How long had he been out of it?

Still so dark. But then the gloom around it seemed to solidify in places, to take on shapes; light filtered in as the iris expanded, and colors began to appear . . .

And the room snapped into focus. He was in the infirmary . . . sitting up—looking down at himself.

His arm was healed. The slashes were completely gone. Not even a scar.

He stood up, looking for his sister. "Sam?" He turned, found himself looking at his own reflection in the observation window—saw there were now no cuts on his face.

The small room was trashed. Cabinets overturned, debris everywhere. A door—locked before—leading from the observation room to the corridor, was torn open, hanging crazily ajar.

Something had taken her. Had left him alone, thinking he was dead or dying. It had taken Sam and the chances were small, very small, that she was still alive.

Once more—and it was harder this time—he put the grief aside so he could deal with what he needed to do right now. He found his weapon, picked it up, slammed home a clip.

Then he stepped over the debris and headed into the dark corridor beyond, to search for Sam—or what was left of her.

Reaper was carried along on a wave of energy—that humming dynamo was pumping away, churning in his head, powering him like a thousand volts through a jackhammer.

His senses seemed impossibly acute. He could smell blood, distinguishing fresh from blood that had been spilled a few minutes earlier—he could smell sweat and the pheromones in it; he could smell cleaning agents and urine. He heard far too much—his boot steps were like a bass drum pounding, and he could hear the movement of air in the ducts and claws scrabbling in another part of the compound. That's how he knew which way to go . . .

And he could see in the dark—the shrouded look of the place remained, as if black scarves were draped at the edges, but it was as if he had some version of infrared working, and he could see all the details of the corridor rushing toward him; rebar in the debris where a wall had been knocked down; serial numbers on pipes hanging from the ceiling.

The gun felt light as a feather in his hand; the floor seemed to drift away beneath him, insubstantial. He felt no effort in hurrying down the hallway. That's what it was like: almost as if he were standing still, and the hallway was rushing past. That corner up ahead was swinging toward him of its own accord.

And then a high-pitched screech—a scream of fury, not of fear—came from around that corner. Reaper reached the branching hallway and spun to see the genetic demon running full bore toward him, a half-turned soldier, uniform in tatters: squalling, as it came on, like a bird of prey.

It was already leaping at Reaper—no time to get the gun into play, so he met it with a fist smashing into its chest and it was flung backward as if struck by a piledriver, spinning away like a broken doll into the darkness it came from.

Reaper stopped moving for a stunned instant, amazed at his own power.

Another hallway off to the right—a sound down there. *Scrape . . . tick-tick. Scrape.* An ordinary man wouldn't have heard it. But he could see nothing down there . . . maybe a rat.

Reaper turned away, then heard the thump as the creature dropped from the hole in the ceiling, all the way from the floor above, howling jeeringly as it came. He spun and a female imp loomed over him— she had grotesque parodies of breasts, a gnarled sketch of a vagina: the effect was obscene.

She snarled and slashed at him—he dodged the talons with ease, again surprised at his own speed.

He seemed superior to the genetic demons—faster, smarter, more powerful.

It was the work of an instant to shove his gun up under her chin and pull the trigger—she jerked backward, the top of her head flying off.

Before the body hit the floor he was moving away—then heard a scuttling sound, turned to see the imp's tongue, detached from her head and moving with a will of its own, on a blind mission of reproduction; it was writhing along the floor toward him like an awkward snake, rearing up to strike at him, to inject him with the genetic ejaculate that would try to make him the other kind of Carmack creation.

He sidestepped its strike—the long, absurd tongue was as fast as a cobra, but Reaper was faster—and fired, blasting it into red scraps.

Reaper heard a groan from behind, turned to see a half-turned stumbling toward him—it was moaning, clawing at itself, seeming to implore him for help. Reaper hesitated—and the thing pointed at his gun, then at its head . . .

It wanted him to put it out of its misery—there was a lot of humanity left in this one. Could it be someone he knew? Was it possible, somehow, to save this pathetic thing? Unlikely but he continued to hesitate—until, as if to push him into it, the demidemon charged, snapping at Reaper's throat, and he shot it point-blank in the face.

It sank to the floor with a grateful sigh.

There was a sizeable room to one side—something moving there. Reaper switched on his gunlight and probed its shadows, moving slowly, carefully through the door, looking at the ceiling for gaps as he came, scanning the floor for unexpected holes. The room was a modest cafeteria, with pillars here and there, and large tables; a kitchen, gleaming with copper and steel, at the farther end. The smell of cooked meat was strong in the room; and the smell of blood.

Nothing moved. Had he imagined it?

There—something slipping in and out of shadow. A skulking movement—almost certainly one of them.

He was reluctant to shoot, though, without getting a clearer sight of it—it was not impossible that Sam was alive somewhere. Improbable, but he hadn't given up hope completely, and after all—

The thought was snapped off by the demon leaping at him from the gloom—snarling at him with its dripping jaws. He jumped back behind a pillar, circled, came up behind the thing and fired, nearly cutting it in half. He fired another burst where its tongue would be coiled up, just to make sure it wasn't going to come at him once he turned his back on the body.

Slapping another clip in his light machine gun, Reaper searched the room. Found a dead man on the tile floor behind the counter, his genitals ripped off and shoved into his mouth, one of his legs missing, his arms turned around backward; found another dead man crammed into an oven, face outward, shoved into a space far too small for a human body, as if into a trash compactor. Someone had switched it to high. He was completely cooked, eye sockets emptied, mouth charred back to expose his teeth. Here was the source of that smell of cooked meat.

Reaper searched the remainder of the kitchen and cafeteria—nothing alive remained.

He heard distant roars, coming from another room, opening off the far end of the cafeteria—they cut off abruptly, to be replaced by gibbering . . .

Reaper drifted across the room—still feeling strong, moving mercurially, with thistledown ease—and kicked through the double doors that led to an even darker room . . .

His gunlight was fading, its battery running low. The room seemed almost to resist its thin illumination.

Something chattered at him without words, in the far corner of the room. Keeping the gun leveled, Reaper felt around in his ammo pack, found the flare he'd noticed there earlier. He snapped the flare into ignition, tossed it hissing into the darkness.

The flare burst into a bright light, briefly illuminating ten, maybe twelve genetic demons—the living dead, imps, and the Hell Knight—crouched near the farther wall, blinking, babbling to one another, as if trying to communicate, cursing like the builders of the tower of Babel.

Then the light went out—just as he saw them tensing to spring at him, teeth bared—and he fired, spraying the room with an arc of lead, the gun jumping in his hand, the air billowing with gun smoke.

He stopped firing for a moment, unsure if he was hitting anything—and the gun spoke to him. He'd had the prompter thumbed off before, but it must've switched on again, because the gun said:

"Low . . . ammo . . . warning . . ."

Just before he ran out of bullets.

He pivoted, fired the last shots into a wall-mounted fire extinguisher, which blew up like a bomb, shrapneling the four demons in the lead as they rushed at him from the darkness.

Three half-turned went down, but the Hell Knight, standing amongst them, didn't seem to feel the explosion. This was the biggest creature he'd seen yet—just enormous, so large it was hard for it to squeeze through the door. It loomed over Reaper, all exposed muscle and neckless head and vast jaws; gazing eyelessly down at him. It seemed to savor the moment—as if it were anticipating eating him alive.

And to Reaper's astonishment, the Hell Knight grinned at him. An evil grin, but a human one, too.

Then it reached into the shadows—and brought out something from a set of shelves he hadn't noticed before, in the dark room beyond the cafeteria: a chain saw. So they could use weapons—or some of them could.

Its grin widened as it started the chain saw and slashed it at him—Reaper jumped backward, smelling the motor oil and feeling the wind of the whirling blade just missing his right ear.

Reaper backed away from the Hell Knight as it raised the chain saw to strike at him again.

The Hell Knight was toying with him, he realized, stalking him. It slashed the air near his face with the chain saw and he jerked back—Reaper smelled sparking metal, hot with friction, as the whirring chain just missed his nose.

The chainsaw—a big device looking like a toy in its massive paws—was roaring itself, like a predator hungry for a kill.

Then the creature squatted—and Reaper realized it was going to jump on him. Land on him while he was flat on his back—pinion and crush him, then, if he were still alive, it would go to work on his face and neck with the chain saw . . .

Heart hammering, Reaper leapt to one side, sprawling. The Hell Knight thudded where he'd been a moment before, turned to lash out at him but Reaper scrambled to his feet, ducked behind a pillar. He dropped the empty weapon, his fingers closing over a familiar metallic shape in his ammo pack.

He sprinted across the room, dodging between tables, his fingers finding the controls on the device, dropping it in what he hoped was the Hell Knight's path . . .

The Hell Knight paused to gleefully cut a table in half with a single swipe, then rushed after him, its bellow mingling with the roar of the chain saw.

Reaper darted around another table—but his way was suddenly blocked by the one the demon kicked at him, tossing it in his way as if it were made of cardboard. He stumbled into it, turned to see the creature looming over him with the chain saw raised to slice down into Reaper's head . . .

Then the timed mine Reaper had dropped went off just behind the demon—Reaper was too close to the blast himself, had to shield his eyes with his arm. The powerful explosive blew the genetic demon into gristle and raw meat. Its body became shrapnel, its head came flying like a cannonball right at Reaper's eyes, still grinning though it was severed from the body—

Impact. It struck Reaper in the forehead and he flew back into spinning darkness. He lay stunned, blinking, in a pile of debris.

Tearing pain jolted Reaper back to full awareness, his sight clearing to show him a genetic demon of a kind he hadn't seen before gnawing at his right shoulder. A thing with a boarlike face, with tusks and tiny eyes and great blunt snout, was trying to eat him alive.

Reaper recoiled from it as the thing snapped at him again, trying to get its enormous jaws around his neck now. He flailed for a weapon and his hand closed over a metal pipe. He jammed the pipe vertically in the boar-demon's mouth, so it couldn't close its jaws. It rocked back, howling in fury, raced erratically around the room, trying to claw the pipe free from its mouth—and Reaper realized, seeing the thing's lower half, that it had been Pinky. The boar-demon was grafted into a cyberchair. It roared and squealed, eyes wild, drooling, prying at its bloody jaws. The pipe wasn't going to keep the Pinky-thing at bay for long.

He spotted the chainsaw on the floor, still whirring away, in the puddle of shattered flesh where the Hell Knight had been, as if the machine were hungrily trying to chew up the remains, sputtering black blood . . . and then it shut down.

Reaper got his feet under him, feeling strength and coordination returning to his souped-up body, and scooped up the chain saw, started it, again revving it up and delighting in the roar of power as the Pinky-thing chomped down on the pipe, sending it ripping through its upper jaw.

It charged, and Reaper jabbed the chain saw at it, missing aim and cutting only through the extruding pipe. He sidestepped like a bullfighter, and raked at the Pinky-thing as it came back around, clawing and snapping—and this time Reaper connected, catching it just above the cyberchair.

The boar-demon was stuck on the chain saw, unable to advance, slashing but missing Reaper as the blade chewed down again and again, slicing deep, until the Pinky creature went limp in the cyberchair and fell into three sagging segments of bloody flesh.

The saw sputtered to a stop, choked with bone and sinew.

Reaper—a bit horrified at how little he felt at what he had just done—dropped the chain saw in disgust and turned to hurry from the room, distantly aware that his own upper half was liberally splashed with blood from the Hell Knight and Pinky . . . and from his own ravaged shoulder. He glanced down at it—the wound was already healing.

He stopped at the door, turned for one last look at what remained of Pinky. *I put the poor bastard out of his misery.*

Right now he had to find Sam . . . and if he was going to get to her alive, he was going to have to arm himself.

Reaper ran back to the shelves where the Hell Knight had found the chain saw. Felt around on them, found a handheld plasma cannon—then remembered the other demons that'd been crouching in that room.

He hadn't gotten them all with that pressure blast from the fire extinguisher. They'd been waiting in the darkness as he fought the Hell Knight and Pinky— waiting for the outcome. He heard them chattering, rushing toward him, and brought the plasma cannon into play just as they charged him from the dark corners of the storage room.

He fired three times fast, the first blindly, the

second and third using the light from the plasma cannon to place his shots. The creatures were caught in the energy beams at close range, their limbs melting away, heads frying, brains boiling out their eye sockets, dancing with agony—and collapsing.

Reaper tried to fire once more to make sure—but the plasma cannon announced that it was out of power. He dropped it—and looked around till he found the light machine gun he'd dropped when the Hell Knight had charged him. He found a couple of clips in his ammo pouch, reloaded it, and returned to the corridor, looking for the elevators . . .

There they were. The elevator lobby. The lockdown indicator flashed red. They were still inoperable.

That's when he heard a shout. Someone farther down the hallway, calling his name.

"John!"

It was his sister's voice.

TWENTY-ONE

REAPER STOPPED DEAD, staring at a scene of blistering carnage.

The hallway wall here was broken down, opening out into an impromptu charnel house, choked with bodies. The crust of the wall steamed and smoked and glowed; beyond the wall, what light there was came from embers and sparks raining from the broken ends of dangling electrical wires twitching against one another. Looking closer, Reaper decided that the walls had been *melted* down. The BFG had done this.

Corridor was blended into room and piled high in both were bodies. Human and demons, mixed up in heaps, tangled, united in blood—black blood swirling with red.

It was a prophecy of human destiny: men and monsters intermingled, fused in death. Great holes were melted in the ceiling, too—molten metal, from cooked pipes and ducts and wires, dripped down on the layered heaps of bodies, a mercuric icing on a grisly cake.

Sam's voice had come from in here somewhere.

"John . . ."

There it was again. But where was she? He aimed his gunlight into the shadows—and spotted her, slumped against a wall.

"Sam!"

He ran to her, jumping over bodies as if they were rocks on a path. He reached her side, hunkered down, taking her hands in his—making her wince. She was bruised, bloodied, her hands skinned to raw flesh. She looked up at him weakly, trembling, relief, even happiness in her eyes—but also warning.

"You're alive . . ." she whispered.

"Don't talk. Please . . ."

Sarge's voice came from behind. "Last man standing, Reaper . . ."

Reaper stood, turned to peer into the shadows. Sarge stepped forward into the fluttering, multicolored light. He'd been using Sam as bait.

Sarge chuckled, as he said, "Think she needs medical attention . . ." As if there was something funny in the remark.

Reaper could see the wound on Sarge's neck; the beginning of the change in his face. "Where are those survivors the Kid found?" Reaper asked.

"I took care of them." Sarge smiled faintly. "Just dotting the i's." He glanced at his watch. "Quarantine's almost over. Power should be back on any minute."

Reaper got it now. He knew where he stood with Sarge. "You killed the Kid . . ."

"We're all killers here, Reaper. That's what they pay us for."

Reaper's hand tightened on his weapon. He wondered if he could get a shot off before Sarge did.

But he didn't think there was much hope of catching Sarge by surprise: he was all animal wariness. It twitched in his fingers; it gleamed in his eyes.

The overhead lights blinked, and a female voice intoned from the public address system:

"Quarantine complete . . . All systems to normal. Elevators back online . . ."

The emergency lighting switched off—and with only a flutter of darkness, were replaced by the main lights, going on in sequence down the long hallways.

Sarge glanced at the ceiling. He grinned. "It's finished. What do you say . . . we get some air?"

Reaper stared. What did he mean?

Then it became evident—as Sarge's gloves split open, like fruit swelling in the heat, with the sudden deformation of his hands. The skin splitting open . . . Sarge going rigid with the agony of transformation . . .

Now, Reaper told himself. *Kill him now, before he's done changing. While he's distracted by the pain . . .*

But he couldn't bring himself to shoot Sarge down in cold blood like that; like the way Sarge had killed the Kid.

"Sam," Reaper said, keeping his eyes on Sarge, "can you get to the elevator?"

"I'm not sure . . ."

293

"Try."

Sam got wearily to her feet. Reaper sidled between Sarge and the door Sam was going to have to go through, to cover her escape.

All the while Sarge was mutating. Growing. Muscles pushing through his clothes. Skin going raw; hands becoming talons; jaws widening . . . eyes reddening . . .

Something inside him, Reaper thought, *is coming to the outside. That's what it's all about . . . The interior demon finally coming out . . .*

Sam slipped out the door behind Reaper. The moment had come . . .

Sarge stopped trembling. Ducked his head like a bull, looking at Reaper from within cavelike sunken eyes. His voice was an inhuman rumble: "You going to shoot me?" Asked as if unconcerned. Almost amused.

"Yeah, I was thinking about it," Reaper admitted.

Sarge looked at Reaper's gun. "What have you got left?"

Reaper glanced down at the weapon. "Half a clip. You?"

Sarge checked the indicator on the big energy weapon in his hand and smiled. That smile, all fangs and sickly glisten, was a nasty sight. "Only got one round."

One round from the BFG was like hundreds of rounds from other energy weapons, converged into one . . . this room was proof of that.

Sarge aimed the BFG.

Reaper leapt to one side, rolled, coming up running, as the torpedo-like bolt from the BFG flashed by him. It struck the floor, eating instantaneously through floor and wall where he'd stood a moment before—and seemed to pursue him: the destructive energy coursing through the floor, the bodies, everything between him and Sarge, trying to catch him, to eat its way through him.

But Reaper had the power of his own transformation in him, and he moved in a blur of speed, outdistancing the ripple effect of the BFG, ducking into the shadows.

Sarge lost sight of Reaper in all the smoke and energy flare.

Then a short burst from Reaper's weapon cued him in, the rounds slapping the wall just beside his head, and he threw himself flat, tossing the now-useless BFG aside.

The air in the room undulated with heat and smoke . . . somewhere in there was Reaper, getting a bead on him.

All Sarge had left was his pride in his work. He wasn't a Marine anymore; he wasn't a Privine; he wasn't even human. But he was still a soldier. And his whole purpose, now, was to find an adversary . . . and destroy him. That's all that mattered anymore. Orders? No. Just . . . find the enemy and fight to the death.

If he thought about anything else, he'd have to blow his own brains out. Smash them out the way Goat had. And he wasn't going to do that. That's the way pussies went out.

A sound from the left . . .

Sarge got his feet under him and leapt to cover behind a heap of debris and bodies, then, crouched, sprinted for the door that led to the Ark chamber.

Two more shots from Reaper, somewhere in the shadows, cracking past Sarge's head—one of them grazing his neck, doing no real damage.

The Ark. Get to the Ark . . . it seemed fitting to end the fight there. On the brink of the gulf between two worlds . . .

Reaper checked his ammo. Two rounds left. No time to scrounge for other weapons.

He got up and started after Sarge . . . headed for the Ark chamber.

When Reaper got there, he found most of the lights had been shot out. The room had been wrecked by some fight between imps and the half-turned. Debris and bodies here, too.

There was no sight of Sarge, big though he was, amongst the pillars in the chamber. But Reaper knew he was there. He listened and his preternaturally acute hearing picked Sarge's breathing up, off to the left, near a heap of rubble.

Reaper slipped behind a pillar, keeping to his own

shadows. But if he knew about where Sarge was, Sarge knew where he was, too.

"Only got two left, Sarge!" Reaper called. Seemed only fair.

He glided to another pillar, his head low. Could be Sarge had found another gun somewhere.

Reaper kept moving, low and slow and quiet, training enhanced by his superhumanity, and spotted Sarge, suddenly, moving to the place he'd occupied a few moments before—Sarge with a big long chunk of ragged metal in his hand. A serrated club.

Reaper aimed . . .

Sarge seemed surprised that Reaper wasn't there, hesitated only a second—then ducked behind a pillar as Reaper, gun set to semiauto, squeezed the trigger. The bullet smacked into the wall just behind Sarge.

"One!" Sarge yelled, rolling into the shadows.

Reaper sprinted in pursuit—and came up short. Sarge was gone.

He heard a noise behind him, spun to see Sarge coming from up high, smashing through the Ark memorial plaque, like the Ark dead demanding remembrance in person, the plaque shattered to translucent shrapnel by the inhuman force of his arrival. Skidding to a stop Sarge roared, *"Semper fi, motherfucker!"*

Reaper took one step back—just one, so he could plant himself for the fight.

"You and me, Reaper," Sarge said. "Old school."

Making himself clear, Sarge unclasped his belt, letting his knife and unloaded pistol fall with it to the floor. He looked at Reaper expectantly.

Reaper sighed inwardly. He knew he shouldn't do this. There were bigger responsibilities here . . .

But he was who he was. And he couldn't lose the chance to take Sarge out hand to hand. Not after what he'd done to the Kid. Reaper had liked that stupid kid . . . And all those people the Kid had tried to save. Sarge had executed them . . .

Besides—one bullet probably wouldn't take Sarge out. Not the way Sarge was now . . . on the cusp of the dark transformation.

So Reaper fired his last round into the ceiling, then threw the weapon aside, dropped his bag of grenades, dropped his knife . . .

And he started toward Sarge. They circled each other slowly, taut with wariness, then moved more rapidly toward one another, tensing as they came, hands ready to grapple.

The two poles of human nature, face-to-face, fighting it out. Not so simple as good versus evil. More like unselfish versus selfish; reason versus appetite; human versus animal instinct.

John Grimm versus Sarge. They rushed each other—and Sarge caught Reaper with a hard, piledriver right, sending him sprawling. Reaper kept rolling, turned it into a movement that carried him onto his feet, spun a kick as Sarge came, catching him square in the chest and sending him flying into a wall. The wall cracked behind Sarge—but he came immediately back at Reaper . . .

And the two warriors began hammering on each other toe-to-toe, with more bludgeoning than artifice. Reaper's blood was up now, his speed was almost bullet-fast, and he blocked nearly every one of Sarge's blows, landing counterblows in return. Slamming Sarge back with mallet blows to the chin, the ribs, the side of the head. Bones cracked with the impacts as Reaper drove Sarge back, stumbling back, into a pillar, close to the Ark itself.

And it was as if the confrontation triggered something in both of them—an outpouring of sheer power, issuing from their newly transformed cells.

Sarge rushed Reaper, who used the rush's momentum and his own enhanced power to throw Sarge—and was amazed himself to see how far: Sarge was flung up to a metal catwalk overlooking the chamber. Sarge was momentarily stunned and in seconds, leaping and pulling himself up, Reaper was there beside him, grappling with Sarge, pinning him facedown against the catwalk's tubular metal railing with such force that the railing began to bend, to crack. But it was Sarge's neck Reaper was trying to crack, to choke, as he pressed it against the metal. Feeling Sarge gathering his strength, Reaper braced, but it was like trying to hold down a volcano as Sarge erupted, and Reaper felt himself tossed like a projectile, off the catwalk, to tumble through the air and slam to the floor below.

Stunned, Reaper looked up to see Sarge ripping off part of the broken metal railing, then leaping down at him.

Reaper got his feet under him, jumped back, set himself . . .

And then stared, as he saw Sarge bending the long chunk of metal in his hand, effortlessly twisting it around his lower right arm, wrist, and fist, making a gauntlet edged with ragged metal.

Reaper's reactions were a little slow—he was still slightly stunned from the fall. Sarge was on him before he could sidestep, slamming into him with the improvised gauntlet, pummeling Reaper, throwing him against the wall, hitting him and throwing him once more, so that Reaper felt like he was inside a cement mixer, tossed back and forth between unforgiving slabs of metal and stone . . .

Reaper blocked what blows he could, landed in ways that protected him from the worst of the impacts, waiting for his chance—and it came when Sarge tripped, fell, blinking, black blood running from a dozen wounds in his face and neck.

Reaper set himself for a final, killing blow, planning to dropkick Sarge's head into the pillar behind him.

Then Sarge looked up at him, holding Reaper's

eyes with his. Making him hesitate that fatal split second . . .

And Sarge grinned as he said: "Welcome to the new school . . ."

Reaper stared, fascinated, as Sarge began to change—the transformation that had begun in him thickened his skull, deepened his eyes, turning them demon-yellow; his hands grew claws.

Reaper knew he had to take the offensive, and he lunged at Sarge—but Sarge reacted with superhuman speed, catching Reaper's fist in his claws, digging his talons into his wrists, pushing back . . .

And they held the pose, straining there, the two warriors, human and inhuman, going eyeball-to-eyeball. The two of them struggling to overbalance the other, turning like dancers—so that the Ark, with its ever-shifting mercurial droplet, hung in the air right behind Sarge. Reaper reached deep inside himself for strength and braced, then threw Sarge to one side—just long enough to reach over and stab the buttons activating the Ark.

Reaper turned to see Sarge twisting a piece of metal on his gauntlet into a spike, and he lunged at Reaper, who sidestepped, but not fast enough to avoid a slash from that improvised dagger. He threw a hand out to block it and Sarge plunged the raw blade into Reaper's right hand—and through it. Reaper reeled with pain, as Sarge pressed the blade, and Reaper's hand, back toward Reaper's head, his other hand clamping Reaper's left . . .

Reaper tried to put all his strength into his left hand, but it was like he was trying to stop an on-rushing rhino.

A voice spoke from a nearby comm screen:

"ARK ACTIVATED . . ."

Reaper had one second and in that one second, one chance. "Like the Kid said, Sarge . . . Go to hell!"

He shifted to his left foot, pivoted, ignoring the pain, and body-kicked Sarge hard with every ounce of strength left—so hard that Sarge was propelled backward, the spike and Sarge flying back . . .

And Sarge was swallowed up by the Ark.

Reaper stared at his injured hand—the change in him had already absorbed much of the injury, and the pain was fading.

He smiled thinly, then reached into a pocket, pulled a grenade, activated it—and tossed it into the Ark after Sarge.

Roaring with rage, Sarge spun and whipped and plummeted between worlds, falling and flying both . . . to tumble, at last, into the Ark facility on Olduvai . . . on the planet Mars.

Sarge, at the other end, leapt to his feet, roaring with fury at Reaper's success. He was blind with rage, looking for his enemy.

Then he stared at something that clattered from

the Ark, following him through from Earth, rolling to a stop right in front of him. Inches away from his foot.

Reaper's grenade, pin missing.

Sarge opened his mouth to curse, but the curse was already spoken and the grenade exploded, consuming Sarge and the Ark in a ball of flame . . . that only got bigger. And bigger.

The chain reaction grew exponentially in heat and velocity, a quantum–fusion reaction expanding to culminate, to fulminate, in the power of an unleashed thermonuclear warhead.

The wormhole chamber on Mars, the atrium, the entire facility—all traces of Carmack's experiments—were consumed, vaporized in the growing fireball. It was a white-hot fiery roar of rage, a conflagration that seemed to express, all at once, the horror and fear and anger at what had taken place here: a blinding light of thermonuclear catharsis.

Instinct, enhanced psychic sensitivity, led Reaper to his sister. She was only dimly conscious as he picked her up, murmuring to soothe her, carrying her to the elevator. It rocketed upward, carrying them to the surface of the facility at Papoose Lake, to the glorious open air of the Nevada wilderness. The explosives he'd set would destroy the last of the genetic demons.

Looking up through the open top of the elevator,

he could see the sunlight reaching down to greet them.

He looked fondly down at her. The sunlight streamed across her face.

"Almost home, Sam . . ." he said.

She smiled up at him—safe in her brother's arms.

ABOUT THE AUTHOR

JOHN SHIRLEY is the author of numerous novels, including *Crawlers, Demons,* and *Wetbones,* the recent motion picture novelization of *Constantine,* and story collections including *Really Really Really Really Weird Stories* and the Bram Stoker Award–winning collection *Black Butterflies*. He also writes scripts for television and film, and was co-screenwriter for *The Crow*. The authorized fan-created website is www.darkecho.com/JohnShirley and his official blog is www.JohnShirley.net.